A Bachelor's Lessons in Love

A Bachelor's Lessons in Love

BACHELORS OF BLACKSTONE'S

SALLY BRITTON

In all honesty, with thirty-odd titles, it's difficult to know who to dedicate things to anymore! So this one is for you. Write your name on the line or mentally insert it.

This book is dedicated to _____, because without a reader, what would even be the point?

-SB-

Chapter One

FEBRUARY 20, 1817

I t was a cold Thursday afternoon, and Colonel Edward Halstead stood alone in the garden of his estate, staring at the bed of roses. The bushes were stripped bare by winter's hand, their branches skeletal and dormant. He brushed his gloved hand carefully along one stem, avoiding a large thorn.

"Sleeping the winter away," Edward murmured aloud, his voice the only sound in the quiet of the well-manicured garden. "I miss the vibrancy you bring to this place. Enjoy your rest, but come awake again as soon as you can."

He ought to have been in his study, poring over the reports from his man of business, making financially responsible decisions for the care and keeping of his home, his accounts, and the people who relied upon him. Instead he found himself lost in thought, his mind tangled with the same familiar worries which had plagued him all winter.

The rhythmic crunch of shoes on gravel broke into his thoughts before they could take him down a familiar and unproductive path. Edward turned to see a footman approaching, the servant's breath clouding in the frosty air.

"Sir, a letter has arrived. The messenger said it is of the utmost importance." The young man extended a thick folded paper, sealed with deep red wax, his gloved hand trembling slightly from the cold.

"Ah, thank you, Samuel. Is the messenger still present?" Edward accepted the missive and studied the unfamiliar seal, a stylized P with a laurel wreath encircling it..

"No, sir. He went on his way, quick as anything." The young man stood at attention, and Edward almost chuckled. He never asked his servants to act so similarly to the soldiers he had once commanded. He supposed it was something about himself which brought it out in them.

Breaking the wax with a snap, he unfolded the letter and studied its contents. His jaw tightened as he reached the heart of the matter: the death of Mr. Anthony Price, a man who had saved his life on the battlefield—and the unexpected news that Edward had been named in the man's will as guardian to Price's only daughter, Daphne.

The words blurred slightly as Edward's grip on the paper tightened. He had not seen Price in…goodness, near a decade. The man had been a good soldier, and almost impossibly, a better friend. Price had left the military long before Edward had dared do the same, and the last two years of his civilian life he had spent putting everything in order. Had put off seeing old friends. He had, in fact, buried himself in other responsibilities. And now, from beyond the grave, he had left Edward a most daunting responsibility.

A child. But what did Edward know about children? Especially the female sort?

Edward read on. The girl was to arrive at Briarwood House in three days' time, accompanied by a female relative. The solicitor's tone left no room for negotiation, nor any time to protest the decision. Edward's guardianship was not a request, but a legal obligation.

He exhaled heavily, the cold air stinging his throat. "A child," he muttered aloud, folding the letter with deliberate care. When he had last seen Price, had the man mentioned a daughter? Yes. He had. And his wife had passed away. Edward sent his regrets to the family, in the midst of a battle that had nearly seen him captured. Details had certainly slipped away from him.

Dash it all. His life had gone through too much upheaval, he had been injured too often, to remember the details of other men's lives. Did that make him a monster? Perhaps. Here, Price had left Edward the most important thing a man could have—a child bearing his name—and Edward could not even remember the particulars of Price's life.

He owed Price his own life. The man had saved him from certain death with a well timed push. Edward would not refuse, even if the option were presented to him in that moment.

"Send word to the housekeeper," Edward said to the waiting footman, his tone brisk. "I must speak with her at once. We'll need to prepare rooms for two guests—one of long duration."

The footman bowed and departed, leaving Edward once again alone with his thoughts and the hibernating roses.

This would change...everything. Briarwood had always been his haven, the one place where he could escape the weight of his past. Now, it seemed, it would become a household of responsibilities, a new little face, and unknown challenges.

Edward turned back to the garden, his thoughts heavier than the gray clouds overhead. What had possessed Price to leave a daughter in the care of an old soldier like Edward?

He winced. "I am hardly in my dotage, I suppose," he muttered to the gravel path beneath his boots. At eight and thirty he had his health, a strong physique, and mental fortitude. Many a man his age began new ventures surely far more daunting than caring for a child. He could likely find a governess or a school for the girl, if he couldn't provide what was needed in his own home.

"Poor little mite," he muttered, tucking the letter into his coat. "Losing her father, having to come live with a stranger." And here he was, already thinking of how he might send her away.

The letter had mentioned she would arrive in the care of a female relative. Having another person intrude in his home caused him the briefest moment of annoyance. He could send the woman on her way, he supposed, but it seemed cruel to deprive Daphne of all family mere days after she lost her father. Perhaps he could convince the woman to stay—take responsibility for the child.

He frowned and pulled the paper out once more, reading over it to see if the relative had been named. But no, the solicitor had left out that detail.

What could that mean?

Edward shook his head and put the letter into his pocket again, striding toward the house. Mrs. Lane would be waiting for him in his study in short order—after all, the woman ran his household with the strictness of a sergeant. She would know how to efficiently prepare for Miss Daphne Price's arrival.

As he entered the house, handing his winter things to a footman, he looked about with new eyes. His home suited him, of course, in its simplicity. But what would a little girl think of the place? Was it too dark? Dreary? He marched down the corridor to his study, his gaze sweeping along the walls.

He had bought the house at auction two years ago, and most of the trappings had been sold separate from the dwelling. He hadn't bothered to fill the house with much, either. A soldier for most of his life, he'd learned to travel light, live sparsely, and place value on things necessary for the day-to-day. Because of this philosophy, his house did not have the same comfortable feel to it that his friends' homes did. Would it matter that he did not have paintings of meadows and sheep along the corridor? That he had not painted the deep green walls a more fashionable shade of…whatever was currently considered fashionable?

A child could not care for such things, surely.

As long as he set up a well-appointed nursery and school room, things would surely be fine. He would fill the child's rooms with everything she could want—the rest of the house would hardly matter then. He owed that to Price, at least.

Edward's thoughts swirled as he entered his study, one of the only rooms he had taken time to fill with things that brought him comfort, the faint scent of leather and aged paper greeting him like an old friend. This was the one room in Briarwood where he had allowed himself the luxury of comfort. The deep green walls, lined with shelves of books collected during his travels, instantly comforted him. He'd never been one for frivolity, but books— those were necessary. Histories, treatises on war, scientific explorations, even a few novels he knew most men wouldn't admit to owning—were all neatly arranged with military precision on his shelves.

A roaring fire in the hearth kept the room warm, the flickering light casting long shadows over the dark wood furniture. His desk, a sturdy oak piece inherited from his father, was free of unnecessary clutter, save for a silver inkwell, a neat stack of correspondence, and a small brass carriage clock. A single chair, upholstered in worn yet supple brown leather, stood behind it. That chair had molded to his frame over countless hours of reading accounts, answering correspondence, and studying documents. It was now as much a part of him as his own clothes.

To the left of the hearth stood a battered armchair with a matching footstool, its upholstery faded from years of use and blistering sunshine. A woolen scratchy blanket, a relic from his days in the army, was draped over the back. It bore the faint scent of campfires and distant memories, and though it had no place in such an elegant room, he could never bring himself to part with it. The place was as close to a sanctuary as it was possible for a mortal man to make.

Edward walked toward the hearth, holding his hands out to warm them as he waited for Mrs. Lane to arrive.

His gaze flickered, unsettled. On the mantel above the fire a handful of mementos were arranged with care: a small framed sketch of his parents' estate, a miniature of his mother, and a carved wooden horse gifted to him by a fellow soldier. Each item had a story, though he rarely indulged in retelling them, even to himself.

His gaze roved on. The windows, framed by heavy velvet curtains, overlooked the garden. By day, they allowed light to spill into the room, but now that dusk had fallen the panes reflected only the flames from the fire and the faint, ghostly outline of his own face.

This was his retreat, a place where the weight of the world could be set aside—at least for a time. As he took his usual place at the desk, the letter in his pocket sapped the room of its familiar warmth. Soon, this quiet refuge would no longer belong to him alone.

His gaze shifted to the large armchair by the fire. Would a child consider it comfortable? Would the stories on his shelves hold any appeal to a girl? He shook his head, dismissing the thought. This room was his alone, and it would remain as it was— a sanctuary of order in a world of chaos. Daphne would have other rooms in the house and people to wait upon her needs there. He would see to that.

A knock on the door had his shoulders relaxing. Mrs. Lane's direction would be most helpful, indeed.

"Come in."

Price had trusted Edward to care for a daughter. Edward would prove himself worthy of that trust easily enough—and there was always the woman coming with Daphne. Surely she would not mind giving him some advice before going on her way again. Between the three of them, they could make certain Miss Daphne Price had everything she needed to begin life at Briar-wood. It would not be all that difficult. One little girl would fit quite easily into his home, and it was ridiculous of him to fret.

"Mrs. Lane," he said, putting a confident smile in place as his housekeeper bobbed a curtsy. "We are expecting guests."

Everything would be fine.

"EVERYTHING IS *NOT* FINE," FELICITY PRICE SAID TAUTLY, TRYING TO keep her tone calm despite her overwhelming desire to shout at the disinterested man behind her late brother's desk. The solicitor barely looked up from the papers in front of him to acknowledge that she had spoken. "Fine, indeed! You are sending my niece to live with a complete stranger, a *man* she has never met before. A bachelor, too, from all accounts. She has never known her mother, she lost her father a fortnight ago, and she is at a delicate and important age—are you listening to me?"

She curled her hands into fists in her lap, trusting the folds of her skirts to hide that detail from Mr. Vole, her brother's solicitor and executor of the modest estate left behind. He barely looked up at her when she asked her indignant question. She had learned long ago how little her protests meant when a man had already made up his mind. Once, she might've believed herself capable of persuading someone to wait, to stay, to choose her.

But that had been a long-ago foolishness.

"Why can she not remain here, in the home where she grew up? She will inherit it upon marriage or her twenty-first birthday, and I can remain here and look after the household. I could send you weekly reports or you can visit monthly or..." Felicity's voice trailed away as the man shook his head at her.

"That is not how the law works, Miss Price, surely you must know that. Your brother left explicit instructions in his will. It is my duty as his executor and solicitor to see that everything is done according to his wishes and within the bounds of the law." The man cleared his throat as his gaze dropped to the paper before him. "Miss Daphne Price is now under the guardianship of Colonel Halstead. Everything will be held in trust for her. *You* received an adequate sum from your late brother's estate to set up a household of your own. After you accompany the younger Miss Price to meet her new guardian, the matter is no longer your concern."

Though the solicitor was in truth a handsome enough man of

fifty, Felicity had never felt so repulsed by a person. His words alone made her wish never to see him again.

Unfortunately it was not likely to be fulfilled.

"No longer my concern?" she repeated incredulously. "Daphne is my niece—my flesh and blood. She will *always* be my concern. How can I possibly hand her over to a stranger as though she be nothing more than a parcel, and leave her to an unknown fate?" Her voice rose enough toward the end of her question that Mr. Vole's expression changed from disinterest to disapproval.

"Come, Miss Price, there is no need for dramatics. An unknown fate? Colonel Halstead is apparently quite respectable, and if your brother trusted him with his daughter's care, you can have no objections."

Oh, she had plenty of objections; just none that this man would hear. Why hadn't her brother told her when he took ill what his plans for Daphne were, should the worst happen? Why had she found out a week ago during the reading of the will that her niece would be ripped from her?

"Dramatics?" she repeated, reminding herself to stay calm. "Sir, I assure you, I am not being dramatic. My niece's whole future is at stake."

There was no reason, apart from male stubbornness, why she and Daphne could not continue to live in this house, her home, and live their lives. Daphne was due to come out in Society—had already made her debut locally—and had looked forward to spending a few weeks in London with her father and aunt at the end of the Season. She was a lively, beautiful girl with her whole life ahead of her.

Until this moment, it seemed.

"I am certain Colonel Halstead will be mindful of your niece's needs," Mr. Vole said vaguely, looking down at the papers again. "He will prove an adequate guardian. If there is nothing else, I have more to attend to with the estate and your niece will need your help to pack. Good day, Miss Price."

The disinterested dismissal hit her as a slap in the face, making

Felicity draw back and press her lips closed. Living with her brother for the last several years, she had grown used to being spoken to with naught but respect—listened to, even, when she had an opinion on a matter. For a time she had forgotten that her status as an unmarried woman marked her as someone with barely more self-governance than a child—and less legal right, now, than her own niece.

Felicity rose and offered only a shallow curtsy to the top of Mr. Vole's head before leaving her brother's study. Once the door shut behind her, she rubbed at her temples. She felt one of her headaches coming on, but she had to fight it.

Daphne needed her.

With a stiffening of her spine, Felicity went to the staircase and ascended, ignoring the soft winter light streaming through the large windows. The sunny skies were a lie, for the moment one stepped out of doors they would be shocked through with the bitter cold of a February afternoon.

So much of life was like that. Shiny and bright in appearance, but cold and unkind in truth. Felicity had learned that with some difficulty. Now she was determined to protect her niece from the same.

But how would she manage that if this interloping stranger, this Colonel Halstead, took over Daphne's care?

"I simply cannot allow it," Felicity whispered, her hand on the latch of her niece's bedchamber door. She took in a deep breath. She had to give the news to her niece that she hadn't managed to persuade Mr. Vole even an inch. They needed to pack—and then there was the carriage ride. There was time enough to come up with something, some way of sparing Daphne the miseries of living with a bachelor who knew nothing of women and their needs.

Heavens, the man might try to marry Daphne off to the first ill-mannered fortune-hunter who asked for her hand!

Felicity knocked softly before she entered the room, knowing already she would find her niece in the same place Daphne had been when she'd left a half hour before. Sure enough, Daphne reposed in an armchair by her hearth, legs curled beneath her, a blanket wrapped around her shoulders, staring into the fireplace as though hoping the meager glowing embers would hold the comfort she desperately needed.

With a heavy heart, Felicity forced a smile. "Oh, this will not do, Daph. You're going to freeze yourself through!" She hurried to the hearth, picked up the poker, and stirred things about before reaching for the coal scuttle. "You must keep warm. Catching a chill now will make our carriage ride to Briarwood House rather miserable."

Daphne's head lifted slowly. Even her strawberry-hued curls looked dull and lifeless, her gray eyes tired. "We are still going to my new guardian's home, then?"

"Yes, my dear. I am afraid so." Felicity barely kept a grimace from her countenance. "But it will not be all bad. I believe I will stay with you for a time, to help you settle in. I doubt the man will wish to have the care of a vibrant young woman left to him all at once."

At seventeen, Felicity had thought herself to possess the same vibrancy that, two weeks ago, her niece had exhibited. There had been years ahead for laughter, courtship, the sort of promises whispered beneath moonlit trees. But years turned quickly to obligations, and duty, and waiting for someone who never returned the way he said he would.

Daphne wrinkled her nose. "Vibrant? Aunt Felicity, we both know I am hardly that—especially at present."

"You *are* vibrant, and charming, and an engaging young lady. At present, of course, is an exception. You are in mourning, and that is perfectly all right." Felicity knelt at her niece's chair and laid a hand on her arm.

"Everything…hurts," Daphne murmured. "I cannot think there will be any warmth to the world again."

"My dear girl, I know it hurts. I miss your father terribly, and I remember losing my own far too well." Felicity pushed aside the pain she had learned to live with. "The ache in your heart means you love him, and he was deserving of that love. Anthony was a wonderful father, and he did all he could to ensure you would be safe and happy, did he not?" She watched her niece carefully, hopefully.

"He did." Daphne sniffled and nodded, a little smile turning her lips upward. "Papa did his best to give me a good upbringing. We were so happy."

"Then we must trust that he left you in the care of someone he in turn trusted to do the same." Felicity gave Daphne's hand a gentle squeeze, attempting to convince herself in the bargain. "Your father would hardly sentence you to life with an ogre for a guardian."

A soft laugh escaped the young woman. "No, he certainly would not do that. He spoke often of Colonel Halstead in the past. He genuinely liked him."

Felicity had no recollection of Anthony mentioning his old army friend, but she was not about to say so to her niece, not when Daphne wore a smile for the first time that day. But if her brother had liked the man so much, why had he never made certain Daphne met him?

"There, now. That is most reassuring, is it not? And I will be with you as long as you need me." She hoped that was not a lie. Colonel Halstead might very well scoff at her suggestion that he needed help with handling and housing a young woman.

Packing up Daphne's things in anticipation of her journey did not give Felicity much time to think. The poor girl needed to weigh the decision of what to take and what to leave in her home, what to send into storage, and what to give away. The child—and even though Daphne was in many ways out, Felicity could not help but think of her darling niece as a child—managed to keep her tears at bay remarkably well for some time, but several hand-kerchiefs were drenched before the maid brought up a tray of dinner for the two of them.

Felicity tucked her niece into bed as she had when Daphne was much younger, placing a kiss on her forehead. "I love you, Dilly-Daph." It was a silly old nickname, sprung from the word daffodil, years and years before...but it felt right in this moment.

"I love you too, Aunt Felicity." Daphne smiled up at her in the dim candlelit room. "Thank you for looking after me. Truly, I do not know how I would manage all of this without you."

Withdrawing to her own bedchamber, Felicity readied herself for bed without calling for a maid. It took her mere moments to cast off her somber black mourning gown in favor of a comfortable, warm nightgown. She slipped beneath the cool sheets and shivered a moment before the heat from her body warmed the bedding adequately. The maid must have forgotten the bed warmer. But then, given that the household had been turned upside down, and it had been all Felicity could do to console the three maids who were now without employment, she could not bring herself to do more than sigh over the cold sheets.

Felicity turned over on one side, then the other, trying to find physical comfort while her heart hurt far too much. She had lost every member of her family, all except Daphne. Her parents, years ago, her sister-in-law upon her niece's birth, and now her brother a fortnight before.

"I cannot lose my little one, too," she murmured to the ceiling. She had already lost too many pieces of her heart.

But what was she to do? After she delivered Daphne to her new guardian, the man might send her packing. She had no legal recourse to stay with the girl she had raised.

Felicity's jaw set. She had to prevent that. She absolutely could not allow him to think, not for one moment, that Daphne could do without her aunt—that he, Colonel Halstead, could manage to look after a girl on the cusp of womanhood.

And so she plotted against the man who had, quite without knowing it, become her adversary.

Chapter Two

E dward stood at the base of Briarwood House's steps, arms folded tightly across his chest, the wind tugging at the edges of his greatcoat. The afternoon was as bleak as he half expected the meeting ahead to be, the sky a dull sheet of grey, the air thick with the damp chill of late winter, no promise of a brilliant spring.

In his gloved hand, he held a doll.

It was a small thing, made of mere cloth and wood, its painted face slightly faded with age. Mrs. Lane had produced it from one of the attic trunks, assuring him that it was still in fine condition. "Little girls like dolls," she had said with a knowing nod.

A little girl.

His whole life would soon change with the arrival of the child. He would devote himself to her protection, her care, her upbringing. That was what his friend had expected of him. He would not let Anthony Price down; failing his old friend wasn't an option. The little girl would find herself a haven at Briarwood—no matter how ill-prepared he felt.

His imagination supplied him with the image of a timid child of no more than eleven or twelve, weeping at the loss of her father, clutching at presumably her aunt's skirts, terrified of being left in the care of a complete stranger. He had steeled himself for the encounter, even prepared what he suspected were awkward words of comfort. Despite the days he'd had to ready himself, Edward felt heavy with the uncertainty of how to handle a child who likely wanted nothing to do with him.

As the carriage rolled to a halt before the house, he took in a deep breath and forced a bright smile onto his face, moderating it slightly as he recalled the circumstances which had led to such an occasion. The loss of his friend.

The footman moved swiftly to lower the steps and open the door. Edward's jaw tightened as not one, but two fully grown women emerged. Both dressed in heavy mourning attire, shrouded in grays and blacks, their expressions as cool and impenetrable as the sky overhead.

And this was the moment he realized his expectations had been entirely wrong.

The elder of the two had stepped down first, graceful and unhurried, and Edward knew at once she was no mere chaperone. She moved with calm authority, her spine rigid, her chin lifted. She took one sweeping glance at him, and the weight of her judgment settled like a stone on his chest.

She looked up at him from no more than three feet away, her head tilted back, as though she disapproved of his height, firstly, and the rest was a matter of course.

Edward's jaw tightened. He couldn't help being taller than average. He had no wish to stand out as he did, but most women looked at him with admiration for a height he could not control.

This woman did not.

The aunt. She had to be the aunt. Her somber expression and mature style of dress marked her as someone with authority in the girl's life. A spinster—yet she did not appear all that old. There were no lines upon her forehead or around her mouth, no wrinkles at the corners of her eyes. Her skin still held warmth and there was a sprightliness in the way she had descended the carriage. She could not even be of an age with him, he would wager; she was surely younger than his eight and thirty years. By how much, he could not tell.

The second figure emerged more hesitantly, her gloved hands gripping the doorframe before she set foot onto the frozen ground. She was younger than her traveling companion, her form slight, her manner clearly subdued. But even from a distance, Edward could see the resemblance between the two—the same elegant bearing, the same delicate features, the same deep brown eyes carrying the weight of recent grief.

Daphne Price. Daphne Price was no child. She was nearly a woman grown.

And Edward, standing there like a fool with a doll in his hand, had never felt more unprepared.

He cleared his throat, shoving the toy behind his back with a swift, sharp movement. *Bother.* "Miss Price," he said, inclining his head toward the younger woman. "I am Colonel Edward Halstead. Please accept my deepest condolences for your loss. Your father was a good man." Then, turning his gaze to the elder, "And you must be—"

"Felicity Price," she supplied, her voice crisp as winter frost. "Daphne's aunt."

Edward pressed his lips together at her tone, at the way her gaze flicked over him, assessing, unimpressed. She was not what he had anticipated, either. He had imagined a quiet, soft-spoken companion, a woman who might cower in the face of change, who might be eager to relinquish responsibility to him and leave the child in his care.

This woman was none of those things.

She was unflinching, unreadable. If he was not mistaken, she had already decided that he was entirely unfit for the role he had been given.

Though he had agreed with her at every waking moment since learning of his new charge, Edward could not help but bristle. She knew nothing of him—yet her eyes passed judgment coolly. But on what grounds?

Miss Daphne Price, for her part, said nothing. She stood close to her aunt, hands clasped before her, gaze averted. It was not the shyness of a child, nor the petulance of a youth. It was the quiet reserve of someone who had lost too much too soon.

They had both lost much, Edward reminded himself of that with sternness, and the presumably long carriage ride could not have improved their humors. He had a responsibility to them, as host and guardian, to provide what they needed to regain their equilibrium.

Edward exhaled slowly, schooling his expression. "You must be cold after your journey," he said. "Please, come inside."

The elder Miss Price hesitated only a moment before she nodded, wrapping her arm around Daphne's and guiding her forward. Edward gestured them through the door and into the small entryway of his home, acutely aware of the tension hovering between them like an approaching storm.

This was not going to be simple.

But then, he supposed, nothing about his life ever had been.

The servants waited in two rows, all of them wearing expressions of welcome as Mrs. Lane had admonished them to look friendly so as not to intimidate the newly arrived child. Edward saw the expressions flicker, however, when the housekeeper, butler, valet, cooks, and maids saw the newcomers, looked behind them as though to search for the missing child, then turn their attention to him; waiting for an explanation or, at the very least, clarification as to what had gone wrong.

As the footmen took the ladies' cloaks and gloves, he handed the doll to one of them with a wince and the hope that neither woman saw the toy disappear between the folds of their cloaks.

"I should like to introduce my staff to you both," he said, eyes going first to his charge. She mattered a great deal more in the moment than her aunt did. "Miss Daphne Price, our butler, Mr. Jones, and our housekeeper, Mrs. Lane." He calmly went down the list, introducing the ten members of the household staff as they bobbed bows or curtsies. "I will introduce you to the outdoor staff at another time."

The aunt stood still during the entirety of the introductions, her body stiff beside her niece, her expression marble. Finally, Edward gestured to her with a slight lift of his hand. "And you are most welcome as my guest, Miss Price. I hope you will be comfortable during your time here."

Her chin came up at the same moment her lashes lowered, as though she was unimpressed by him. Or perhaps, offended? "I am certain we will be well enough, Colonel Halstead."

What on earth had he done to so swiftly earn her disapproval? He'd worn one of his finest suits of clothing, attended to his grooming with extra care, yet she looked at him as though he'd appeared in muddied boots and fraying trousers—or bore himself like a cutpurse rather than a gentleman.

Squaring his shoulders, Edward stepped back. "Mrs. Lane will show you both to your rooms. There is time to rest before the dinner hour, at which point I hope to have the pleasure of getting to know you both better."

He'd originally thought the formal meal would prove a treat to a young girl unused to eating with adults at a large dining table. Now, he realized, it would simply prove a matter of course to his charge.

"Thank you, Colonel Halstead," the aunt said, voice unbe-traying of any emotion other than frosty politeness. "We will see you at the evening meal."

Mrs. Lane curtsied to him, then gestured to the corridor that would lead to the staircase. "If the misses would follow me, please. We will see you comfortable in your chambers in a trice."

The women followed, and as he watched them disappear around the corner, his valet Randall sidled up to him. "Not a little girl then, sir?"

"Apparently not."

"How old is she, sir?"

"I haven't the foggiest idea. Nearly full grown, I think."

The valet nodded sagely. "That's both good and bad, I s'pose."

Edward looked down at his most loyal servant and former batman. "Both?"

"Aye, sir." Randall winced slightly. "She'll be fully grown and gone sooner, which means less worries for the raising of her. But...you see you'll have to actually find her a husband? Not an easy task, I wager. It'll mean going out. Into Society. London."

A low, uncomfortable throb pulsed through Edward's head. Into Society. London. To find Daphne Price a husband.

"Blast it," he muttered. The valet was right—and there was nothing Edward abhorred more than making a spectacle of himself for the upper-crust of London. He turned on his heel and stalked out the front door, snatching his coat from the lad who held it and throwing it on in a whirl of heavy wool.

He needed a good, brisk walk in cold air to clear his head and form a new plan of action.

His charge wasn't a child, but a woman of age to enter the marriage mart soon, if not immediately.

"Blast, blast, blast."

He had even less idea of how to manage a woman-grown than an innocent girl, and that was before one considered the *aunt*. The woman looked as though she'd happily pitch him out a window the first time he proved an inadequate guardian.

Which he surely would within hours.

Not only did Edward have to determine how to be a protector to a young lady, he also had to win over the only person who might prove helpful to that cause. A woman who did not appear as though she wished to be won over.

He went to the rose garden, sat on a cold stone bench, and gave himself over to thought.

MRS. LANE INFORMED THEM OF WHAT EACH ROOM WAS AS THEY passed, making certain to give directions to the dining room as well. The corridors were rather austere, as were the rooms Felicity was able to peep into. The house was large and stately enough, but it felt rather...empty. Most of the walls were bare. The carpets they walked across were tidy, but plain.

It was clearly the home of a bachelor, functional rather than welcoming, clean and well-kept but lacking the soft touches of a woman. Trimmings were few, if not altogether nonexistent. The housekeeper was kind and thorough, her tone appropriately warm yet respectful for a servant addressing two gentlewomen.

Then Mrs. Lane brought them to the wing of bedrooms. She gestured to two doors on one side of the corridor. "These are for your use, Miss Price and Miss Daphne. The chambers have a door adjoining them, as we thought...er. We supposed you would want a close connection." The housekeeper appeared momentarily uncertain, but opened the nearer door. "This will be Miss Daphne's room."

They walked through to a room with curtains open, a fire burning in the hearth, and a variety of trappings that made Felicity stiffen at once. The room did not appear at all ready for a young woman about to enter Society, but looked intended for a child of half Daphne's age.

There was a dollhouse on a side table, its delicate furniture and miniature figurines arranged neatly inside. Toy horses stood guard along the mantel. A selection of children's books, thin volumes with brightly covered covers, filled a shelf near the bed. A bed with a quilt in a riot of colors. A large painting over the mantel depicted children playing with puppies and kittens, a piece better suited to a nursery than to the room of a seventeen-year-old young woman.

So, the man truly has no idea what he is doing, Felicity thought, shaking her head in dismay. Men rarely did, she reminded herself. They promised futures they couldn't be bothered to build, left rooms and hearts half-furnished...half-forgotten.

Mrs. Lane cleared her throat, and when Felicity turned sharply at the sound, she felt a momentary pang of guilt when the housekeeper winced. "Dinner is two hours from now, Miss Price. I will send a maid up to assist you both a half hour before. If you have need of anything, there is a bell-pull beside each of your beds." She curtsied. "A pleasure to serve you both, Miss Price, Miss Daphne." She had backed out of the room and shut the door before Felicity had recovered her tongue.

Daphne walked listlessly to the dollhouse, lifting a small chair from inside. "What...what is the meaning of this? I haven't played with dolls in ages. This is more like my old nursery than my bedchamber at h-home." Her voice wobbled on the last word, and Felicity hurried to wrap an arm around her niece's shoulder.

"You are quite right, my darling." Felicity led Daphne with gentleness to the bed. "I am afraid your guardian is out of touch with what a young lady requires. But never mind, this is why I am here—to put matters to rights and make certain you are well cared for."

Daphne nodded rapidly as she sank down, sitting on the edge of the bed. "Yes. Please, Aunt, you cannot leave me to this. He obviously knows nothing about women, and I cannot even think of what I could say to repair the situation." She looked about her with dismay. "This is awful."

"There is nothing to fret over, Daffodil." She sat next to the young woman, her heart breaking yet keeping her face calm, as best she could. "Men like Colonel Halstead, bachelors, they rarely have need to think about what young women need. They simply assume. Perhaps he thought these things would make you comfortable. I doubt there was any malice in the room's preparation. Everything would be quite lovely...were you a decade younger." She tried to inject humor into her tone, but her words did not calm her niece.

"Papa wouldn't have made such a mistake. This man is a stranger, he doesn't know me, and I am supposed to live in his home?" Her niece sniffled, her eyes full of tears. "I like novels, and music, and drawing. Not—not whatever all of this is." She gestured around her helplessly.

Mention of Anthony made Felicity's throat tighten. She had to clear it, softly, to keep her own tears at bay. "You will not be alone in this, Daphne. I am here. I will not leave you."

"But what if he sends you away?"

Felicity forced a smile, though her stomach knotted most uncomfortably. It was a challenge, to hear her greatest fear vocalized by the person she cared for the most. "He will not, my dear. I have a plan. We are going to prove to Colonel Halstead that he cannot do without me. That *you* cannot do without me." She smoothed the sleeves of Daphne's gown, then tugged a handkerchief from her own and pressed it into her niece's hand. "Dry your tears, my dear. Lay down for a time. Rest before dinner." She kissed Daphne's cheek before standing. "I will go inspect my room and hope I do not find it full of tiny tea sets and Indian rubber balls."

That made Daphne's smile appear, though only in brief. "I should prefer rubber balls to all of this."

"Then if I have any, I will share." She went to the door that joined their two rooms. "All will be well, Daphne. You will see."

Felicity entered her room and barely spared it a glance as she marched to the trunk which had already been brought and left at the end of her bed. She knelt on the floor, glowering as she opened the lid to her things.

"Edward Halstead is ill-equipped for his new responsibilities," she muttered as she found a dress for the evening that would suit her, the gray of mourning adorned with cream-colored embroidery at its hem. "And it's my duty to ensure he doesn't ruin Daphne's future." She took in a deep breath as she held the dress to her chest. "Even if I have to fight him for control over it."

She went to the bellpull and gave it a tug. She needed a maid to press her gown long before it was time to dress. Her brother, Anthony, may have been a soldier, but she knew well how to dress for the sort of battles only a woman could fight and win.

Looking around the room, Felicity shook her head. Her niece's chamber had been filled with things that were, while not appropriate to her age, at least pretty. Her own room was sparsely furnished. It was not a welcoming chamber for a guest, let alone one closely related to the gentleman's new charge.

It felt all too painfully familiar. She knew what it was to be given the bare minimum of care, just enough to suggest she was remembered, but not enough to feel wanted.

Once had been enough. She would not endure it again.

Biting her lip, Felicity shook her head. "You will not rid yourself of me by making my room unwelcoming," she said sternly to her absent host. "I am here to stay as long as Daphne needs me."

She had sworn it to herself, and to her brother's memory. Felicity would do everything in her power to ensure Edward Halstead realized how much he needed her at his side.

Chapter Three

The drawing room nearest the dining room hadn't ever received much of Edward's attention, as he rarely spent any time within it. Bachelors rarely entertained, for one thing, and he took most of his meals wherever was most convenient to him, for another. His desk, his room, the library, and even the garden saw him enjoying his dinners more than the dining table ever did. Thankfully, the staff still kept the rooms neat as a pin. The nearly bare mantel had no dust upon it. The large velvet curtains covering the windows did not smell of damp.

The stiff furniture looked practically new, though he'd purchased it used when he'd come to the house. All in all, there was nothing about the room to make a guest uncomfortable, nothing that would make anyone question his ability to maintain a household—yet the instant the ladies entered the room, he saw the disapproving sweep of Miss Price's gaze take everything in before they settled on him.

The single clock on the mantel ticked loudly in the quiet.

The blunder with Miss Daphne's age rolled about in Edward's mind like an unruly hound, refusing to come to heel and let him put the matter aside. He looked to her, the one who should most concern him, to find the young woman pale and her eyes lowered, the gray circles beneath them standing out all the more thanks to the matching color of her gown. Her shoulders were rounded, making her look quite small and helpless beside her much-more composed aunt.

She was not as young as he expected, but she was a child who had lost a father. The poor mite was hurting.

Edward cleared his throat and bowed, then held his hands out in a friendly gesture to gesture at the drawing room. "Ladies, good evening to you both. Please, do make yourselves comfortable. Dinner ought to be announced in a few moments."

"Thank you," Daphne murmured with a small dip of her head.

Miss Price settled on the settee, and Daphne beside her. That left him the chair across from them, which he settled into with less than his usual grace. He had always been rather large, too tall and too broad, but as he looked across at the woman before him he felt positively ogrish.

Well, he had to make a start. "Perhaps we might use this time to come to know each other better," he ventured.

"A thoughtful suggestion," Miss Price said, tone neutral, her gaze on the hearth instead of him.

He felt well and truly dismissed. In his own home. Edward curled his fingers around the armrest of the chair. "I trust your accommodations are satisfactory?" A host ought to ask such a thing, surely.

Miss Price glanced at her niece, then examined him when the younger woman made no answer. "My room is tolerable." She tilted her chin up somewhat. "Daphne's, however, has some rather unexpected furnishings which are not quite appropriate for one of her age and station."

The girl did not so much as twitch, as though she had not even heard her aunt speak, or did not care.

He settled his gaze on Miss Price, his jaw tightening as he prepared to admit the error he made. "I was given the impression that Miss Daphne was much younger." The girl shifted as he said her name, and he caught a slight wince. What a fool he was, attempting to defend himself. "I apologize, Miss Daphne. I will have the things you do not like removed at once, and we will replace them with anything you wish. I know you have trunks from home, too. You must feel free to decorate the room—your room, to your own tastes."

Daphne met his gaze for the first time since entering the room, a brief flicker of curiosity in her eyes, before the girl nodded. "Thank you, Colonel Halstead."

That was something. The aunt hadn't expressed gratitude for much since her arrival.

Edward gave Daphne an encouraging smile. "Do you enjoy music?"

Her eyebrows raised. "I do. Very much. Have you a music room?"

Why had he asked that question? Now he had to admit, "No. No, I do not have a music room. But—" he added quickly, when the young woman glanced toward her aunt, "—I will send for anything you like, first thing in the morning. Being so near London has its advantages. We can obtain nearly anything in no more than a week's time. Would you like a pianoforte? A harp? A violin?"

"Ladies do not play the violin before others," the aunt said, her voice soft velvet covering steel. "But the other things…" She looked at her niece. "Yes?"

Daphne nodded slowly. "If…if it is not too much trouble. I did bring my favorite musical arrangements."

"It is not too much trouble, not in the least. I will arrange for it tomorrow," he said quickly, a sense of relief making him exhale with a smile.

That relief was short lived.

The aunt's gaze had narrowed. "And what else will you be arranging for her, sir?"

Why did she sound so suspicious of him? Hadn't he just offered her niece a kindness—an expensive kindness, to boot? It made him hesitate a moment. "I will see to whatever is necessary."

"Really?" Miss Price lifted her chin. "Necessary for whom? You, or Daphne?"

He blinked, opened his mouth to answer—when the door opened.

The butler came inside. "Dinner is served, Colonel Halstead."

Edward rose. He ought to take Miss Price's arm to guide her in, but he wondered if she would allow for such a thing. He approached as cautiously as he would a cobra, then held out his elbow for her to take. She looked at his arm, a small wrinkle appearing at the bridge of her nose, before she gingerly took it. He led her through the door, across the corridor, and into the dining room. Daphne followed behind them, silent, pale, and graceful as a ghost.

Things were not going as well as he hoped.

After they were settled around the dining table, which was meant to hold at least a dozen people, Edward found himself devoid of anything to say or ask. There he sat, at the head of the table, and there they were, on either side, in the middle. Halfway down from him. Across from each other. Quietly eating.

The silver gleamed in the candlelight. The sounds of forks and knives softly scraping the plates barely broke the silence.

Finally, Edward cleared his throat, then immediately took a drink of his wine when Miss Price's gaze snapped to his, brow furrowed with disapproval. Putting his glass down again, he addressed her directly. "Miss Price, have you spent much time in London?"

Her expression remained unreadable. "A fair amount."

With a smile, he tried to lighten the moment. "Then perhaps you will find Briarwood rather too quiet by comparison."

She reached for her own wine glass. "It is quiet. And rather... sparse."

Rather what? He tilted his head to the side. "Sparse? In what way?" His house wasn't enormous, but it was a respectable size for a gentleman of his means. It suited him, quiet as it was. What complaint could be levelled at it?

"It feels rather empty. Cavernous." The aunt shuddered before taking a small sip of her wine. "It concerns me, given that a house is often a reflection of its master. Are you a miser, I wonder, or merely frugal? I wonder if you will think to provide the things that Daphne needs to be comfortable, let alone happy. How will she prepare for her formal entrance into Society in such an unwelcoming place?"

His jaw fell open as the woman spoke, but he did not realize it until he had to snap it closed again to speak his own answer. "You speak quite critically and freely of another person's home, Miss Price."

"You asked what I thought," she said, her tone as cool as it had been from the first, utterly unruffled by his poorly concealed anger. "And as these things concern the future happiness of one who is dearer to me than my own life, I will not feign polite indifference." Her chin came up as she sat her glass down.

Edward stared at her in some shock. No one had spoken to him that way in...well. He could not remember when. A flash of curiosity sparked through him, but he pushed it away to focus instead on her words. "You seem determined to find fault with my household, Miss Price. I assure you, though you find it 'sparse' in trappings, such a thing does not mark me as an inadequate guardian. I am capable of and committed to providing for my ward." He inclined his head to Daphne, whose eyes had widened somewhat as she glanced between the two of them.

"Capable, perhaps. But aware?" the aunt asked, challenge in her tone. "Understanding? That remains to be seen."

He exhaled, slowly, a suspicion in his thoughts, so he gave it voice. Why not? Miss Price did not seem willing to keep anything back. He ought act the same. "You believe yourself better suited to the task, do you not?"

"I believe my experience in the realm of what young ladies require far outstrips your own, and my being intimately acquainted with my niece speaks for itself." The barest curve of her lips made him stare. Had she almost smiled? At him? Surely not. Unless she was smiling at the thought of his demise.

Before he could respond, Daphne's soft voice spoke. "Please, Aunt. Colonel Halstead. We...we can discuss this another time, surely?"

The child must not be as used to speaking her mind as her aunt was—nor hearing others do the same. Edward cleared his throat. "Of course, Miss Daphne. You are quite right. We are all overwhelmed from the events of the previous days, most likely. This is hardly a time for debate or making decisions."

Miss Price nodded to her niece. "That time will come later, I imagine."

She wasn't finished with him, then.

Edward narrowed his eyes. The time would come the moment he could speak to the woman alone. He had hoped to convince her to stay long enough to make Daphne comfortable. Now, he wondered if that was still a good idea. The woman was antagonistic, to say the least.

Daphne resumed picking at her food, gaze downcast and quiet. Every time he glanced at her aunt, the woman appeared to be watching him from the corner of her eye. His frustration mounted.

Why did it feel like he had a battle ahead of him? He lifted his glass and took another slow sip of wine. Miss Felicity Price did not trust him. Daphne, his ward, was grief-stricken and understandably listless. And he was somehow meant to broker peace with the elder and make the younger feel at home.

A curl of excitement slowly unraveled in his chest.

He did love a good challenge.

THE EVENING MEAL ENDED IN STRAINED SILENCE, AND FELICITY couldn't help but feel she had won a victory, however small. When the servants took the last of the plates away and Colonel Halstead stood, she did as well.

"Come, Daphne. It has been a long day. You ought to retire early." She walked around the table and held a hand out to her niece.

Daphne took the hand gratefully and curtsied to her guardian. "Thank you, Colonel Halstead. The meal was delicious."

"You are most welcome, Miss Daphne." He bowed, before his gaze moved sharply to Felicity's. "Miss Price, if you have a moment, I should like a word before you retire for the evening."

She felt Daphne's hand tense in her own. She expected this, of course, after their verbal sparring over the meal. But so soon? She had long learned that her place in a household was safest when she remained indispensable. A woman who made herself useful rarely found herself shown the door. Perhaps pleasantness should have been her first method of attack, not possessiveness.

"Of course, Colonel Halstead. But first, I will see my niece to her room." She tilted her chin up again, daring him to deny her such a simple thing.

"I will be in the drawing room," he answered. Then bowed to them both again, dismissing them with all politeness.

Felicity led Daphne down the corridor, arm in arm, her mind whirling, trying to organize her list of reasons why he was an unfit guardian for her niece. All the reasons he needed Felicity to remain, to oversee Daphne's education and entrance into Society. She was so lost in thought, she did not realize that Daphne had slowed their walk to a stop until the young woman spoke.

"Aunt Felicity? Please, do not push the Colonel too hard."

Felicity blinked and looked into her niece's eyes. They were the same height now. When had that happened? "Push him?" She shook her head. "In what way could I push that man?"

Daphne glanced down briefly, swallowed, then met Felicity's eyes with an earnest expression. "I know he does not understand —I know he should. But if he sends you away, I will be alone here." She swallowed. "I do not want to be alone. I do not want to lose you so soon, not after losing Papa."

Felicity's heart squeezed in sympathy, her own grief tightening in her chest. "Oh, my darling." She wrapped her arms around her niece. "I know, Daffodil. I do. I am not going anywhere. You needn't worry. I promise."

Though Daphne nodded, she did not appear reassured. "Thank you. Only...only be careful what you say to him."

"I am not going to insult him further." Though Felicity was not entirely sure she could keep her word on that matter. "I am not trying to prove him incapable. I am trying to ensure he will understand the responsibility and honor of caring for you."

"Yes, Aunt Felicity." Daphne kissed her cheek. "I hope everything goes well." She opened her bedroom door and slipped inside, giving her aunt one last, tremulous smile before closing the door.

Releasing a heavy sigh, Felicity turned to retrace her steps to the drawing room. "I am not going anywhere," she repeated to herself in the quiet corridor. She had to be strategic, for Daphne's sake. This battle would not be won through sheer force of will. "I must not be ruled by frustration." She paused before the drawing room door and finding it already open, the fire crackling again, the candles still lit. Edward Halstead stood with his back to the door, elbow on the mantel, staring deep into the embers.

He had been in the military—served his king and country. Anthony's commanding officer. If her brother had admired him, Colonel Halstead was not a bumbling fool, but likely an intelligent man who had simply never been around women. She had to find a way to position herself as indispensable to him rather than intrusive.

Once again, Felicity let her eyes sweep across the room. It was stark, masculine, practical. No fripperies. Nothing to delight the eye. But it wasn't dirty, the furniture was sturdy and well made— like the man himself. She glanced at his broad back, his tall form slightly hunched, was still imposing. Truly, she ought to be intimidated at the mere size of him.

But she could not afford to be. Felicity tried to calm her rapidly fluttering heart. He was hardly to blame or to credit for his size, though he had lived a different life from hers. One of battlefields, not drawing rooms.

Felicity cleared her head of thoughts and entered the room with a purposeful stride, the soft heels of her slippers making only the slightest click on the wood floor. "Colonel Halstead. You wished to speak with me?"

He turned at the sound of her voice, his green-brown eyes meeting her gaze without hesitation. "I did." He paused, then nodded to her. "This may take a few moments. Please, sit."

For a moment, she considered where to settle. Not the settee again—that might make the man think he could sit beside her, and she would look small, unimposing in a seat made for two. So, she chose the chair where he had sat before. She went to it directly, sat and smoothed the skirts of her gown, then looked up at him. Eyebrows raised. Expectant.

One corner of his mouth ticked upward, as though she had amused him, but he sat on the settee across the rug from her. He looked calm rather than put out, though he clearly did not regard her with complete confidence. Why would he? He draped one arm along the arm of the settee and reset his other hand on his thigh, tapping his fingers for a moment.

Then he exhaled, the sound heavy. "You do not approve of my guardianship."

She had to give him credit for his directness. A statement, then, not a question. "I do not approve of your inexperience."

A flicker of something crossed his eyes. Amusement? Frustration? Or perhaps some odd combination of both. "I have managed estates, commanded men, navigated war. And yet you believe I cannot manage one young lady?"

Her niece's plea at the forefront of her mind, Felicity kept her tone even. "It is not about managing her, sir. It is about understanding Daphne—and you do not understand what it means to prepare a young woman for Society. The fact that she is grieving only complicates matters."

He leaned back slightly, and the fingers on the arm of the settee tapped softly against the upholstery. "Then perhaps you will enlighten me."

A skip to her pulse made Felicity stiffen, though with surprise rather than displeasure. Had he really invited her to educate him? How unlike a man. Men, in her limited experience, did not often ask for a woman's opinions. They took what they needed, left when they were done. If this one thought to dismiss her after a polite hearing, he would find she had built her arguments to be not only persuasive—but permanent.

Felicity tilted her head to one side. "Do you truly wish to learn, or are you humoring me?"

The Colonel's lips twitched, and she almost grew angry. How dare he laugh at her?

Yet the anger dissipated into caution as he nodded deeply. "I wish to learn, Miss Price. Whether you are capable of teaching me remains to be seen."

The opportunity to outline all her reasons for remaining close to Daphne, as a companion if not a guardian, had arrived far sooner than she thought it would. It appeared he was not going to ignore her, nor dismiss her without warning. He was asking for her to present her argument, the same one she had prepared from the moment she learned Daphne would not come under her protection.

She had prepared for this. Now all she had to do was perform.

Tucking her emotions carefully behind a mask of calm, Felicity launched into her list of arguments. "Daphne's education is sufficient for a young lady of her station, but there is much she has not learned, things a gentleman would not even consider. A governess has taught her literature, languages, art, and such things are important—but Daphne knows nothing of the nuances of Society. Only another woman can guide her on how to behave in

London's drawing rooms, ballrooms, and markets. It is not sufficient to be well-mannered. One must also be perceptive, discerning, wise in choosing one's company."

Colonel Halstead raised his eyebrows at her. "You have experience in these places, of course. I cannot argue that." He tapped the arm of the chair again. "You speak, in part, of her maintaining a respectable reputation."

"A reputation is all a lady has to rely upon most of the time, Colonel Halstead," Felicity stated with a firmness he could not dare to argue with. "My niece may now be an heiress, but that brings with it more dangers than protections. A woman's reputation is everything. Every part of her is considered when she enters Society, the clothes she wears, the music she plays, the theatricals she attends, and the company she keeps. To stay abreast of all of it is a demanding task. Not one for a mind divided between her and other matters, such as businesses and estates."

The corner of his lips tipped up again. "You propose delegation?"

An argument, a metaphor he might understand entered her mind, and Felicity spoke it at once. "There is a reason one man alone cannot command an entire army, sir, so he relies upon officers to see to matters he cannot attend to himself."

The Colonel leaned back somewhat. "Point taken. What else ought I to know about Daphne's entrance into Society?"

"Oh." Felicity folded her hands in her lap, gripping her own fingers. He was...actually listening to her. She could not afford to stumble now. "Goodness, where to start. There is more to it than simply attending a few balls and simpering at dinners. It is a strategic endeavor, one that requires careful management." Calmly, or at least far more calmly than she had thought possible, she explained, "A young lady's first Season is crucial. Besides keeping her reputation spotless, her suitors must be well vetted. Her name must be introduced in the right circles. Daphne must learn how to reject unwanted advances without causing offense, to recall the names of those she should associate with and those she must avoid—all without causing gossip. She must recognize the difference between a charming rake and a steady, respectable man—"

"And you know the difference between two such characters?" Colonel Halstead interrupted.

She could not tell if he was amused or mocking her, only that his smile was more on display than before. Felicity swallowed back her irritation. "Despite the fact that I am an unmarried spinster I can, in fact, judge character with some success. I also know who to ask when I cannot find the answers on my own." It pricked her pride to mention her unwed status. Yet what else could he have alluded to, with a question such as that?

His expression swiftly sobered. "I did not mean any insult, Miss Price. Forgive me if I have caused harm."

She waved aside his polite apology. "My feelings are unimportant, it is Daphne I am concerned about. You would not send a soldier into battle without training. Would you send your new ward into Society unarmed?"

He slowly shook his head. "I would much prefer not to."

Good. She had gained some ground, Felicity could feel it. "A young lady with too much time unstructured and unsupervised is open to scandal and gossip. Boredom is a dangerous thing for a young person. Daphne must be encouraged to fill her days with worthy pursuits. Music, art, charitable endeavors, friendships with those of her rank and breeding, not idleness nor foolish friendships."

The Colonel folded his arms across his chest, appearing somewhat skeptical. "You would *schedule* her into good behavior?"

"Not as such," Felicity accepted with a shrug. "But I would look after her time, ensure she does not spend it on entertainments of little to no value. If left to her own devices, Daphne—any young woman might gravitate toward anyone who provides her companionship or amusement, regardless of their character." She leaned forward, hands spread before her. "Her friends will shape her reputation as much as her own conduct. Do you know which ladies of Society she should avoid? Or who will bring her invitations to the right houses?"

Slowly, he shook his head, his gaze never leaving hers. No, of course he did not.

"And that is not a failing on your part, sir," Felicity said, gaining confidence. She had to win him over, and if that meant giving him excuses to avoid taking a more active role in Daphne's life, she would do that. "Men do not have to concern themselves with the things women must think of daily." She moved to the edge of her chair. "Have you ever had to navigate a ballroom where smiling at the wrong person could invite not merely gossip, but a whisper of scandal?"

"No. I have never had to consider such a thing." The Colonel clasped his hands before him and leaned toward her. "I have not concerned myself overmuch with what Society thinks of me. I did my duty to my country, I conduct myself with as much integrity and honor as I know how. That has been enough." Here a measure of seriousness came into his tone, as though he thought of a specific thing that weighed on him.

"It may have been enough for a gentleman, but for a lady..." Felicity took a deep breath. "Even if you do not care for Society's opinion, Colonel Halstead, I assure you that Society cares about you. If Daphne is not properly introduced into Society, it will reflect poorly on you as her guardian. If she stumbles into her Season ill-prepared, she will suffer—perhaps for the rest of her life. But it will not truly be her failing. It will be yours."

He sat back abruptly, arms moving up again, now crossed against his broad chest. Her brow contracted.

Had she offended him or worried him?

Felicity rushed forward, hoping she had not said the wrong thing. "Even with all of this, above it all, Daphne has lost her father—a child who hardly knew her mother. She needs someone familiar in her life. Someone who knows her, loves her, who can ease this transition for her. You, Colonel Halstead, are a gentleman—but you are also a stranger. If she feels vulnerable or uncertain, do you think she would come to you? If she is unsure as to a course of action, would she seek your counsel...or attempt it alone? Would you truly send her out into this world of judgment with only yourself for guidance?"

Colonel Halstead stared at her for a long, uncomfortable moment. The silence stretched on for an eternity, and the blasted clock on the mantel was the only sound Felicity heard other than the pulse in her own ears.

Why did he not speak? Was he not utterly convinced?

Finally, she dared to prod him one last time. "If you wish for Daphne to thrive, allow me to ensure her success. Let me help you in this responsibility." There. She gave him the choice, or at least the illusion of it. If he rejected her offer after all she had presented, even obtaining his agreement in some places, it would make no sense.

"And what," Colonel Halstead said, his words low and unhurried, "if I do not believe I require your assistance?"

Her heart froze. *No.* After all she had presented, how could he not understand how important she was to her niece's future? She swallowed her first indignant answer, the temptation to cut with words forced down. She had to think of Daphne. She had to do whatever she could to stay near Daphne.

"Perhaps this is a thing to consider, rather than decide this evening. Any hasty decision can hardly be the correct one." She forced a smile but felt it wilt immediately under his stare. "Daphne is my last remaining relative, Colonel Halstead. I helped to raise her. She...she is my only family, my darling niece. I love her, I want her to have happiness and success. Please—if you consider nothing else, think on that. You must understand, I want what is best for her."

Colonel Halstead stood, hands dropping to tuck behind his back. "You make many assumptions about what I do and do not understand...but I suppose we shall see. Thank you for sharing your concerns with me, Miss Price. This has been educational. I look forward to discussing the matter with you again. Perhaps tomorrow."

It was a dismissal.

Felicity rose slowly to her feet, confusion clouding her thoughts. She had thought he would understand. All her feelings led her to believe he would agree with her; the way he had listened, the way he had respected her arguments, made her think she had succeeded.

Had she miscalculated?

It had happened before. She had believed herself wanted—needed—and had still been set aside. It was a lesson she thought she'd learned well enough not to repeat, but here she was, heart trembling with the old fear that no effort would ever be quite enough to make her essential.

Felicity dropped into a shallow curtsy. "Good evening, Colonel Halstead."

"Good evening, Miss Price." He turned his back to her, staring once more into the embers in the hearth.

Felicity withdrew, doubt creeping into her heart and making her far colder than the winter wind ever had.

If she failed Daphne, she would never forgive herself.

Chapter Four

E state matters and a pile of correspondence took up the better part of Edward's morning, remaining in his study through the afternoon and taking tea at his desk as he read a report from his steward. Then he went over his financial accounts, checking all was in order. He even wrote a brief note to his man of business regarding an investment opportunity with a contact in Spain.

In his study the world was orderly, structured, and efficient. The man, however, was struggling to maintain his usual focus. His mind remained preoccupied with his new ward and her earnest, concerned aunt.

He had sent Mrs. Lane to the ladies earlier in the day, hoping the delegation—he almost laughed—would take the thoughts of them from his mind. Despite the housekeeper's capabilities, he couldn't help feeling he ought to have gone himself. The tactical decision kept him from another verbal sparring match with the aunt, at least. He wasn't ready to let her know his decision regarding the length of her stay in his home.

That Mrs. Lane had not yet returned with a list of Miss Felicity Price's demands concerned him. Either they had been so minimal that the housekeeper did not require funds, or they were still producing a list after hours of conversation.

Neither of those outcomes seemed ideal.

Edward stood from the desk and stretched, looking at the clock on the mantel, before opening a drawer and taking out his favorite pipe, crossing the room to the window that looked out over the sleeping rose garden. Once the pipe was lit, he took the stem between his lips and puffed at it for a moment.

He'd taken up smoking a pipe in the military. It was one way to get warm on cold nights, and it distracted from the feeling of an empty belly when rations were low. It wasn't the most ideal habit, and he rarely indulged it anymore but in moments of duress. Having two women beneath his roof, women he would have to take some measure of responsibility for, women who did not appear to wish for his help, guidance, or even presence, certainly qualified as distressing.

"What does a bachelor know of such things?" he muttered, watching a bird descend to land on the slowly sprouting rose bushes, bobbing up and down on a thorny branch. "Especially a near recluse."

Well, he wasn't precisely a recluse. The people in the little village nearby knew him, and most seemed to like him. But he rarely went into London, and had avoided Society for years. While he attended the occasional dinner party, it was only those held by old friends from the military or business acquaintances made after his return from the war. All his correspondence was with the same sort of people.

Thinking back, Edward tried to remember the last time he had danced in a ballroom. Goodness, it had to have been a decade past. And paying court to a woman? At least as long. He hadn't been part of London's social whirl in any meaningful way in years.

"This is going to be a problem." He tapped his reflection in the window with the stem of his pipe. "You, old fellow, are a hermit. How did I come to this?"

If Daphne were to make a proper entrance into Society, she needed introductions. Invitations. Sponsors. Connections. Edward had no sisters, no female cousins in London to help smooth the way. He'd thought there was a decade or more ahead of him before facing such a challenge.

Felicity Price was right about what her niece needed—and she was right when she said Edward could not handle such matters on his own. Admitting that he needed her was the right thing to do, and yet he felt a strange reluctance to give in to her demands completely. He had his limitations, but Miss Price undeniably had her own. She wasn't married, she had no other family, she had admitted to as much. A maiden aunt with no connections of under thirty years of age—she had to be less than thirty, if he guessed aright—had just as little business sponsoring a young lady's entrance into Society.

Why *was* Miss Price unwed? Anthony had come from money, from memory. A dowry had likely existed for her at some point. Besides, she was rather pleasant to look at, when her expression wasn't stiff as stone.

She had lovely blue eyes, her hair an indeterminate color between gold and umber. Her skin was clear, her figure healthy from what Edward could tell, and she moved with a confidence that intrigued him. All in all, a handsome woman such as she, with obvious intelligence, ought to have been married to a discerning gentleman years ago.

His reflection in the glass smirked, and Edward quickly wiped the expression from his face. He had no business thinking of Miss Price as an attractive woman. Not when his ward, her niece, needed his full attention.

A soft tap at the door pulled his thoughts away from that particular set of troubles, and he called out, "Enter."

One of the footmen came in, bearing a silver tray with the afternoon post. "Letters for you, Colonel Halstead."

Edward thanked the young man as he accepted the folded missives. He sorted through the three of them, knowing from whence they came by the handwriting. The first two held little interest for him, but the third—

He broke the seal immediately and read the far too short letter with a deep frown.

Sir—

I have found at last a woman who worked at Miss Goodie's School for Girls. She was a nurse there, two decades past, and kept records in personal journals of the women who came to them in distress. She has granted me access to her journals for a small fee. She did not know the name I gave her, but she believes most of the women were cared for under assumed names to protect their families and reputations. I will do my utmost to uncover more information from these journals.

I have included a list of my expenses to this point, for your information and an accurate accounting of the use of the payment and fees already allotted for my use. I remain optimistic that I will discover that which you bade me to find.

The signature of the man he had hired ended the note, with a post script detailing how Edward could contact him.

He slowly folded the letter, denying himself the hope that his paid investigator would finally succeed in his task. Two decades separated Edward from his quarry. Two decades of secrets and misdirection.

He closed his eyes and sighed. All those years ago, when his family had sent him away, none of them had known how the gossip would fester in his absence. Perhaps his parents had hoped the war would wipe his sins from the minds of the gentry. Instead, he had returned home at the end of Napoleon's defeat to find old family friends no longer sought his company. Few of his former friends came to call. His parents had passed on. There had been nothing left of his old life.

Would Society ever forgive him? Did they still whisper about him? Did they still lower their voices when his name was mentioned?

He hadn't been publicly shunned; not exactly. When he had attended places, however, those first few years, there had always been an edge of polite reserve in certain circles. He hadn't tested the waters in years, of course. Not since the last time he had come home on leave, a decade before.

What would his reputation mean for Daphne?

All his concerns regarding the young woman in his care came rushing back to the forefront of Edward's mind as he squared his shoulders and looked to the door. Daphne depended on him. He was her protector. Her guardian. Avoiding the aunt would do little to solve the difficulties facing him when it came to providing for the girl.

He took a step toward the door and at the same moment a soft knock sounded on the wood. He paused, cleared his throat, and tucked his pipe behind his back. "Enter."

The door opened and Mrs. Lane came inside the study, her expression somewhat stern. She held the book in her hands where she made note of household needs and routines. "I have just come from speaking with Miss Price and Miss Daphne."

Something about the set of his housekeeper's jaw made him wonder if she'd switched allegiances. He really, truly did not know much about women, a fact that settled heavily upon his shoulders as he gestured for his housekeeper to sit at the desk while he resumed his own seat.

"I am eager for your report, Mrs. Lane."

Her chin came up and her gaze was steadfast—brooking no opposition.

Yes. She'd joined up with the opposition. And for some reason, that made him want to smile.

AFTER THE HOUSEKEEPER GAVE THEM A TOUR OF THE HOUSE, AND then had a thorough conversation detailing what Felicity and Daphne required for settling in, she left them in a well-lit room which faced the front drive of the estate. With windows from floor to ceiling, and a comfortable couch before a well-lit fire-place, Felicity found herself content to remain there.

"This would be a most excellent music room," she mused, looking at the tall shelves and empty half of the room. "A pianoforte would sit beautifully there, with the light on the keys. The shelves are perfect for holding music sheets and books. What do you think?"

Daphne bit her bottom lip as she took in the same things her aunt looked at, and nodded somewhat reluctantly. "I think so, too. The lighting is perfect." She glanced at the door. "Mrs. Lane was kind."

Barely keeping in a snort of amusement, Felicity agreed. "Indeed. At least *someone* in this house knows how to manage things."

The housekeeper had listened, nodded, and asked intelligent questions of them when they had made their requests, giving them clear signs she intended to act on what they asked for, even advocate for some of the more inconvenient things on their long —and still incomplete—list.

"She reminds me of Mrs. Talbot at home," Daphne murmured, the smile on her lips not at all making up for the sadness in her eyes. "I do like her."

Felicity nodded, having felt a great deal of affection for the woman who had looked after her brother's home. "A housekeeper with a good deal of sense is worth her weight in gold." At least the Price estate had been able to keep on Mrs. Talbot, who would care for the shut up house that Daphne would one day inherit.

Mrs. Lane clearly knew the same truths about making herself dispensable as Felicity did. Felicity had lived the last decade that way, quietly ensuring that she provided enough value to her late brother that he never thought to ask her to leave.

The Colonel's housekeeper would make a fine ally when it came to seeing to Daphne's needs.

The requests they had issued that afternoon were not small ones. They had not merely asked for comforts in their rooms, but for everything Daphne would need to prepare for her opening Season. Felicity went over some items again in her mind, hoping she had left nothing of true importance out.

A music and dance instructor

A pianoforte, expertly tuned

A visit to a seamstress with a list of reputable establishments

A modiste

A milliner

A cobbler

A list of invitations they would need to secure for Daphne

A list of people she needed to meet, including the local vicar and his wife, and any nobility in the environs

Several outings in London to familiarize Daphne with the city, and city manners

Proper stationery and calling cards for social correspondence

A ladies' maid specifically for Daphne

The Price jewels to be secured from the bank

Felicity tapped her finger on the arm of the couch as she went over each of those things, then the list of things Daphne needed for her bedchamber and in the household in general. Now they were listed out, she could see that it would cost a small fortune to set up the young woman for success and comfort.

As though reading her aunt's thoughts, Daphne asked softly, "Do you think Colonel Halstead will comply with everything we asked for?"

She certainly hoped so. The man seemed so reasonable the evening before, up until the moment he had dismissed her. Given Daphne's somewhat uncertain expression, Felicity decided it was best to make light of the situation. "Oh, I believe so. Colonel Halstead seems to pride himself on being capable. We will likely receive everything so he can make his point."

Daphne's smile appeared, brighter than it had been in weeks. "I think he would rather suffer a thousand battle wounds than appear incapable."

Felicity patted her niece's hand. "Then we most certainly will get our dance instructor."

"Aunt Felicity? Did you hear what Mrs. Lane said, after we talked about needing to visit points of interest in London?" Daphne tilted her head to the side, her eyebrows raised. "What do you think she meant?"

Mrs. Lane had muttered as she made notes in a little book, and Felicity had not thought the woman meant for them to hear, "It's about time the master gets dragged out of this house. Back to the land of the living."

Turning those words over in her mind, Felicity finally shook her head. "I haven't the faintest idea. Perhaps he has not ventured into Society much since the loss of his parents." That had to be it, did it not? "Most likely, Colonel Halstead isn't an entirely sociable person. It happens, you know, with confirmed bachelors. They become rather settled in their ways and see no reason to step outside of the place where they are most comfortable."

"He seemed perfectly polite, though." Daphne folded her hands in her lap, her gaze turning to the rather bland painting of a meadow above the fireplace, the only décor of note in the entire room. "One would think someone set in their ways would be a miserable grump rather than a kind gentleman."

"Kind gentleman?" Felicity repeated and laughed. "That is quite the opinion to form when you have only seen him twice, once when we arrived and once at dinner."

"Mrs. Lane likes him." Daphne shrugged one shoulder upward. "And he was kind at dinner."

"He has avoided us all day today, though." Felicity frowned at the painting, its colors all drab browns and muted greens. "Hardly the sign of an attentive guardian." He had not been at breakfast, had not sent them a note to excuse himself, and had sent the housekeeper in his stead. Where was the man?

The door to the room opened without a courteous knock, and

Felicity turned her head to see who had walked in with such authority. She ought to have guessed, of course, that only Colonel Edward Halstead would move through Briarwood with such confidence. She hurriedly came to her feet, as did Daphne, and both curtsied to him.

"Colonel Halstead," Felicity said, keeping her tone everything that was polite. "Good afternoon. How pleasant a surprise, to see you at last."

The gentleman bowed slightly, and a slight twitch to his lips surprised her. He'd taken her jab with good humor. Interesting.

"Miss Price. Miss Daphne. I have reviewed your requests." He gave Felicity a rather pointed glance as he paused, and her stomach twisted somewhat unpleasantly. "They are...extensive."

An argument rose to her lips, but before she could give it voice, he continued in a low, measured voice.

"However, I see no reason why they should not be met." He smiled broadly at Daphne, and the smile made him look less a stern military man and more a kindly benefactor. A handsome one, too. "You will have your instructors, your seamstress, and all the rest. The pianoforte was ordered this very morning."

Daphne gave a happy gasp and took half a step forward in her joy. "Oh, thank you, Colonel Halstead. Truly. This is wonderful news. I promise we will be mindful of the costs—"

He waved a hand to gently interrupt her. "Nonsense, Miss Daphne. It is my duty to look after you, and I will happily spend whatever necessary to make certain you are comfortable and well turned-out—as is my duty." He glanced at Felicity again, tucking his hands behind his back. "As it so happens, I must tend to some matters in London myself. I will escort you both to Town in two days' time. We will check off as many things from your list as we can, and schedule another visit after that. If such a plan is agreeable to you?"

It could not be more clear that he was asking for her opinion, and not his ward's. Felicity hesitated only a moment before adding her gratitude to her niece's. "That is very kind of you,

Colonel Halstead. Thank you." She curtsied, then put a hand on Daphne's arm. "We must carefully plan for the occasion to make the most out of it."

She glanced at the man, wondering if he would correct her—if she was meant to come with them on this London outing, or if she was meant to remain in the home at all.

But he merely continued to stand there, smiling. Pleased with himself. Why?

Asking him outright if she was staying would not be wise, especially in front of Daphne. He had to know she yet waited to learn her fate on that matter. Until Felicity knew, she would be horribly off balance. "I...I appreciate your willingness to see to Daphne's needs, Colonel Halstead. It is most reassuring."

She still wasn't certain she trusted him to look after Daphne. But this was a start.

His lips quirked upward, and a flash of amusement went through his eyes. "I am relieved, then, for I should hate to disappoint you, Miss Price."

She narrowed her eyes at him, confused by his smile and doubly so by his words. Disappoint *her*? Whatever could he mean? She wasn't accustomed to being anyone's concern. Disappointing people required them to expect something of you first. It was easier, safer indeed, to be the one anticipating needs, not the one whose feelings others measured.

As a woman, and a single one at that, she had long since learned that the only way to assert herself in male company was to use directness to her advantage, and Felicity had no hesitation in doing so. "Your housekeeper said the most interesting remark as she left us earlier. I am therefore quite surprised at your eagerness to escort us to Town."

Daphne blanched and turned to look at her, but Felicity kept a serene smile on her lips. She knew what she was doing.

"Did she?" Colonel Halstead gave a subtle shake of his head. "I cannot imagine what that might be."

"She said something about...oh, let me see." Felicity tapped her chin as though having to search to remember the words that were on the tip of her tongue. "Dragging you back to the land of the living? I think that was it."

Releasing a slow exhale, the gentleman shook his head as a soft laugh escaped him. "Mrs. Lane has never been one to hold her opinions quietly, and I have always respected her for that."

She lowered her hands to her sides, curiosity swelling. "What, precisely, did she mean?"

Though he kept his gaze on her, the Colonel did not immediately answer. His expression remained friendly enough, but his eyes seemed to darken and look through her. "I have been absent from Society, Miss Price. That much is true." His gaze sharpened on hers once more. "And that is the extent of the tale."

An evasion? How curious. The man was hiding something—but what? Would his reasons for keeping away impact Daphne's chances at a good match? If he would not reveal the truth to Felicity... She would have to find out for herself. Somehow.

Daphne took another step forward and a little in front of Felicity, her disapproval of her aunt's prying apparent in the movement. "I look forward to our trip to London, Colonel Halstead. Thank you."

The man inclined his head. "I imagine it will prove...educational. To all of us." His eyes flickered over Daphne's shoulder to meet Felicity's, and her chin came up.

"Indeed. I expect it will be," she said, tone perfectly polite.

He looked from one woman to the other. "I will see you both again at dinner. Perhaps you will have an itinerary for our London trip by this time tomorrow?"

"Of course," Daphne agreed quickly. Then looked at Felicity with raised eyebrows. "We will have it ready, will we not?"

Felicity gave her niece a reassuring nod. "Yes, darling. We will."

"Good. Until dinner, then." Colonel Halstead bowed as they curtsied, smiled at Daphne, sent one last curiously amused glance to Felicity, then left the room.

"Educational?" Daphne looked to her aunt. "What do you think he meant by that?"

"I suspect he wasn't referring solely to your lessons." Felicity retook her seat, with as calm an expression as she could manage.

Did she trust Colonel Halstead? No. Not yet. But he was proving himself by degrees. What troubled her at that moment was the tickle of curiosity she felt at the back of her mind. Curiosity about him.

Yes, she definitely wanted to know more about Edward Halstead.

Chapter Five

The Black Swan Coffeehouse had changed nothing about its interior or menu in years, which was one reason Edward enjoyed visiting on the infrequent occasions that he came to London. They still had the board up with information on stock and trade, updated daily, as it had been in the days when all such business was conducted in coffeehouses. It still smelled of roasting coffee beans and gossip. There was still the same liveried men moving calmly about the place, delivering orders to tables. Edward took a seat at a table near the front window, his hat on a stand nearby, and ordered coffee and toast for himself.

He had ridden in the carriage with the ladies in relative silence, and left them at a seamstress's shop with promises to meet them for tea in a few hours' time. Miss Price had nodded curtly, Daphne had given him a shy smile, and both had disappeared inside the business without a backward glance.

Somehow, he had to win their trust. Daphne, sweet as she was, did not seem ready to trust him while her aunt held back—which marked the girl as intelligent, measuring her response to him by someone who she already knew had her best interests at heart. It was Miss Felicity Price he needed to convince of his suitability as a guardian.

Her, and all of London.

The bells above the door chimed, and Edward looked with hope for the friend he intended to meet, but it was not him, merely two other unknown gentlemen who doffed hats and took seats, talking about a boxing match with enthusiasm.

Edward wrinkled his nose in distaste. After years spent fighting, he had little love for fisticuffs, or hunting. Truly, most of the sport other men enjoyed made him feel somewhat ill. He did not begrudge them their entertainment or exercise, he merely wished for more peaceful forms of it for himself. One of the men speaking glanced his way, and only then did Edward recognize him. He nodded. The other man turned his head and hesitated before doing the same, then pointedly gave no word of greeting and back to his conversation with his companion.

Not everyone would forget his name tied to past scandal, it would seem, despite the two decades between his youthful indiscretions and the present. He focused on his coffee, ignoring the weight of the past pressing upon his chest.

This was precisely why he was here. He needed advice—guidance—in navigating London Society's twisted paths, for Daphne's sake. Even if he'd rather stay at home, tucked away in the countryside, where life was simpler.

The bells jingled again and this time it was his friend, Frederick Baker, who entered the room. Baker raised his hand the moment he spied Edward, and called out a cheerful, "Halstead, here you are at last!"

Edward rose, exchanging a hearty handshake with his old army friend. "Baker, good to see you again. What's it been? Five months?"

"Eight, you rascal." Baker slapped his shoulder with his free hand and took his seat as Edward did the same. After a staff member took Baker's order, he continued as though without interruption. "It is good to see you leave your hermitage on occasion. Your letter yesterday afternoon gave me a great deal of entertainment, you must know. I told my Hannah when I read it, 'You'll not believe what's happened to poor Halstead.' She laughed and said, 'Oh, dear. He will not know what to do with any of it.'"

"I am glad I provided some amusement to your lovely wife and you." Edward smiled, despite the jest at his expense. "You know me better than most, so it seemed natural to turn to you."

"Ha! Truly, you ought to have asked Hannah to coffee. She is the one who manages our family. Three children, two of them girls! Aye, Hannah would be the best for advice on taking a young female into your home."

"I have no doubt of that." Edward lowered his coffee cup to the table, taking in his friend's relaxed posture and cheerful grin. "But I told you that my ward, Daphne, came with someone who knows how to manage."

"The aunt? Yes. How grim, to be saddled with a spritely youthful ward and a grim miserly spinster as companion at the same time." Baker shook his head with some show of sympathy. "I suppose the aunt will do well enough for now, especially with Miss Daphne Price so near an age to be wed. Yet your letter spoke of needing advice—so how might I advise you?" Baker folded his arms and leaned back in his chair, a crooked grin upon his face.

Edward shifted in his chair, feeling his size more than usual as his knee knocked against a table leg. He managed not to wince, a control gained from practice. "I have been out of Society for so long, I must make my own re-entry before I can even hope to introduce Daphne to the people who matter, let alone receive invitations to the best parties and balls."

"Have you gone to the clubs yet and put your name down? Or the Assembly Rooms?" Baker asked, eyebrows raised.

"No." At this point, Edward truly wished he might shrink himself. The most he could do was hunch his shoulders. "I...I must confess that I have not. I am not certain how such a thing would be received in the Assembly Rooms, especially since it was made quite clear some time ago that I am not welcome at either Brook's or White's."

At this, Baker blinked. "What's that, man? Not welcome? But you must know many of their members, and you likely served with many, too. You must surely qualify for entry on your military record alone."

Edward had to shake his head. He lowered his voice, wondering whether a more private conversation may have suited better. "I attempted, eleven or so years ago, to join both. Members put my name forward, seconded my request. I was rejected."

"Blackballed," his friend said, the word a whisper. "But who would do such a thing?"

Edward had sworn to keep the important secret, not for his own sake, but for the sake of another. Anything that touched on that secret he did not dare speak of, lest he break his word and bring harm to another. At White's, the father of the girl he had loved had, anonymously, vetoed his membership. At Brook's, it was the man who had married that girl after Edward's father had sent him away and told his son to forget about her. Neither story could be told.

He evaded the question. "Does it matter? I am not permitted to join either of the most well-respected and well-known clubs in London." He rubbed a hand across his forehead and heaved a sigh. "What else might I do to move into better circles for Daphne's sake?"

"You certainly cannot simply throw her into the Season and hope for the best." In the long moment of silence between them, Baker's coffee and a table of biscuits were delivered to the table. His friend turned his coffee cup one way and then the other, then sipped at it. "You are right. You need invitations, connections. Friends. For that, you must be seen and known by the right people. You will have invitations to my home and small entertainments, of course, but as you know, none of my children are old enough to enter the marriage mart. There will not be suitors for your ward in my home."

"A shame." Edward looked at his toast which had cooled in the time he had waited for his friend, and briefly debated eating it. The dry bread would likely stick to his throat. Perhaps he'd choke. That would gain attention from everyone in the room, at least. "It is a pity there are not more places for a man to find himself the right sort of friends."

"Oh." Baker sat up straighter. "There is another club."

"Boodle's? I do not think—"

"No, no. Blackstone's."

Edward considered the name a moment. "The name that sounds familiar, I am not certain I remember many details about that club."

"It is located at the edge of Mayfair and St. James's." Baker brightened considerably. "And it is a respectable enough establishment, even if it is known for collecting members who are a bit... well. Varied, might be the safest word to use."

Frowning, Edward tried to remember what he had heard about the club. "Blackstone," he murmured, picking up his coffee. "The proprietor is a lord, is he not?"

"A viscount, yes," Baker said with a slight nod. "Must be somewhere in his sixties now. He is an interesting fellow. His club members do not vote on new entries, it is Lord Blackstone alone who decides if someone can join."

"I cannot recall with any clarity how reputable this club is. How can I be certain a membership there will be a help to Daphne, rather than a hindrance?"

Baker sipped at his drink. "Lord Blackstone is respectable, for all that Society knows he is eccentric. He is a viscount, and a wealthy one at that. He donates to worthy causes—there is nothing questionable about his reputation. Those associated with his club are deemed to be of similar ilk—well bred, with sufficient funds, but with no interest in being in the fashionable set. It is well known he has ousted men from his club for acting as scoundrels or for ill-mannered behavior. If you are in his good graces, others will regard you as a comfortable guest, if not a highly sought after member of a party."

Comfortable. That sounded perfect. Especially for one as out of practice with the fashionable set as Edward.

"Some think the club is a place for misfits, of course," Baker said with a dismissive wave of his hand. "Others, the more open mind sort, see it as a club for independent thinkers—for men with varied interests. You would not be the first soldier to join, for instance. You would not feel at odds at Blackstone's."

Edward found himself nodding. "Yes. It sounds like I ought to at least find a way to meet Lord Blackstone."

"I can arrange an introduction." Baker's grin reappeared wider than before, a hint of pompous delight in his air. "My wife's brother is a member of that club."

The weight of responsibility pressed upon him again, all the heavier for the conversation and realization of how much depended upon him impressing this 'eccentric' Lord Blackstone. Edward was not a man to rely on others; even this request of coffee with Baker had been a hard letter to write. He turned his coffee cup slowly in his hands. "I never thought I would have to re-enter Society at all. Much less for the sake of another."

Baker appraised him without pity. "That is what guardianship is. You are not merely managing an estate, Halstead. You are shaping the future for your ward—her future."

The words landed upon him like lodestones. He swallowed the last of his coffee and set the cup down with deliberate care. Daphne's future was in his hands. If he mis-stepped, if he failed, what would become of her?

Miss Price's dire warnings echoed in his mind.

Failure was not an option.

"There's more to this reluctance of yours than time away from your hermitage, isn't there?" Baker mused, watching Edward's fingers tighten slightly around the handle of his cup.

Edward chuckled, rolling his shoulders to ease the tension in them, but made no reply.

"A man doesn't spend two decades avoiding Society without reason," Baker continued, his tone turning speculative. "A man of your caliber doesn't get turned down from one, let alone two, clubs. Just what happened to you all those years ago, Halstead?"

"Nothing Society would care to remember," he finally muttered, and before Baker could press, he added, "But since I must make my return, I might as well do it somewhere I still have a chance." He met Baker's gaze and forced a smile. "When can you introduce me to Lord Blackstone?"

THE BELL ABOVE THE DOOR CHIMED AS FELICITY AND DAPHNE stepped into Keller's Fine Stationery & Engraving, the warm scent of ink, pressed paper, and beeswax polish greeting them like an old friend. The shop was small but elegant, refined and respectable, with high shelves stacked with bound ledgers, writing folios, and reams of paper in every shade from crisp white to a deep blue.

A clerk in a modest coat and dark blue waistcoat looked up from a glass counter where he was arranging gilt-edged invitations. He gave them a practiced bow. "Good afternoon, ladies. How may I be of service?"

Daphne glanced at Felicity for reassurance, and she gave her niece a small nod. They had discussed this errand at length before leaving Briarwood, and Felicity wanted Daphne to feel a sense of ownership over her preparations. It would also give her greater confidence, to speak to shopkeepers herself. It would not be long before she would have to impress much greater personages.

"I wish to order calling cards," Daphne said, her voice carefully composed but bright with repressed excitement. "On the account of Colonel Halstead."

"Ah, yes. We received a letter from his agent yesterday." The clerk perked up considerably upon understanding who would pay their bill. He had seemed polite before, but now he wore a rather warm smile.

"We will also need stationery," Felicity added smoothly. "A lady requires the proper materials for correspondence, after all."

"Of course," the clerk said, stepping from behind the counter. "Would you care to browse our selection of papers? We have a variety of finishes—smooth vellum, woven, laid—"

"Oh!" Daphne's eyes lit up as she drifted toward a polished wooden case displaying thick paper stock in shades of ivory, pearl, and pale blue. She ran a gloved fingertip over the embossed edges of a soft pink sheet, a touch of longing in her expression— an expression Felicity had not seen in weeks. "This is lovely. What do you think of this one, Aunt?"

Felicity followed her gaze. The paper was delicate and charming, suited for a young woman with romantic sensibilities...but not exactly practical for formal occasions.

"It is very pretty," she agreed, keeping her tone neutral. "But it may be best to select something more traditional for formal correspondence. You want to make a refined first impression, not a frivolous one."

Daphne hesitated, then turned toward the clerk. "What is the most common choice for a young lady to send letters?"

The man folded his hands behind his back, considering. "Cream or ivory, miss. They are the most elegant and timeless. But younger ladies who prefer a touch of charm favor a refined pink."

Daphne's brow furrowed, clear indecision flickering across her face.

Felicity softened. She remembered what it was like to be seventeen, caught between youthful fancies and the rigid expectations of the world. Her fancies had never been indulged by her parents. They had always insisted on practicality over sentimentality. Besides, it was not as though she had been in Society recently; perhaps habits had changed. Perhaps a little frivolity for her niece was no bad thing.

Which made her feel somewhat guilty as she said, "Perhaps a set of each? The pink for private notes to friends, the cream for formal correspondence?"

Daphne's face brightened. "That is an excellent idea!"

"Very well, then," Felicity said, turning to the enthusiastic clerk. "We will require a selection of writing paper in both shades. We will also need a set of calling cards in each as well—engraved, of course—with Miss Price's name and direction. A set of fountain pens, ideally engraved with her name, and a set of pencils, too. And a blotter. And an inkwell set. And some ink."

Well, if the Colonel was in earnest about establishing Daphne for the Season she deserved...

The clerk smiled. "A fine choice, miss. And what will you require for yourself?"

Felicity hesitated a moment before giving a polite but firm shake of her head. She had no need for calling cards—she was not in Society, nor did she have many acquaintances outside of those who already knew where to find her. Besides, it was not her life that Colonel Halstead had agreed to fund. "Only Miss Price today."

As the clerk made note of the order, the bell above the shop door chimed once more. A tall, stately woman swept into the shop, her gown of deep blue silk rustling as she moved. A maid followed behind her, carrying on her arm a small reticule and an ivory fan.

Felicity instinctively straightened, recognizing the quiet air of importance that a lady of high standing exuded as naturally as breathing. Daphne, still flipping through paper samples, hadn't yet noticed the newcomer.

But Felicity had a feeling this woman had already noticed them.

The newly arrived lady glanced around the shop, taking in the shelves, the clerk, and finally, Felicity and Daphne. There was no immediate smile, no recognition, merely a calculated sweep of the eyes, the sort of look a seasoned Society matron gave when assessing the worth of her surroundings.

But Felicity recognized the Countess of Kendal immediately.

The lady moved forward, her posture effortlessly regal, her dark blue silk gown skimming the polished wooden floor. A string of pearls lay at her throat, her gloves pristine, her bonnet framing a face which had once been undoubtedly beautiful, now retaining beauty but refined with age and experience.

Daphne, oblivious for a moment, continued sorting through the samples.

The lady's gaze lingered on her, then shifted briefly to Felicity. *And there it was.*

The moment of recognition, followed almost immediately by dismissal. A flicker of politeness, but no real interest. Felicity had seen it many times before. She was a genteel spinster, and in the world of the ton, that made her invisible.

Once, long ago, she might have harbored hope that a woman of standing would see her as something more than a chaperone. A friend. An equal. But unmarried women of a certain age were ornaments of naught but practicality, noticed as far as they were useful and then summarily ignored. She had learned to carry that invisibility like a shawl, worn tightly and without complaint.

Daphne, however, was young, fresh, and eligible, untainted by the world's critique or censor. That made her worth attention.

The woman turned slightly, addressing the clerk in a voice that was pleasant but carried quiet authority. "I came to see if the sample for my daughter's stationery is ready, Mr. Keller."

The clerk bowed immediately. "Of course, Lady Kendal. I will have it brought at once."

Lady Kendal. A widow, two daughters, one of them just older than Daphne's age, the other a little older, from Felicity's memory. She had met the woman when she had come out, ten years before. The countess hadn't been impressed with her then and would not be impressed with her now. But it was not her own reputation she wished to impress.

Lady Kendal turned her piercing gaze back toward them. "Miss Price. It has been a long time. I do not believe I know your young companion," she said smoothly.

Felicity resisted the urge to stiffen, not from nerves, but from years of ingrained experience. She already knew what was coming.

"Lady Kendal," she said evenly. "May I present my niece, Miss Daphne Price?"

Daphne, to her credit, curtsied immediately and gracefully. "A pleasure to meet you, my lady."

Lady Kendal's lips curved slightly, and though it was not quite a smile, it was close enough to pass for one. "Another Miss Price," she said, giving her a slow nod of acknowledgment. Only then did she return her attention fleetingly to Felicity.

"And you are her chaperone rather than her sponsor this Season, *Miss* Price?"

The words were delivered lightly, but with an air of certainty. Felicity's cheeks burned. She was still a miss: she hadn't corrected the countess with a husband's name, and she wore the drab, modest clothes of a matron in mourning.

But she smiled, smooth as ever. "For now, yes. Her guardian, Colonel Halstead, supports that decision."

Lady Kendal expression flickered with surprise, followed by a moment's recalculation. "Ah. Colonel Halstead. I am somewhat familiar with that name. A gentleman soldier, is he not? Well, well. I had not heard he had a young lady under his care."

"It is a new development," Felicity said, tone even. "The death of my brother was unexpected. We are both grateful for Colonel Halstead's willingness to take his duty seriously."

The Countess returned her gaze to Daphne. "When will you be out of mourning, child?"

"My guardian and aunt believe it will be appropriate to attend events the first week of March," she answered demurely, after a quick glance at her aunt. "Though I will keep some reminder of my father on my person for a long time to come."

She touched the necklace she wore, a simple pendant on a black ribbon.

"There are no strict rules of how long one ought to wear black, of course," the countess said, glancing at Felicity's all black attire. "Let there be no doubt that you loved your father, my dear, and most will understand."

"That is wise counsel, Lady Kendal." Daphne kept her eyes lowered, and Felicity could not help feeling proud of her.

Yes, there were those who would comment about Daphne's abbreviated time in black, but there were no true rules written about when one could cast off mourning without someone thinking it too soon. Besides, Daphne's father would not want her to waste away in shadow when she was so young and full of life.

"Hmmm. And is this your first time to visit London?"

"Yes, Lady Kendal." The young lady braved her own question, and Felicity tried not to smile in quiet pride. "Are you often in Town?"

The lady nodded stiffly. "Yes. It is my primary place of residence. My youngest daughter, Lady Louisa, is only a year older than you, I believe. She will make her debut in court this Season."

Daphne lit up, genuine pleasure in her smile. "How lovely for her."

Lady Kendal's gaze assessed her in a way that Felicity recognized too well; appraising, weighing pedigree, manners, and potential connections. Then she smiled slightly, a hint of satisfaction in the curve of her lips. "It would be well for young ladies of similar age and experience to become acquainted before the Season begins properly," she said smoothly. "I shall mention you to Louisa and see if we might arrange a time to meet."

Daphne looked to Felicity, eyes shining, as if seeking permission.

Felicity, despite the sting of being so thoroughly dismissed, gave her niece a nod of approval. It was down to her niece, now, to start forming these connections.

"That is most generous, my lady," Daphne said pleasantly.

Lady Kendal barely acknowledged her response. Instead, she returned her attention to the clerk, speaking as though neither of the other ladies were there at all. She looked over the stationery with gold embossed lettering, nodded, and gave direction for a few adjustments. "Do be sure my daughter's stationery is prepared before the end of the week, Mr. Keller. We will require it in time for several important invitations."

Felicity's hands folded carefully in front of her. This was Society; a place where youth mattered more than intelligence, and breeding mattered more than good sense. Where marriageable young ladies were seen, and spinsters were merely tolerated. She had long since accepted that this was her place in the world, but the sting of it never fully faded.

Daphne, however, was delighted. When Lady Kendal remembered them long enough to bid them a courteous farewell and swept from the shop, Daphne practically hummed with excitement.

"Aunt Felicity, can you believe it? She wants me to meet her daughter—Lady Kendal! A lady! Oh, this is a good first step, is it not?"

Felicity forced a smile, smoothing a hand over her jacket. "Yes, darling. Wonderful indeed."

Because it was. For Daphne. That was all that mattered.

But as she turned back to the counter to approve the engravings for Daphne's calling cards, Felicity found herself unable to shake the reminder—yet again—of precisely where she stood on the rungs of London's fashionable set: as close to the bottom as one could be before actually becoming a servant.

It was a thought she pushed far from her mind as they continued on to other errands until the time came to rejoin Colonel Halstead for tea. The tea shop he had suggested was warm and bustling, the scent of fresh bread and spiced cakes mingling with the sharp notes of steeping leaves. Felicity and Daphne arrived just before the appointed time, the weight of their parcels slightly burdensome but nothing they couldn't manage. They had ordered most things to be delivered to Briarwood House, but a few items had seemed important to keep with them. At least, Daphne had wanted to keep them, and Felicity could hardly deny her such a small thing.

She spotted Edward Halstead at once. He sat near the window, an untouched cup of tea before him, his broad shoulders making the delicate chair seem far too small for his frame. The sight of him in such a genteel and feminine setting, amid painted porcelain cups and cream cloth-draped tables, doilies covering every spare inch amidst the soft pink of the wallpaper, was almost amusing. He looked like a soldier placed in the middle of a garden party, yet he wore the scene well, appearing at ease despite his incongruity.

Daphne hesitated only a moment before moving toward him, fingers clutching the fabric of her skirt in a nervous gesture Felicity recognized. It was strange how easily Daphne had engaged with Lady Kendal earlier, yet now, in front of Colonel Halstead, she turned shy again.

"Colonel Halstead," Daphne greeted him with a small curtsy.

The gentleman rose immediately, bowing with precise courtesy before gesturing for them to take their seats. "Miss Price, Miss Daphne." His gaze flickered over the packages they carried. "I see the day has been productive."

Felicity settled into her chair, careful with her movements. It was a small effort, but after hours of standing, walking, and enduring subtle slights, she felt the ache in her legs and shoulders. Her gown was still tidy, her bonnet and hair still in place, but the strain of the day draped around her like a too-heavy shawl she could not take off.

"Very productive," she said lightly. "Daphne now has her calling cards and writing paper ordered. She has been measured for a new wardrobe appropriate for a young lady of her station. We were even given the unexpected honor of meeting the Countess of Kendal."

Colonel Halstead lifted a brow. "An honor?"

Daphne brightened, though she cast a quick glance at her aunt before saying, "She was very kind. She suggested I might make the acquaintance of her daughter, Lady Louisa, before the Season begins."

Colonel Halstead's expression gave nothing away, but Felicity caught the way his gaze flickered over Daphne, assessing. Was there anyone in Society who wasn't measuring up their neighbor? "That is good fortune, indeed," he said quietly. "Lady Kendal is well respected in London."

"Yes," Felicity murmured, lifting her teacup to her lips to hide her wry smile. *Well respected, indeed. And well practiced in the art of social dismissal.*

Colonel Halstead's attention shifted to her. "And you, Miss Price?" His voice was as even as ever, but there was something in the way he regarded her which made her straighten slightly. An unexpected flicker of interest in his eyes. What did it mean? "How did you find your day?"

Felicity took a breath, composing herself. There was no point in lingering on old wounds. She was accustomed to them, after all. "Quite satisfactory," she answered, choosing her words carefully. "We accomplished a great deal. Miss Daphne was the focus of our time, as she should be."

Colonel Halstead said nothing at first, only stirred his tea absently before speaking again. "That does not exactly answer my question."

Felicity's fingers tightened around her cup. *Observant man.*

Before she could formulate a response, Daphne leaned forward slightly, her shyness giving way to earnest enthusiasm. "Aunt Felicity is being modest. She has been guiding me all day, and has helped me choose the best of everything—and she never once thought of herself, though I did try to have her spend at least some of her own funds on something pretty or even useful for herself. She would not take even a moment to consider doing so— but then, she never does."

The gentleman's gaze sharpened on Felicity, something unreadable in his expression.

Felicity forced a small smile. "It is a chaperone's duty to ensure the young lady in her charge is properly provided for. Besides, I have no personal needs at present. That is all." It had been years since anyone expected Felicity Price to indulge in anything simply for the pleasure of it. That was a privilege for young women with futures ahead of them. Her days of acquiring pretty things for herself had ended when she realized there was no one left in the world who cared whether she wore pink roses or daisies in her hair.

A silence settled between them for a moment, but before Colonel Halstead could speak again, a server arrived to take their order. Grateful for the reprieve, Felicity changed the topic the moment the server left, keeping Daphne engaged in sharing her thoughts about London thus far. Though she caught Colonel Halstead's gaze on her several times, his expression somewhat worrisome, he appeared to study her for a purpose. Perhaps trying to determine whether she would be invited to stay or told to go.

How could she convince him he needed her to remain in Daphne's life?

Chapter Six

The next day, Felicity helped Daphne rearrange the furniture in the room they'd chosen as their primary place to pass the afternoon. With the cool winter sun coming through the western facing windows, the room had enough light and natural warmth to make the small hearth enough to keep them comfortable. Together, despite her niece's suggestion that they request the assistance of a footman which Felicity had sternly declined, they shifted the settee to sit between the window and fireplace, then moved the three chairs to make the sitting more cozy if they welcomed guests.

"Pardon me, Miss Price." A voice from the doorway had Felicity turning to see one of the young footmen there, his brow furrowed in curiosity as he looked around the room.

"Yes, Peter? What is it?"

He blinked and his expression became neutral once more. "Colonel Halstead has asked that you come to his study, Miss Price. To discuss an important matter, he said."

"Oh." She looked at Daphne with raised eyebrows and a limp smile. "I wonder what he could need now. Why don't you find a book to read, dear? I am certain I won't be long." Despite her words, her stomach twisted with worry.

Was this it? The moment when he would tell her he would hire a suitable companion, that her presence was no longer needed? True, it was somewhat unconventional for her, a member of Daphne's family, to stay in a bachelor's home. But surely it made a great deal more sense to keep her than it did to hire someone else to chaperone Daphne—another stranger?

Felicity made her way to the study, walking through the bare-walled corridors, her steps echoing off the walls far too loudly. When she came to the study, the door was already open. Still, she hesitated on the threshold.

This was surely the moment where she would discover her fate.

Colonel Halstead sat at his desk, head bowed as he made a notation in a book. His red-brown hair fell across his forehead in loose waves, his brow furrowed as he concentrated on his writing. He wasn't wearing a coat. It looked as though he had cast it off on the back of the chair, leaving him in white shirtsleeves. Somehow, the absence of the dark fabric made him look even larger than usual. Broader.

She had never particularly noticed the breadth of a man's shoulders before, certainly not when they were hunched in concentration over estate accounts. Her brother had been... Anthony. She had barley registered his appearance. But there was something...steadfast about the Colonel. Solid in a way that unsettled her, as though this house's weight rested entirely on his shoulders.

"Do come in, Miss Price. I will not bite." He spoke without looking up.

Felicity stilled in surprise. He had to have heard her coming, of course. There was no carpet outside his study.

She entered quietly, approaching his desk. There she stood, waiting patiently for an invitation to sit. Though the abrupt sound of his voice had startled her, he had not spoken harshly. Indeed, his deep voice was low. Gentle, even. It struck her that she had not yet heard him raise it, nor speak harshly to man or beast.

68

He put the pen down on the blotter and looked up at her, his green eyes somewhat less bright than normal. "Oh do sit, Miss Price. You need never stand on ceremony with me. I had quite enough of that during my time in the army."

She complied, sitting in one of the comfortable chairs across the desk from him. "You do not speak of that time often, sir. Not at any of the meals or conversations you have had with Daphne and me." She looked down at her lap, clasping her hands there. "Anthony rarely spoke of such things, either. He once told me that the less a man spoke of his time at war, the more my brother respected him."

A moment of thoughtful silence passed before she heard Colonel Halstead's sigh. "I agree with your late brother." Felicity glanced up to see him pass a hand over his eyes. "War is nothing to speak of lightly, nor are there as many glorious moments within it as old ballads and tales would have you believe. It is a violent, heart-breaking time, and no man who sees a battle can ever be the same as he was before."

Here was more revealed to her about him than she had heard before, and Felicity could not let that be all she learned. Carefully, keeping her voice soft and tone polite, she asked, "How long were you in the army, Colonel Halstead?"

"Eighteen years," he said, gaze focused on her once more. "I became an Ensign at eighteen years old. I resigned my commission shortly before Waterloo." He grimaced, his jaw going tighter. "I am both grateful and ashamed I was not there that day. I had no way of knowing what a battle that would be. How…how it would shape the fate and end the lives of so many men."

The words he spoke were strained, carrying a sharpness that pricked her heart. There was not a person in England who did not understand what Waterloo has cost their nation in blood.

"After so long in the military, half your lifetime, why did you decide to leave?" she asked softly. She would neither soothe his conscience nor offer him censure. What did she, a spinster with a comfortable life, know of war? She had no right to speak against him, nor enough familiarity to comfort him. Best to merely move the conversation along.

The Colonel cleared his throat and stood, tucking his hands behind his back in a surely unconscious gesture as he went to the window. "In March of 1815, my older brother sent for me. I took leave to return home, for my father was dying. There were things he wished to tell me before he passed. We had spoken little to one another since I became a soldier, you see."

"Did he not approve?" Most men, to her understanding, took pride in their sons serving in the military.

"Oh, he is the one who forced me in," the Colonel said, looking over his shoulder enough to offer her a bitter smile. "It was I who disapproved—at least for the first few years that I served. But, after a time, I saw the importance of what I was doing. I accepted that my father may have understood better than I did how to take the wild, reckless youth I had been and mold me into a more responsible, more honorable man. Still, I often found myself at odds with him every time I returned home. Even that last time, when he was weak in his bed, I was angry with him."

It was quite the confession to make to a near stranger, but it did not make her uncomfortable. If anything, Felicity felt more at ease with the man. It was disarming, this glimpse of vulnerability. She had expected the Colonel to be as rigid as the walls of his study, as sparse with detail as he had been with his décor. Instead, he was proving himself all too human. Besides, Felicity wanted to understand him better, which was a most inconvenient feeling.

Here was another sign of his humanity, his imperfections. "I imagine you had good reason for such feelings. After he passed away, did you forgive him?"

Colonel Halstead turned fully to face her, hands still behind his back, eyes on hers. "Not quite. But I grow closer to that point every day." He gave her a measured look, as though realizing how much he had revealed. "Miss Price, I don't know why I am telling you all of this."

Felicity remained still, uncertain what to say, but he gave a dry, almost self-deprecating chuckle.

"Perhaps because we are about to be comrades in arms of another sort."

She tilted her head to the side as her curiosity and hope flickered brighter. Hope? Good heavens, what nonsense. What exactly did she hope for? Cooperation, surely. An agreement that she was best suited to secure Daphne's future, nothing more personal than that. And yet, when he smiled at her in that quiet, knowing way, the thought lingered, stubborn as a weed.

"Comrades in arms, Colonel?"

He nodded once, decisively. "I have been thinking on it, and I believe it is in everyone's best interest that you remain at Briarwood with Daphne for the foreseeable future."

She drew in a breath, schooling her expression into polite neutrality, but inside—inside she felt blissful relief. Oh, thank the heavens.

"For Daphne's sake, of course," she said aloud, quite certain of herself when it came to caring for her niece.

Colonel Halstead smiled, amusement once again in his eyes. "For Daphne's sake," he agreed.

Her whole body relaxed. He would not replace her with a paid companion or female relative of his own. The Colonel would keep her in his home, where she could see to it that Daphne was looked after, loved, and eventually married well. Then her life's work would be complete.

In that moment, she almost liked the man. Certainly she felt distinct gratitude toward him.

His gaze went down to the desk, and hers followed. The surface was organized, but quite full of stacks of papers, books, and—she noticed for the first time—cloth samples.

"Colonel," she said, looking at all of it with raised eyebrows. "It appears you are under attack."

His posture stiffened, and he shook his head slightly. "I beg your pardon?"

She gestured to the desk. "From matters of business. You look quite overrun." She had never seen her father's, nor Anthony's, desk so littered with papers. "Have you no secretary? A steward, or a man of business?"

"Oh, this?" Colonel Halstead put his hand down on the large stack of books. "It is not so bad as it seems, though there is no secretary, and my man of business keeps threatening to retire. I have been told I ought to consider a steward of my own rather than sharing my neighbor's, but that seems like nonsense considering how small the estate is, and I have only two tenants." He tapped the books again. "These are for my personal edification and enjoyment." He gestured to a stack of paper. "This is correspondence I have already answered and wish to file away." Another stack. "These are bills paid." Another. "Bills yet to be paid." And the final stack of books. "Ledgers for the income of the estate going back to before I bought the place a few years ago."

Hearing he bought his home rather than inherited it did not surprise her. Many a man had made his fortune during the war and returned to England in a far better financial position. He had told her about his father and older brother but moments before, too. What had they been, in Society's rungs? "How do you find being a landowner, Colonel?"

A smile with a somewhat rueful tilt grew upon his face, and Felicity caught herself returning it as he said, "Commanding a company of mules would be an easier feat, but this one is arguably more rewarding."

Her laugh nearly escaped, but Felicity pressed her lips together in time to stop such a thing. "And now you have a young lady to contend with."

"She does not seem so fearsome a foe." He retook his seat with his smile still in place, folding his arms across his chest and leaning back in his chair, gaze fixed on her. "From all I have seen, she is an even-tempered girl, clever too. Eager to like others and be liked in turn. Though certainly a touch shy with strangers."

"Daphne is still in mourning." Felicity rested her elbows on the arms of the chair, clasping her hands before her. "Her grief will be of a longer duration than the time we limit her to wearing mourning colors—but I do see glimmers of her usual cheerful demeanor returning. Then she seems to remember her loss, and she grows solemn again. I hope you come to know her fully. She is a delightful young lady. Kind, cheerful, and quite talented musically."

"I look forward to hearing her perform when the pianoforte arrives." He looked up at the ceiling for a moment. "I am told the room you wish to put it in is the one above my study?"

Felicity stilled. "Oh. Yes." She looked up at the ceiling, then out the window. Oh dear. "I had not fully realized the positioning…"

"It will be a delight to listen to her play as I work," he said, and she met his gaze again. Though his smile had faded, there was no doubting the sincerity in his tone. "Whether she is as talented as you say, or not. This house is far too quiet. I did not realize it until you both arrived. The servants walk as silently as ghosts, which leaves only me to stomp about it most of the time. It eases something, to hear the muffled voices of others in the house, to hear footsteps on the stairs. The house feels more alive with you both here."

Felicity blinked at him, and for some strange reason, she felt heat creeping up her throat and into her cheeks. Surely, she was not blushing? Not at her age! She was too mature for such things. Too…well. Too much a spinster.

Really. He hadn't said anything especially flattering, either.

"A dog or two would accomplish a similar thing, you know," she said, trying to keep her tone light. Uncaring. "Most gentlemen keep hounds about, I believe, for companionship."

The Colonel chuckled. "You are not the first person to suggest a four-legged companion. I fear I do not have it in me to hunt, so most good dogs would be rather wasted on me. They are bred for such a life, and I would not take in a creature only to keep it from its purpose."

That idea ticked at her thoughts. A man who did not hunt was one thing, but to think of the preferences of an animal in such a way… She did not know what to make of it.

"We were speaking of Daphne, though," Colonel Halstead said, before she could think of a thing to say. "I think another foray into London is in order, and soon. I wish to show her some of the sights she mentioned in the list you gave me—you likely have more purchases to make, too."

She nodded. "Though I want to assure you, Colonel, that I am aware of the monthly stipend from the trust for her upkeep. I promise to keep well within the budget of that amount."

"I have every confidence in your practicality, Miss Price." He continued to seem relaxed, even a little more amused by her. "You do not strike me as a spendthrift—though I have an important matter regarding finances to address with you. You may find it indelicate for me to do so, but as you are going to be a member of this household, and therefore part of my responsibility, I hope you will see why I feel the need to speak so openly on the matter at hand."

Felicity's heart stuttered. A member of a new household. She truly was to stay. "I understand, of course. What is it you wish to address?"

He did not seem unduly upset. Previous experience warned her, however, that when a man discussed finances with a woman, it was most often to express disapproval over how money slipped from her fingers, despite her clear frugality.

Slowly, Colonel Halstead unfolded his arms to put his elbows on the desk, leaning forward. "Miss Price, I am aware of Daphne's situation with her father's trust, the amount of pin money she is used to, and the size of her dowry. I have been informed, too, of her inheritance, the house and other particulars. She was well cared for in that regard by her father, though I will certainly add my own funds to support her upkeep, especially with regards to making this house a home for her."

"Thank you for that," Felicity said, her voice soft. For Daphne's sake, she would always be grateful.

He moved his hand, flicking his fingers almost as though to both acknowledge and dismiss her words. Not disrespectfully. Merely efficiently. A soldier's habit. "What I do not know, Miss Price, is whether *you* have funds enough to keep yourself comfortable and living in the manner with which you were accustomed in your brother's household. When Daphne expressed displeasure that you did not make purchases for yourself while we were in Town, I realized I know nothing about your financial situation. It may be crass, but I see no way to discover what I need to without being blunt. Forgive me, but is there enough money set aside for your needs?"

It was, indeed, an indelicate question. Inappropriate in many ways, too, she well knew...yet he had a point. And stranger still, his concern wasn't patronizing. He did not seem to pity her for her unmarried state nor see her as an inconvenience to be managed. He simply wanted to ensure she was comfortable.

How rare. How unexpectedly kind.

Felicity swallowed. She supposed that as a member of his household, even if she was not precisely his responsibility, he had a right to concern himself with such matters. Even if the discussion was a little...unsavory.

"I am not a pauper," she said, hands tightening around the arms of the chair. "I have my own monthly stipend from the inheritance my parents left me, along with a generous gift from my late brother's will. It is a modest amount, all told, but it is enough to set up a small household for myself, or procure rented rooms in a respectable neighborhood in Bath, if I should wish."

"Hm." Her host regarded her seriously for another moment. "There is an amount set aside, in Price's will, for a paid companion for Daphne. If you would benefit from receiving such funds—"

"No, I thank you," she said at once, interrupting him with a flush to her cheeks. "Daphne is my niece. It is my duty to look after her so long as I am able—I would never, I could never dream

SALLY BRITTON

of accepting a wage for such a thing." Felicity shuddered, the mere thought repellent. "Leave it to go to her when she weds."

"You truly have enough?" The man regarded her with an expression which had likely served him well in the army. It was serious. A lesser woman might have ducked her head beneath such a grave stare.

Felicity tipped her chin up. "More than is necessary, Colonel Halstead."

"Just Halstead is fine," he said, then continued before she could protest that familiarity. "If that is true, Miss Price, then I am content. But should you need anything at all, I will gladly lend my assistance. I understand Daphne must attend all manner of events, and I know female wardrobes are far more extensive than a man's, so you will likely require as much in the way of gowns and finery as she will. You must both be turned out in your best to impress the families of potential suitors."

That thought had not occurred to her, and the realization that her own modest attire could reflect poorly on Daphne silenced the protests rising to her lips. *Bother.* "You…you may have a point, Colonel."

"Halstead," he repeated quietly. "Please."

She shook her head, the suggestion utterly at odds with her feelings. "I cannot possibly be on such familiar terms with you, sir."

"Everyone outside of this house, all the servants, call me by my rank," he said, his voice low. Almost sad, she thought. "At times— well, it feels as though I have never left the army. And besides," his tone changed to something lighter, though it struck Felicity as a false levity. "We are comrades in arms now, joined by our cause. That makes us equals, Miss Price, so I must insist, call me Halstead. At least when we are in this house, or when others cannot hear us."

The request was a simple one, and it was the only thing he had asked of her when she had demanded so much of him. True, Felicity had done it all for Daphne, not to earn the man's good

opinion; but he was a good man, and he had agreed to do everything he could for his new ward.

Including keeping Felicity in his home.

"Very well," she said at last. "Halstead. Will you call me Price,
then?"

"That was what I called your brother." His smile reappeared.

"And what his other friends called him," she said, her heart
aching at her loss. She knew from experience that the ache would
never fully go away, merely lessen with time. "I suppose it must be
Felicity, then. I have no other names or titles."

"I could give you one. You would make a fierce captain."
Though he said the words without a smile, his eyes twinkled, and
she realized he was…teasing her.

The stoic, proper colonel, teasing her!

Truly, she ought to insist on being Miss Price and nothing
more. That would be the proper, respectable thing to do. A very
spinsterly thing to do…which made her very much not want to do
it. "Very well," she said sternly, attempting not to smile. "I will be
Miss Price in formal occasions, and you may call me 'Captain' in
company and 'Felicity' in the house."

A broad grin broke out across his face, making an already
impressive visage suddenly quite attractive. It was dangerous,
how a grin transformed him. Dangerous because it made her want
to see it again.

Good heavens. The man had the sort of rugged attractiveness
to him that British ladies thought all soldiers ought to have.

Felicity felt the blush flooding up her neck again, and quickly
jumped to her feet. If she moved quickly enough, she might
escape before the heat made it into her cheeks. "Thank you for
letting me stay for Daphne, Colonel. Halstead. I mean—yes.
Thank you. I will let her know the happy news at once." She curtsied as he rose to his feet, whirled around and hurried to the
door.

"Of course," she heard him say. "I will see you both at dinner?"

Felicity paused in the doorway, barely looking over her shoulder. "Yes, of course. Until then." And did not wait a moment more to disappear from sight.

Blushing! Her! How could her body betray her so? And why? Of course, he had said kind things. And he was a handsome man. But that was no reason for her to flush like an addlepated schoolgirl.

How silly of her. Perhaps she had merely been overexcited by the good news. Yes, that had to be it: she was staying with Daphne. Relief had strengthened her reactions. And the Colonel—Halstead, that was. Halstead had been the source of the good news, so of course the blush had come on in his presence. It would not happen again.

At least, Felicity hoped it would not happen again.

Chapter Seven

Blackstone's Club stood where St. James and Mayfair collided, an unassuming building of similar construction to its neighbors. Edward stood on the pavement outside of the address, looking at it with the same trepidation he had felt when first summoned to a superior officer's presence. In his jacket pocket he possessed a letter of introduction from Baker's brother-in-law, a member of the club, vouching for him. That same gentleman, a Mr. Harold Marlowe, had sent a letter to Lord Blackstone to request that the viscount meet with Edward at his earliest convenience.

The summons had arrived the evening before, one week after Edward had met with Baker. The viscount was prompt, he would give him that.

Edward walked sedately up the few steps to the large black door of the Palladian style building, a private residence at some time in the past, and stared at the knocker for a moment. It looked like a crow's head. How...unusual. He had barely tapped the door before it opened, a man near his own age standing there, dressed in all black except for a crisp white cravat.

"Do you have an appointment?"

Edward blinked at the doorman, then nodded. "Yes. I was

invited to a meeting with Lord Blackstone." He reached into his jacket and held out the letter with Blackstone's seal. "I am Colonel Halstead."

The doorman looked at the letter, then took a book from beneath his arm—Edward hadn't seen it before that moment. He opened it, turned a page, ran his finger along the paper, then nodded and snapped the book shut. "Yes, your name is on my list. If you will follow me, Colonel Halstead?"

Edward stepped inside, where a footman stood ready to accept his hat and coat. He doffed the hat easily enough, but as he was slipping his arms free of his heavy coat, he froze as his gaze collided with the black glassy eyes of a rather large ram.

Or the head of the ram, at least. A stuffed head, mounted on the wall of the entry hall. And the ram wasn't alone. No, hunting trophies covered the walls, taxidermies of every conceivable quarry met his gaze and made his throat tighten.

Was this a gentleman's *hunting* club?

Swallowing back his discomfort, Edward finished taking off his coat and followed the doorman up the stairs, past more stuffed species than he cared to count, through a parlor, then down a narrow corridor filled with glass cases of yet more deceased creatures. Some of them were a little...well, odd. He noted a fox with spectacles on its nose, for one thing, and an owl with a university cap upon its head. He tried not to look at anything else too closely.

The servant knocked on a door, then opened it when a voice called for them to enter. The servant went first, bowed, then gestured to Edward. "Colonel Halstead to see you, my lord."

"Yes, yes. I've been expecting you, young man!" The voice, chipper in tone and possessing the somewhat rough quality that came with age, belonged to a man of small stature standing behind a large desk. He wore a smile, the sort with warmth more common in a friend than in a stranger. His brown eyes took Edward in with a sharpness that suggested either intelligence or a measure of madness. Perhaps both. His gray hair stood on end at the side of his head, though it was combed neatly on the top.

Edward attempted a formal tone. "I have not been called a young man in some time, Lord Blackstone."

The doorman had vanished, leaving Edward alone with the viscount.

"Eh, we are all young at heart when we have a measure of passion left in us, are we not?" The man gestured to the chairs across the desk from him. "Do sit down, do—we must conduct the interview with at least some measure of decorum, I suppose." He settled in his own chair, and Edward caught sight of the large painting behind the viscount.

It was a portrait unlike any Edward had seen before. It was a badger. A badger, wearing some sort of jacket. He blinked at it, then looked directly into the Viscount's eyes, hoping to avoid seeing anything else startling in the room.

The Viscount was stuffing a pipe. "I prefer to smoke when I conduct these things. Keeps me settled and on task, giving me something to do besides sit still and listen." He raised his eyebrows. "Do you smoke a pipe?"

Slowly, Edward nodded. "Yes. I took it up during my time in the army."

"As good an excuse as any." He lit his pipe, then puffed at it with a gleam of satisfaction in his eyes. "So long as you see to the hygiene of it, you know. Have to clean your teeth. Scrub out your beard, if you have one. I can't abide tobacco stains on teeth and in beards. Positively indecent. And what lady would want to kiss such a man?"

Edward blinked. "Erm." What sort of a question was that? "I cannot think of any of my acquaintance, my lord."

"Of course not. And you would know, it's a most practical concern for a bachelor." He narrowed his eyes at Edward. "Mr. Marlowe said you are unmarried in his letter. We've a fair number of unattached men in the club, you know."

"I did not," Edward said, shifting in his chair. At least it wasn't a delicate piece of furniture. It seemed sturdy enough that he wasn't worried about breaking it with one wrong move. "I am a bachelor. Is that a problem?"

"No." Lord Blackwell puffed at his pipe again. "Not for me. I wonder if it is a difficulty for you? Eight and thirty. Impressive military career. Financially independent. A landowner. Usually a man of your age is at least looking for a wife." He tapped his desk with a finger as he named each item. "I also confirmed from a friend that the members at White's and Brook's blackballed you, a decade past. Not Boodle's, though. Have you never applied there?"

An unpleasant heat crept up Edward's neck. So it was to be that sort of interview "I have not, my lord. I thought it best not to, a decade ago, as I am certain there is at least one man there who would disapprove of my joining."

The older man's gaze softened, his expression turned understanding. Even kind. "It is a difficult thing, to face rejection. You need not tell me the particulars, but I must ask a few questions. Do you know why men at those clubs rejected your application for membership?"

Edward lowered his gaze to the desk. "I do, my lord."

"If the reason became known to the general public—"

"It will never come to that, my lord." Edward raised his gaze, meeting the Viscount's with fervency. On this, at least, there would be no quarter given. "Never. I am not the only one invested in keeping it a secret, and I swear it will never be a problem in the future. I was rejected for a youthful indiscretion which would have consequences impacting the reputations of others, should it become known. But I would rather die than hurt those people, even though they have made it a point to exclude me from their circles from that time until now."

He did not falter in his gaze, his tone remained steady and firm.

It was true. Those who knew the secret of his shame would rather die than reveal it, all to protect the woman they loved.

None of them would expose Pamela, now Lady Rothman, for her part in the almost-scandal of their brief, youthful affair.

Silently, Lord Blackstone observed him. He blew a puff of smoke that formed a ring before it dissipated to float in the air above them, a cloud of tobacco-scented mist forming. "You have letters of reference?"

Edward reached into his jacket and took out letters of character, written by military peers and commanders after he had resigned his post.

Lord Blackstone picked them up, barely glancing at more than the signatures before folding them and handing them back. He opened a drawer and took out a large book that looked like the ledgers Edward had in his own study. He also took out a sheet of paper he held out to Edward. "Our code of conduct and agreements." He opened the ledger to a page half-filled with names, dates, and amounts, took out a pen, and dipped it in ink.

After a glance at the paper, Edward looked up again, half in shock, half unsure. "I am admitted to your club?"

"On a probationary period, yes." Lord Blackwell kept at his work, writing something down. "You will pay your dues, of course. I prefer a year's worth at once, but not everyone can afford that. I make the books public at the end of each year, of course, so the members can see where their funds go. Special events we host will require the purchase of vouchers. You are permitted to bring guests, provided they abide by our rules while here. We also have rooms on the second floor that our members may make use of for a small fee, to cover costs of laundry and the servants' wages. You may use the club as a reference of character of course, too, after your probationary period ends."

Hardly believing his good fortune, Edward asked, "How long is the probationary period?"

"Three months, I should think." Lord Blackstone turned the ledger around. "Sign here, please." He tapped a line beneath the entry for Edward's date of membership.

Edward signed, hardly able to believe the whole interview was, to all intents and purposes, over. "I will pay the dues at once, my lord. A year's worth."

"Excellent. Now, let me take you on the tour, and I will introduce you to those currently within our walls." He stood, picked up his pipe, and gestured to the door. "If you have questions, do ask."

Edward glanced at the badger's portrait behind the desk, then at the shelves full of animals. "Well. There was one thing that concerned me, Lord Blackstone. I have noticed all the hunting trophies. I have to confess, I do not enjoy the sport, and have not taken part in a hunt since my days in the military."

Lord Blackstone's chest puffed up. "I have not hunted in an age, either. These fine specimens you see here are not from hunts." His eyes twinkled, and he looked about himself with no small measure of pride. "I have a great fondness and affection for animals. Everything you see in this club is here because of that fondness—they have all died natural deaths. I make it a point to ensure it is so before I obtain a specimen."

Though Edward immediately doubted such was the case, he nodded with solemnity. "That is a relief, my lord." He looked at the fine feathers of a red bird on one shelf. Lord Blackstone could believe whatever he wished about his collection.

"Wait until you see the giraffe," the Viscount said brightly as they left his study. "Enormous thing. I could only fit it in the billiard room from the neck up. Looks like it's coming through the floor." He chuckled. "Though I am thinking of having it moved. I can never settle on permanent places for anything." He pointed to a leopard's head as they passed it in the corridor. "I think this fellow would be better suited behind a door, for one thing. Can you imagine the surprise of closing a door to have that beauty snarling at you from behind it?"

"It seems the sort of surprise that may cause shock, my lord," Edward admitted, studying the teeth of the creature as they passed. The animal would startle him if he came upon it unexpected, alive or dead. "At least, the very first time."

"Shock, awe, and amazement," Lord Blackstone said with a chuckle. His delight seemed innocent enough, though.

The tour took the better part of two hours, in part because Lord Blackstone introduced Edward to at least a dozen members, but also because the Viscount enjoyed pointing out the most exotic creatures in his collection. He was especially proud of a full-sized emperor penguin just outside the water closet. Then Lord Blackstone gave Edward cards from the club, invited Edward to the theater and a dinner hosted by himself, and finally took his leave to attend to another appointment in his study.

It had been easier than Edward anticipated, joining the club. His name was in the ledger, and in the guest book, and he had introductions to other gentlemen in Society well underway. He had an invitation not only to a private dinner but a public outing, and cards in his pocket that would aid him in future introductions. He returned to the room on the first floor, ordered tea, and made himself pleasant company to the others present.

Edward leaned back in his chair, the scent of fresh tea mixing with the faint musk of old fur and polished wood.

He had done it.

His name was on the ledger, it was official. His introductions had begun. If all went as planned, Daphne would soon have the connections she needed. It had been easier than he anticipated; easier than White's, easier than Brook's, easier than any of the doors that had closed to him a decade ago.

Edward took another sip of tea, settling into the odd comfort of Blackstone's club. His gaze drifted across the room, past a gentleman reading the Times, past another pouring brandy, and landed on a rather large glass case near the door.

Inside sat a stuffed squirrel on a fabricated tree. Holding a miniature cane. Wearing a top hat.

Edward exhaled. Well, this was his life now. A strange host, and even stranger environs.

And yet, as he lifted his teacup, he couldn't quite shake the feeling that Blackstone's was exactly where he was meant to be.

Chapter Eight

MARCH 21ST, 1817

I n the weeks since her agreement with Halstead that she would be remaining at Briarwood for the foreseeable future, Felicity devoted all her attention to Daphne. At last, on the first evening of spring, Felicity would watch her niece attend a public entertainment. The Colonel would escort them both to the theater.

"I can hardly believe it," Daphne said, pacing before the hearth in the parlor. "My first proper evening out—here, at last."

The parlor was warm with candlelight, the fire burning low, making Daphne's lilac-colored gown glow silver in the soft light. Felicity remained seated in her favorite chair, her keen eye taking in every detail of her niece's appearance.

There was no official timing for mourning to come to an end, except in cases when royalty passed, and the Crown issued a decree on such a thing. Everyday people imitated royalty, of course, but it was still a matter often left up to the family. To individuals. Though she would miss her brother fiercely, Felicity knew it was time for Daphne to step into the next stage of her life, as dear Anthony would have wished. The fabric draped smoothly over Daphne's form, the neckline low enough to suggest maturity while still maintaining modesty, and the spray of rosebuds in her hair brought out the natural beauty of her soft blush and shining curls.

"The theater is a perfect place to begin, both to see and be seen." Felicity folded her gloved hands in her lap. "An excellent preparation for attending your first ball."

That would be the moment in which Daphne truly stepped into Society; the moment when she could do more than visit museums and theaters, more than attend private events. She could go to balls. Receive offers of courtship. Perhaps even a voucher to Almack's, if Halstead came through.

The man had spent a great deal of time in London of late, even spending nights at his club. He kept Felicity and the staff apprised of his comings and goings, should they have need for him, but he had barely been at Briarwood...which had been something of an unexpected frustration for Felicity.

He ought to spend more time with Daphne—or at least spend more time concerning himself with Daphne's future.

"Are you certain the color of the gown is all right?" Daphne stood looking into a small oval mirror over the writing desk in the corner. "I know I am still in mourning..."

"It is a suitable color for a young lady, and your father would not wish you to wear grays or blacks one moment longer than you must." Felicity smiled slightly. "It is perfectly appropriate."

Besides, she herself wore enough drab gray for both of them. She had on a plain evening dress, modestly cut, in a fabric that would not so much as shimmer in gaslight. Her reticule, shawl, and fan were all black, too. No one would fault Daphne, young and on the verge of courtship, for dressing to attract the eye of suitable gentlemen...and no one would notice her aunt as more than a shadow to chaperone her.

Felicity rose and joined Daphne at the looking glass, standing behind her. She placed her hands on Daphne's shoulders. "You are ready for this, Daffodil. You needn't be nervous."

For a moment, Felicity remembered when she had been the one standing on the brink of womanhood; when she had looked in the looking glass as her mother fussed over her gown and told her the same things. *All would be well.* That she would find her way.

But in Felicity's case, it had all been lies.

She shook the bitter thought away and focused again on her niece.

The time spent preparing Daphne for her introduction to Society had passed far too quickly for Felicity. Not that Daphne needed an excess of time to prepare, of course. The girl had been raised from birth to know how to conduct herself properly, her father had seen to her education, and she had a kind and honest character. The practical matters however had caused concern, especially when the seamstress had fallen behind in her work, the dancing instructor had caught a cold, and the Lady Louisa's friendship came with her mother's judgmental conversation.

"You look elegant," she assured her niece. "Perfectly suited to an evening at the theater. You will look neither ostentatious nor underdressed."

"Lady Louisa will wear blue," Daphne murmured, worry creeping into her tone. "Jewel tones, she said."

Felicity arched a brow. Jewel tones, indeed. "Lady Louisa is making her full debut this Season—and she is the daughter of an earl. You, my dear, are not yet meant to dazzle, only to be observed. Tonight, you must be seen as a young lady of good sense, modest elegance, and excellent manners. Your time to stand out will come."

"Yes. Of course." Daphne nodded slowly. "It is, after all, only the theater," she tried to say breezily, but a tremble in her voice betrayed her nerves.

Felicity smoothed a stray curl behind her niece's ear, giving her a knowing look. "Yes, but it is the first time you will be seated in a place where half of London might turn their gaze upon you. Afterward, the card party will be filled with people who will speak of you to their friends, their sisters, and their sons. How they speak of you depends on your comportment this evening."

"You are not making this easier," Daphne said with a breathless laugh.

"I am preparing you," Felicity corrected fondly. "Which is the best thing I can do for you."

The door to their parlor opened, interrupting the conversation as both women turned to see Halstead enter. He was dressed for the evening in a sharp black coat, deep green waistcoat, and a perfectly tied, snowy white cravat.

It was the first time Felicity had seen him dressed formally. As he met her gaze, she felt her chest tighten and her cheeks warm. Colonel Edward Halstead looked the very image of masculine dignity, and she found she could not think of a man she had ever found more handsome than him.

What an absurd thought. Handsome men were not for women like her.

Not anymore.

His gaze left hers to take in Daphne, and he smiled with approval. "Daphne, you look wonderful. That color suits you."

"Thank you, Colonel." Daphne flushed with pleasure and dipped into a curtsy.

Felicity took a moment to observe Halstead, taking in his appearance again, noting the slight furrow in his brow. Was he nervous, too? Or perhaps merely uncomfortable with going out? He wasn't much in Society, he had told her, though he'd spend near enough every waking moment at that club of his—and he'd promised to make an effort for Daphne's sake.

"Are you ready for the evening?" he asked Daphne politely.

"I believe so." Daphne sent one last look toward Felicity, still seeking reassurance.

Felicity took her niece's gloved hand in her own, giving it a light squeeze. "Mind your posture, keep your voice pleasant, and let your natural charm do the rest."

Daphne exhaled, squared her shoulders, and smiled. "Yes, Aunt Felicity."

Halstead's eyes flickered between them, something unreadable in his expression, though the furrow had deepened. He turned toward the door. "Then let us be on our way."

They walked together all the way out the door to the carriage, where Halstead handed first Felicity and then Daphne inside. She tried to ignore her own nerves as Halstead slid into the seat across from her, facing the rear of the carriage.

"Never was there a man as lucky as I am," he said after the door closed. "Escorting two such charming ladies to the theater. I am honored."

Honored? He escorted two unmarried ladies in mourning, one on the cusp of life and one passed over by it.

A sting of regret for the past caused Felicity to wince and turn her gaze to the night-darkened window. She wasn't flattered, not this time. She knew all too well that her sharp features and tall form well suited the part of a strict spinster. Wearing a gray gown that washed out her features did not help matters; she likely appeared as pale as the moon, if not outright sickly.

But it didn't matter. None of it did. Let him play the gallant if he wished. Only Daphne's future concerned her now, for her own was set. She would see her niece happily settled, then she would withdraw to some quiet village where she could lease a little cottage and live out her days tending to a garden and giving the neighbors something to gossip about.

That was all there was to it.

EDWARD SETTLED IN THE CARRIAGE, ADJUSTING HIS GLOVES BEFORE resting one arm lightly along the seat. He kept his tone light, teasing, but purposeful. "You clearly disapprove of something, Captain."

Miss Price blinked at him from across the dim carriage, her hands neatly folded in her lap. "Do I?"

"Oh, yes," he said, studying her in the flickering lantern light. "That look has been on your face since I returned to Briarwood this evening. Do not think I am unfamiliar with it, as it is the one you wore when we first met, and you disapproved of the entirety of me. I thought we had moved beyond that?"

Daphne looked between them, wide-eyed and uncertain.

Captain—or rather, perhaps Miss Price now that they were about to be out in the world—tilted her chin up slightly, prim as ever. "I would not presume to tell you how to manage your responsibilities, Colonel."

Ah. There it was. She thought him shirking his duties in some way. But why? What could he have left undone?

"You must tell me all about the play we are to see tonight, Colonel. I have never heard of it before. Will it be well attended?" Daphne spoke swiftly, with a look on her face one might wear when leaping between two duelists. The girl did not enjoy seeing the two of them in conflict, however mild. A sweet sentiment, but it made him wonder if she knew how to handle herself in an argument. Perhaps he ought to study her reactions to such things. It would not do for her to enter the wider world without some thought as to how to handle disagreements—nor protect herself from them.

Edward gave his attention to Daphne, and each time he explained a thing to her satisfaction, she asked another question. The clever girl kept him talking all the way through the carriage ride, leaving her aunt to stare at the glass as though she could see through it to the darkness beyond. When they finally reached London's outskirts, with lamps lighting the streets, Miss Price closed her eyes as though resting them from a great fatigue.

What had he done to offend her?

They arrived at the theater, and Edward soon found himself standing on the pavement with both ladies on his arms. They walked through the doors together and the moment they stepped into the lobby, Edward felt the weight of Society pressing down upon him.

A burden he had avoided for years.

Gaslight flickered against marble pillars, chandeliers gleamed overhead, and all around them, London's finest moved in ripples of silk and murmured greetings.

Daphne tensed beside him though she hid it well, her hands tightening ever so slightly around her reticule. Miss Price, however, did not falter. She stepped forward with the practiced grace of a woman who knew exactly how this world worked, opening her black lace fan with a graceful flick of her wrist.

Edward watched her, wondering when had she last been here, at the heart of it all? Why did it feel as though she belonged here no more than he did?

He overtook Miss Price to lead them to the private balcony he had arranged for their use through Blackstone's club. Lord Blackstone kept several choice seats on reserve for the popular theaters, all for the use of club members. It was an unexpected benefit to joining the Viscount's club, and one Edward had happily taken advantage of for this particular occasion.

Daphne sat in a chair at the front of the balcony, and her aunt immediately settled on the chair behind her.

Edward frowned. It was not what he had expected. "Would you not prefer to sit at the front of the balcony, Miss Price?"

"I am content here," she said, folding both her hands and fan in her lap. "You ought to sit next to Daphne, so others know of her connection to you."

Well, that made some sense. He sat down next to his ward, but as she was busy perusing the theater bill in her hands, he turned in his chair to continue conversing with Miss Price. "Perhaps we could take turns. After intermission, you ought to sit here so you have a better view."

Her eyes narrowed as though he had mortally wounded her. "It serves Daphne nothing to be seen seated next to me."

"This is our first outing," Edward said lightly, trying to elicit a smile. "Surely it cannot matter so much."

Her jaw stiffened a moment before she answered. "Everything we do in the public eye will matter from this moment further. You ought not to look too concerned with the spinsterly chaperone, for one thing. I am her companion. I am not your responsibility."

"We both know that is not entirely true. I look after members of my household."

A wrinkle appeared at the bridge of her nose. "Of course."

"Is that skepticism I hear?"

"I haven't the slightest idea how your ears interpret sound, Colonel."

He nearly laughed and instead bit back the smile that threatened to show. With some sympathy for Daphne's discomfort, he stood and went to the door of the balcony, gesturing for Miss Price to follow. "We will return momentarily, Daphne."

"Yes, Colonel." Her shoulders relaxed, and she offered him a sweet smile.

Once Miss Price had stepped into the corridor with him, he lowered his voice. "The implication that there is something wrong with my hearing notwithstanding, you sound put out. Will you tell me what I have done, Captain Price? I doubt I could guess, considering I have politely stayed well out of your way for near a fortnight."

"Out of *my* way?" she repeated, eyebrows climbing higher on her forehead. She had to tip her chin up to meet his gaze in the narrow passage, given their close proximity to one another. "Is that what you call your—your inexplicable leave of absence? Two weeks without deigning to bestow your company on your ward?"

Ah, now they were getting somewhere. "Did Daphne suffer without my company?" he asked, glancing at the door to the balcony curiously. "I think she seemed well enough."

Miss Price bristled like a hedgehog. "Of course, she is well—I have done everything I could to give her the instruction and confidence she needs for her debut." She kept her voice low, hardly above a whisper. The murmurs of the crowd in the theater and the foyer below nearly drowned out her words until he leaned closer. "A guardian who is always absent can hardly say he has done his duty. Daphne needs to come to know you, to trust you. Instead, you disappeared with hardly more than a word! I know bachelors are not used to sharing their quarters with ladies, but fleeing our company was hardly gentlemanlike."

He narrowed his eyes. "Is that what you think? That I was avoiding Daphne? Avoiding you?" Edward shook his head, disbelief and irritation coursing through him. He had spent the last two weeks putting himself in the uncomfortable position of getting to know people; ingratiating himself to gentlemen and lesser lords, pretending an interest in things he cared naught for, like boxing matches and horse races and the blasted hunting.

"Avoiding us? The evidence speaks for itself," she said, her eyes piercing him with indignation.

Edward could not let her misconstrue the situation a moment longer. "Miss Price. While you have been instructing Daphne on the proper way to hold a fan, I have been ensuring she will be invited to the events where she can flutter it."

Her soft gray eyes filled with irritation—and perhaps the slightest curiosity. "And how have you done that, exactly?"

In the army, he'd never been challenged in such a way. His decisions were accepted and respected—at least, by the time he'd made captain. The same went for his dealings with his household staff, tenants, and in his business dealings. He barely knew Miss Price. He barely understood if he was annoyed by her question or admired her the more for it.

Edward exhaled sharply, pressing his lips together before speaking in a calm, measured tone. "I have spent the last two weeks at my new club, Blackstone's, playing cards with men I have no interest in befriending. I have lost money to them on purpose. I have asked questions about their sisters and daughters while pretending to care about the state of the turf at Newmarket. I have listened to men boast of their prospects, their estates, and their politics, and smiled, and bought drinks, and loaned money, and flattered idiots, all to ensure that when the subject of my ward arises, they see her as someone worth welcoming into their ranks."

Miss Price's brow furrowed, as if she had not expected such an answer.

"It is not enough for Daphne to be well-mannered and charming," Edward continued, his voice lower now but no less firm. "She must have sponsors. Invitations, connections, friendly faces —and that requires me to play a game I have never had any interest in. I have dined where I would rather not dine. I have endured conversations I would rather forget. I have worn clothes most uncomfortable and stayed up far too late, and I have done it all so that Daphne's name will be on the right lists when the Season truly begins." Edward leaned forward slightly, his voice dropping to a murmur. "You think I was neglecting my duty, Miss Price? I was doing the one thing I know how to do—something, forgive me, that you cannot. I was securing her future as a soldier secures a victory. By outmaneuvering those who might keep her from it."

After a pause, Miss Price lowered her gaze to the vicinity of his cravat. He saw her throat bob with a swallow. "I...I see," she said finally, her voice quieter than before. "I had not realized..."

Edward watched her closely, tilting his head to the side as he studied the play of emotion on her features. "No. I don't suppose you had."

Her gray eyes flickered up to meet his again, her chin lifted but with less irritation than before. "Then I suppose I must thank you, Colonel. It is no small thing to endure insipid conversation for the greater good."

The unexpected levity in the statement made a quiet laugh escape him. "That, Miss Price, was certainly the greatest hardship of all."

"Men ought to receive medals for such things."

"Indeed."

The slightest smile curved her lips, and Edward found himself watching the movement with interest. Goodness, she had a lovely smile. It appeared all too infrequently. She was a beautiful woman; formidable when she wished to be, but at moments like this—or when she interacted with Daphne—there was a gentleness to her that made him question why no man had wed her.

Edward leaned closer to her, looking into her eyes again. "You know even when I am not at home, you are always welcome to contact me. Write me. Even send for me, if need be. I will always come."

Her gaze flickered downward and back again. Even in the flickering light of the corridor, he saw the pink rise in her cheeks. A most becoming color on her, to be sure. "I-I think I managed well enough in your absence, but I appreciate knowing that. Thank you."

He leaned nearer, lowering his head as his chest tightened. "I am certain you had matters well in hand. I doubt you even missed me."

What was he doing? Looming over her as he was, he was bound to frighten her, to offer insult. He needed to get hold of himself at once.

Step away. Far, far away.

Miss Price swayed toward him just enough that he sensed the hem of her gown brushing the tops of his shoes. "Miss you?" She tilted her head back a little more, bringing the slight smile of her lips closer. "Certainly not."

He chuckled, and another clever retort rose to his lips—

Laughter from the corridor pulled him out of the moment as his head jerked in the direction of the stairs, just as he heard a small gasp from Miss Price. He returned his attention to her as she took a step back, placing her hand on the latch for the door to their balcony seats.

"I ought to return to Daphne. Poor thing will think she's been abandoned." She did not wait for him to speak but opened the door and slipped through—leaving Edward in the corridor, alone, to clear his muddled thoughts.

Had he nearly… No. Of course not. He wasn't about to kiss the aunt of his ward. Most likely, she would run him through if he tried. They had, perhaps, been carried away in their argument;

which, truly, had stopped seeming like an argument fairly quickly. It had almost felt playful, the way Miss Price had spoken to him, the challenge in her voice while her eyes shone with enjoyment.

He shook his head, hoping to clear it, then heaved a sigh, squared his shoulders, and rejoined the ladies in the balcony, seating himself next to his ward. He glanced over his shoulder only once at Miss Price, a few minutes after the entertainment began, and found her staring straight ahead without even the slightest smile on her lovely face.

Edward gave his full attention to the theatrical, letting his mind think on nothing beyond the lights of the stage. That seemed the safest course of action, for now, in any case.

Because if he thought too long on the way Felicity Price had looked at him in the corridor, or the way she had leaned in for a breath of a second, he knew he would find himself in a great deal of trouble.

Chapter Nine

The drawing room in Lord Donwell's townhouse was a glittering display of Society at play, laughter and the quiet murmur of conversation rising over the gentle clink of teacups and the shuffle of cards. It was far livelier than the theater they had just left, and the differences in atmosphere took some getting used to.

Felicity had excused herself from the card tables as most of the chaperones had, choosing instead to observe their charges from discreet edges of the room. Halstead had disappeared into the billiard room with their host and several other gentlemen, which was just as well. Daphne needed space to navigate without her every move being shadowed.

Besides, she herself—if she were being truthful—needed a moment alone. Her fingers toyed with the edge of her fan as she stood near a marble-topped side table, her gaze moving over the room without truly focusing.

She had nearly kissed Colonel Halstead.

The thought made her stomach tighten, though she refused to acknowledge whether it was from embarrassment or...something else. Something more disastrous for a woman in her position.

It had been the smallest of moments, the breath of a second

where her world had tilted dangerously. And she would not let it happen again.

Pressing her lips together, Felicity inhaled deeply, as if she could steady herself with the mere act of breathing. It was foolish to even think on that interlude in the corridor. Whatever had passed between them had been nothing more than a lapse in judgment. A closeness born of a shared moment of humor. A misunderstanding. She might have completely misunderstood the moment!

A moment which must not happen again.

She had not come to London to entangle herself in unwise affections. As a spinster, a maidenly aunt, a chaperone, a woman whose age put her above most of Society's reproach, she danced at the edge of respectability.

Besides, she was here for Daphne's future, not her own.

"Miss Price, is it not?"

Felicity affected a polite smile, turning sharply to find herself face-to-face with a Mrs. Yates, a woman of middling years, impeccably dressed, and possessed of the sort of sharp, knowing eyes that saw more than people wished.

Felicity dipped into a polite curtsy. "Mrs. Yates. A pleasure."

The woman's gaze flickered toward Daphne, who was seated at a nearby card table, speaking with a young gentleman.

"Your niece is charming," Mrs. Yates observed, her tone almost bored. "And in good hands, I believe."

"Colonel Halstead is a most responsible guardian," Felicity replied, nodding her agreement. "He has seen that she has all she needs for her comfort."

Mrs. Yates made a soft, amused sound, tipping her head. "Oh, I do not doubt that he is responsible now. But it is always interesting, is it not, when a man so firmly ensconced in bachelorhood suddenly finds himself with a ward. I wonder..." She tapped a gloved finger lightly against the stem of her wineglass. "Do you know much about his younger years, Miss Price?"

Felicity kept her face a mask of calm disinterest. This was a test. Everything in Society was a test. "I cannot say that I do. My brother spoke highly of him, he saved the colonel's life. I know he served with distinction in the war," she added, tone even.

Mrs. Yates lifted a delicate brow. "Oh, indeed he did. And before that?"

A pause.

Resisting the urge to tighten her grip on her fan, Felicity maintained an air of cool composure. "I cannot say I have inquired much into Colonel Halstead's youth. His maturity is naught but respectable."

"Mmm." Mrs. Yates took a slow sip of her wine, her eyes glinting with the sort of satisfaction one gets from knowing something others do not. Felicity knew it well. "It is all rather old gossip, you understand," she continued with a wave of her hand, as if it were nothing. "And I confess I do not recall the particulars. But I do seem to remember there was a young lady involved, and of a rather important family. The names elude me now—so much time has passed. I recall most thought it a rather unfortunate incident. His family, I believe, sent him to war as punishment. Though, of course, such things are hardly spoken of now."

"How mysterious." Felicity's breath hitched so slightly, so imperceptibly, that she hoped the gossipy woman did not notice. People who spoke so lightly of others' reputations were always looking for a reaction. She would not give Mrs. Yates the satisfaction, if she could help it. "You do not remember the particulars?" she asked, keeping her tone carefully neutral.

"No, no," Mrs. Yates said, sighing in disappointment. "Only that it was a rather delicate situation. A shame, really. I recall he was quite the promising young man when they sent him away. But war made him into something greater, did it not?"

Felicity's stomach twisted. She should brush it off. Dismiss it. And so she did. "Tales that grow so hazy with time are hardly worth ruminating over now, are they? When the details are lost, such things hardly bare repeating," she said smoothly, offering a thin, polite smile. "I prefer to judge a man on the actions of his present, rather than whispers of his past."

Mrs. Yates laughed lightly, tilting her head as if amused by Felicity's response. "A commendable philosophy, Miss Price. A rare one, too." She sipped once more at her glass, then said, "But I wonder how you can afford to think in such a way, with your niece's future in the Colonel's hands?" With that she took her leave, her skirts sweeping the floor as she moved on to some other conversation, some other reputation to weigh and measure.

Felicity exhaled slowly.

She would not let this bother her. Colonel Edward Halstead was a man of good character; she had seen it with her own eyes, but the words curled at the edges of her mind, refusing to be banished.

A young lady. A punishment.

The idea bothered her, yet why should it? He had told her he went to war young, only eighteen. Many a person made youthful mistakes, said or did things their parents did not approve of, at that age. She had given her own parents fits when she refused to have a proper coming out when she turned eighteen. She hadn't wanted to put herself on display. They had kept her home, in the country, for two more years. When she had entered Society for herself, she did it quietly. Not at all like all her friends.

Not at all the way Daphne would take her first steps into the public eye.

Her niece was beautiful. Intelligent. Kind-spirited. She had lived her life protected and loved. She deserved all the beautiful things a true Season brought, Felicity knew, whether this first one ended with a good match or not. London's richness would be Daphne's to enjoy and indulge in. Felicity would see to that.

And Halstead had promised to do what was right and best for Daphne. Thus far, his honorable behavior, beneficence, and kindness had done nothing to warrant Felicity's concern. Though Mrs. Yates had tried to plant a seed of doubt, Felicity need not nurture it by letting her thoughts dwell upon such idle speculation.

That decided, she gave herself a firm nod and then nearly jumped out of her skin when a gentle hand touched her forearm.

"Aunt Felicity? Lady Louisa, Miss Clark, and her brother Mr. Paul Clark have invited me to walk through the portrait gallery with them. The door is over there." Daphne innocently pointed to double doors already open to allow guests the opportunity to walk through and stretch their legs. "Is it all right if I accompany them?"

Felicity cast her gaze to the trio standing a few paces away, all waiting for her decree before they left the confines of the card room. She gave them an approving smile. Daphne needed friends, and what she knew of the Clarks made up for her concerns over Lady Louisa, daughter of Lady Kendal. "Of course, darling."

Moving about would also help Daphne stay awake and bright, as the girl was still unused to the late hours of London Society.

"Thank you, Aunt." Daphne rejoined her friends and the four of them walked to the gallery doors. Lady Louisa on the young man's arm, and Daphne arm-in-arm with Miss Clark, all of them already speaking with animation, as young people did when finding themselves in amiable company.

After they had stepped through the room, Felicity wandered to that side of the room, unhurried, placing herself where she could periodically glance through the gallery doors to be certain Daphne stayed in sight.

She had just gained the best position when she sensed the approach of someone taller, larger than herself. A smile twitched at her lips as she turned to greet the Colonel. "Colonel Halstead. How did you do at billiards?"

His brow was furrowed as he joined her, and he glanced around the room with the air of someone displeased at what he saw.

Was he truly so very against Society and crowds?

"It must not have been a successful game, with you looking like that," Felicity said, keeping her smile in place. If anyone looked over and saw him scowling, they would not suppose it her fault.

He barely looked at her from the corner of his eye. "The game was fine—but where is Daphne? I did not see her anywhere when I entered, and she is not with you. Have you lost her?" The accusation in his tone would have made her defensive, had she not seen the concern in his eyes.

Felicity kept her temper in check, still smiling. "Why, she has only stepped into the portrait gallery with some friends—after securing my permission, naturally. They are taking a bit of exercise after sitting at the card table overlong."

The Colonel's gaze flitted to the doors of the gallery, then focused again on her. "Friends?"

"The Clarks and Lady Louisa." The amount of questions he asked at least proved he made an engaged guardian, but really, she felt as though she were under examination from her old schoolmistress. "Is there something wrong, Colonel? Have you any objection? We have spoken of Lady Louisa, the Earl of Kendal's daughter. The Clarks are from a fine family, Mr. Paul Clark is studying the law and his sister—"

He loomed over her, brows knit tightly together. This closeness wasn't nearly as pleasant as the one outside the balcony at the theater, and when he lowered his voice, it was to a disapproving rather than an intimate tone. "You mean to tell me there is a gentleman alone with Daphne, and you are not with them?"

"The other ladies present—"

"Are mere girls." Colonel Halstead shook his head and abruptly walked away from her, directly to the gallery, through its doors and down the long corridor where Felicity could plainly see Daphne with the others. She took a step in that direction, raising a hand to—what? Stop Halstead? The man was like a brown bear, people stepping out of his way on instinct. She could no more halt him than she could a tumbling boulder.

Standing still and smiling as though all was right with the world was the best thing for her to do, especially since she could not understand his actions. Felicity had thought they were on the same side; that he trusted her.

Apparently, she had been mistaken.

She watched, unable to even make out what anyone said, as he bowed to the little group. He spoke and extended his arm to Daphne. She took it. He brought her back to the card room, to a table. The Colonel helped her into a chair then positioned himself across the table to partner with her in Whist.

Daphne looked over her shoulder but once. Felicity thought she saw disappointment on her niece's face, but the young lady then turned to her hand of cards with a cheerful smile as they played with another couple.

Felicity wove her way through the room again, nodding at renewed acquaintances, until she rejoined a small group of chaperones near one of the open windows. Her cheeks had grown hot as she watched Halstead fetch her niece—as though Daphne were a misplaced doll, or a child in need of constant minding! Thankfully Daphne did not seem to realize the slight. But Felicity...she felt it keenly.

He did not trust Felicity's judgment. He did not trust Daphne's behavior. If he kept Daphne that close all Season, the girl would make few friends, gain fewer introductions, and her prospects would be fewer still. Felicity watched as Daphne bit her bottom lip and stared out the window into the night, but the London sky held as little guidance as it did stars on that cloudy March evening.

What was she going to do about this newest problem?

Chapter Ten

E dward shifted in the leather armchair in the library of Blackstone's, his discomfort less to do with the chair and more the furnishings of his mind, but it did not stop him from muttering a complaint about the width of the seat.

"Ah, I am afraid I did not obtain furniture with giants in mind," said a cheery voice from behind him.

Edward jumped up from his seat and turned to see Lord Blackstone standing there, hands tucked behind his back, his eyes as warm and full of amusement as ever.

"I beg your pardon, Lord Blackstone. I did not see you there."

"Unless you had eyes in the back of your head, I imagine that would be a rather impossible feat." He gestured to a chair that matched Edward's, facing the window at angled for conversation between the two seats. "May I join you, Colonel Halstead?"

"Of course." Edward waited for the older man to seat himself before carefully lowering himself back to his chair. "This is your club, my lord. You need not ask my permission for anything."

"When one wishes for polite company, one must be mostly polite rather than mostly tyrannical." The man put his elbows on the arms of the chair and steepled his fingers together. "Now then. Apart from the lack of Colonel-sized furnishings—which, you ought to know, there are such chairs on the other side of the room —what is it that is bothering you, young man?"

Edward's eight and thirty years sat more heavily upon him when the man addressed him that way. "I know myself too old in the ways of the world to accept such flattery, sir."

"Piffle. You are a younger man than me—my words stand." Lord Blackstone chuckled and smiled almost benevolently. "You are trying to avoid the question. That tells me to tread lightly. Would it help if I promised discretion? If I told you I am not one to gossip?"

"Perhaps." Edward considered the man across from him. "Have you...er...any experience with ladies?" When the old gentleman raised his eyebrows, Edward hastened to add, "I mean—you see, I am a second son. I have no sisters, I have no wife. I barely spent time with my mother. Now I am responsible for a young woman as her guardian, and her companion—her aunt—by extension. I find myself lost. There are no maps or guides for a man in my position."

"Indeed, not. Even if there were, I imagine they would be almost useless since most such things are written by men." Lord Blackstone chuckled with amusement at his own observation. "Women are rather delicate creatures in some ways, but I find they are stronger than they look. Rather like geese."

Edward's mind struggled to understand that particular comparison. "Women...are like geese, my lord?"

Lord Blackstone's head bobbed as he appeared most pleased with himself. "Indeed, yes. Picture one of those lovely creatures on the water of a pond. There it is. Drifting serenely, appearing as delicate as their cousins the ducks. But then, put both creatures on dry land. Send a cat among them. The duck will fly away, if possible. The goose will puff up and hiss. Rather like a cobra. The goose will fight rather than fly. Can you think of any man willing to harass a goose without at least a stick at hand?"

"I cannot. But you must forgive me, my lord. I also cannot imagine how this applies to women."

"They are stronger than they look," Lord Blackwell stated with firmness. "More willing to fight than we give them credit for. Perfectly capable of managing difficulties in all shapes and sizes."

"But...that does not exactly help my particular situation, my lord." Edward wanted to rub at his temples. Lord Blackstone's talk of birds and nature, a topic he had come to realize occurred with great frequency in the club, had done no more than confuse his already exhausted mind. "I must offer a correction to my ward's companion. An admonition. I fear she does not see the danger that I do in her management of her niece."

Lord Blackstone's eyes gleamed knowingly. "And what, precisely, about this situation is causing you such distress, my boy? The girl's safety or her aunt's resistance?"

Edward stiffened. "They are one and the same."

Lord Blackstone merely hummed. "Are they?"

His traitorous chest tightened, but he shook his head. "They are. I do not know the best approach to take."

"Best approach? Colonel, speak to her," his companion said with a lackadaisical shrug. "Make your concerns clear. She will not break or crumble—I find most women are quite logical, though many a man would tell you I am wrong. My experience is that honest conversation with a woman does far more good than skirting an issue or making demands. Though I suppose the latter would come more naturally to a military man."

It would. But the fear of both hurting Miss Price's feelings and causing an emotional display had kept him silent on the matter.

And there was the faint thought that she would defy orders rather than follow them, which had kept his tongue still.

"A direct conversation will serve you better than sitting in my club, ruminating on it, ever will." Lord Blackstone patted the arms of the chair. "Well. That is my advice. Now, I am off to see my taxidermist. He sent word he has the most beautiful North American robin he was bid repair, but the owner did not like the job, so now he must sell it instead. I do not yet have a North American robin. One can never have too many robins, can one?"

He bowed as Edward stood, then went on his way, humming to himself.

Edward remained standing, watching the nobleman go, and heaved a sigh before making his own way out of the library, then the club, requesting that his horse be brought around.

Whether the comparison of women and geese was apt, Lord Blackstone had made an excellent point. Edward accomplished nothing by sitting in the club, miles away from his home. He needed to speak to Felicity—his Captain. The Captain. Bother— Miss Price.

He needed to speak to Miss Price directly.

If she cried when he corrected her mistake, well, so be it. If she defied his instructions, that would be a different matter altogether. He needed to approach the subject of Daphne's chaperonage with logic and reasoning, perhaps with an appeal to Miss Price's protective instincts. He had to make her understand the sort of trouble a girl of Daphne's age could get into if not watched closely at all times.

The sort of trouble that he had caused for another young lady two decades previously. He'd been a careless, foolish youth who thought he knew better than everyone else. He was not a careless, foolish youth now.

He had to make Miss Price understand the sort of trouble a girl of Daphne's age could get into if not watched closely at all times.

Oh, the way Pamela had looked at him that night, eyes wide with trust, thinking he was offering her love when all he had to give was ruin.

Fool.

As he rode homeward, Edward rehearsed what he wished to say in his mind, again and again. Daphne needed protection from men like he had been, he had to make Miss Price see the importance of vigilance. Perhaps he ought to speak to Daphne first. She was his ward, after all, and she was obligated to obey him. If he could gain her promise of strict obedience, her aunt would have no choice but to do as Edward wished.

That seemed as sound an idea as any. Speaking to Daphne, that was what was needed.

That course of action decided, Edward made his way to Briarwood with determination in his gut and his battle-ready mask in place.

<hr />

THE SMALLER PARLOR WAS BRIGHT WITH THE SOFT AFTERNOON SUN, the open curtains letting in the light and keeping out the still too cool air. A steady fire crackled in the hearth, its warmth providing comfort that softened the lingering chill of early spring.

Felicity sat close to Daphne on the settee, the younger woman tucked beneath a woolen shawl, her slippered feet curled beneath her. A cup of tea rested in her hands, the fragrant steam curling up toward her face, and she breathed it in slowly before taking another careful sip. Her cheeks were faintly flushed, a telltale sign of her slight fever, but otherwise, she looked comfortable. Rested.

Felicity turned a page in the book she held, her voice low and soothing as she read aloud.

> *Emma was not required, by any subsequent discovery, to retract her ill opinion of Mrs. Elton. Her observation had been pretty correct. Such as Mrs. Elton appeared to her on this second interview, such she appeared whenever they met again,—self-important, presuming, familiar, igno- rant, and ill-bred.*

Daphne sniffled. "Isn't it interesting that someone as little in the world as Emma can still see how Mrs. Elton is ill-mannered?"

"I think it matters little how much in the world we are, so long as we endeavor to understand it. I think that is what Mrs. Elton lacks," Felicity said gently. "An understanding of the world, and that her place in it is not so important as she assumes."

After dabbing at her nose, Daphne leaned her head against Felicity's shoulder. "Do continue. I want to know what happens with the Eltons."

Felicity resumed reading, the steady cadence of the words filling the quiet room, mixing with the occasional pop of the fire and the faint ticking of the clock on the mantel. She glanced up between sentences, pleased to see Daphne's lashes drooping slightly, her body sinking deeper into the cushions.

"You needn't keep reading if you're tired, Aunt Felicity," Daphne murmured, though she was the one who ill-covered a yawn.

Felicity smiled, brushing a loose curl from Daphne's forehead in an old, familiar gesture. "Nonsense, my Daffodil. What better use have I for my afternoon than reading to you? Besides, this story is far too engaging to put aside just yet. I too wish to know what happens to the Eltons."

Daphne gave a small, drowsy smile and let her head tip against the cushion. "Then I suppose I shall allow you to continue," she teased softly, closing her eyes and settling in against her aunt's shoulder again.

A faint tap preceded the quiet entrance of a footman.

Felicity paused in her reading, eyebrows raised. "Yes, Peter?"

He bowed. "The Colonel summons Miss Daphne to attend to him in the gardens, madam."

Felicity bristled. "Summons?" she repeated.

Not requested. Not asked. But *summoned*—and without regard to Daphne's current state of health? Her niece was a young lady in his care, not a soldier under his command.

Daphne released a soft sigh as she sat up, her brow furrowed. "I will go, of course. I must not displease my guardian."

"You most certainly will not." Felicity rose faster than her niece and placed her hand on Daphne's forehead, testing for warmth. The poor girl still burned hotter than she ought, and her nose was an unsightly red. She was in no fit state to go out into the garden. In March? In reply to a summons? "My niece is unwell

112

and will not be going out into the cold. I will see Colonel Halstead myself."

The footman visibly swallowed as he bowed. "He is in the rose garden, Miss Price."

She nodded her thanks. "Please fetch my niece more tea, and a fresh hot brick." Then she turned to Daphne. "I will return shortly to resume our book. If you are too tired to continue, take your tea to your chamber and have a nap."

"But Aunt Felicity—"

"No." Felicity picked up a shawl from the back of the settee and wrapped it around her niece's shoulders. "He cannot order you about when you are unwell, Daphne. I will not allow it." She stepped to the door and hesitated. "If it is truly a matter of great importance, you can speak with him inside the house later."

Daphne's expression was somewhat pained, and though it hurt Felicity to make her niece uncertain, she blew her a kiss and went out the door anyway. She made her way down the stairs, through the house, and out into the cold air. A brisk breeze immediately pushed against her, stinging her cheeks and snatching at the edges of her shawl.

As she strode toward the garden, the sharp wind biting at her cheeks, Felicity felt more than cold. She felt *erased*. A man she barely knew, summoning her niece as though she were nothing more than a piece on his chessboard. Like a housemaid. As if Felicity hadn't poured years into Daphne's happiness—as if she herself hadn't sacrificed enough already.

Well. He would learn she was not so easily brushed aside.

"No one should be out for garden walks in this weather," she muttered as she made her way gingerly down the damp paths to the rose garden. A rather dismal place at that time of year, given the complete lack of blooms and the small stumps belying great roses come the summer. Why would anyone wish to be in a rose garden in March?

She saw Halstead's head over the sleeping rose bushes, his back to her, wearing his greatcoat. Of course, he had dressed for the weather. Felicity gave a small shiver as she approached, coming into the garden as he walked along one of the stone paths, bending to peer closer at a plant.

The sight of him pacing like an officer inspecting his troops increased her irritation with him, him and his *summons*.

"Good afternoon, Colonel," Felicity called out to him, her voice carrying across the empty space. He stopped walking and turned to look at her with a raised brow. She kept walking until she was within six paces of him, which meant she did not have to look up to meet his gaze, making sure to halt before she stepped too close. "Ought I to curtsy or salute? I am afraid I am uncertain at the moment if you expect a lady or a foot soldier to attend you."

His look of surprise changed to an expression which she interpreted as consternation. "I beg your pardon, Miss Price? What do you mean by those words?"

"Mean? Why, Colonel, I am merely confused. What are the rules of engagement when a commanding officer summons a woman like a foot soldier?"

Slowly, her host shook his head. "I did not *summon* you, Miss Price. I sent for Daphne, and when I ask my ward to join me for a discussion, I expect her to come rather than send an envoy in her stead."

"Envoy?" Felicity laughed, trying and failing to keep back her invitation. "Colonel Halstead, you know full well that Daphne has a cold, a growing fever in fact, and should not be out in this weather."

"A cold?" His mouth turned downward in a frown. "I was not informed."

Felicity opened her mouth, then hesitated. Well, he had not been. She had merely leapt into action that morning, upon seeing her niece with such a streaming nose, and taken care of her.

The Colonel was still frowning. "I merely wished to see how she fared today. Your reaction to my concern is naught but an *over*reaction. A note would have been sufficient."

"Or you could have come to see her."

"I did not know she was incapable of enjoying a short time out of doors," he retorted, voice somewhat more stern than before.

"It is a thing you would have known if you spent any time with her yesterday evening or this morning at breakfast," Felicity argued, pulled her shawl tighter about herself as the cold seeped through the thin fabric. Why on earth had she not requested her pelisse from Peter? "If you were more attentive to her, as a guardian ought to be, you would not need to issue commands without having a full understanding of the situation."

Colonel Halstead turned away from her, then back and came a step closer. "Miss Price, while I respect your role as Daphne's aunt, I must ask you to remember that you are here at *my* home, and by my invitation. You should also remember that I am the one responsible for making decisions regarding Daphne—not you."

Felicity's anger bubbled upward and she took several steps closer, her chin tilting up to better look up into his sharp-eyed glare. She would not be cowed. "It is quite difficult to recognize your authority, Colonel, when you are so distant and removed from the very person you are supposed to protect." Her voice trembled as the cold sank through her slippers. She really ought to have put on a coat before coming outside. "I recognize your efforts in Town, but while you are at home I thought you meant to get to know Daphne? How else will you know what is best for her?"

His eyes narrowed as he glared down at her. When he spoke, his tone was as chilly as the weather. "You do not understand me, Miss Price. That is obvious."

"I understand you enough to know you are exactly like your house." She pointed to the building behind her. "You may look fine enough on the outside, but inside? Inside you are hollow. Unwelcoming. Cold."

Halstead appeared stunned, as though her words struck him harder than she had expected. He looked over her shoulder at the house, then back at her. "What on earth does my house have to do with anything?"

"I told you before, a home reflects its master." Felicity pulled her shawl tighter, ignoring the nudge of guilt against her conscious. Her tongue continued on, sharper than before, as it always did when her temper gained the better of her. "Your home is merely an empty shell, without warmth, without life, without a touch of beauty or comfort inside of it."

The Colonel, clearly affected, tightened his jaw. "Miss Price. You do not know me well enough to pass such a judgment."

Felicity lifted her chin, meeting his gaze evenly, and replied, "Nor do you know me, Colonel Halstead—or Daphne. And until you take the time to do so, I cannot see us working together for her good."

Halstead appeared completely caught off guard by Felicity's accusation, his mouth opening and closing as he struggled to find a response. Instead of answering her outright, he turned away, looking toward the barren rose garden as if searching for answers among the thorns. "I...I'd never given much thought to the house. It didn't seem necessary to fill it with things, living there alone."

Felicity, having spoken more sharply than she intended, felt a stab of remorse, but she could not take back her words. Not when she had spoken them for Daphne's sake. Yet she felt herself softening, somewhat. "You are not living there alone anymore, Halstead."

He said nothing but turned again, staring at her with new regard. Studying her.

Still frowning, though. Still disapproving. But he moved a step closer, brow furrowed, and something about the intensity of his stare made it impossible to look away.

At that moment, an unexpected shiver passed through her. Due to the cold, of course. Felicity would not attribute her sudden intake of breath and tremble of her body to anything else.

Halstead kept moving toward her and she was in half a mind to step back—before without a word, the man shrugged off his coat and draped it around her shoulders before she could protest.

Felicity stiffened, but the sudden warmth was undeniable. The weight of his coat settled across her shoulders, heavier than she expected. Warmer, too, and it smelled of him, of bergamot and leather and ink. She loathed how much she noticed. How easily kindness from the man she meant to scold could unravel her focus. But she would not let it; warmth would not move her. Not his, not anyone's.

Even if it was an unspoken act of care, contradicting her words about him being cold and unfeeling. A thing that made her prickle with awareness even as she pulled the wool coat tighter about herself.

Colonel Halstead gave a sharp nod and looked away before he spoke again, his voice quieter. "I don't know how to make the house more suitable, Miss Price. But I know how to protect what is mine."

She stared at him, realization dawning that perhaps his detachment wasn't the apathy or carelessness she had feared—it was something else. Though she still stood her ground, she did not want to be softened by his gesture. She had to keep Daphne at the forefront of her thoughts...no matter how wonderful his coat smelled. "Then protect Daphne properly, Colonel Halstead. Not like a soldier guarding a post, but like a guardian watching over someone he cares for."

Halstead turned back to her, his expression unreadable, studying her as if trying to decide whether to be angry or impressed. Finally, he nodded. "Very well. But if I do, I expect the same of you."

"I have done nothing but care for Daphne," she countered.

"Then prove to me you are willing to let me do the same. Listen to my wishes regarding her protection."

A beat of silence passed between them before Felicity inclined her head ever so slightly. "I am listening now, sir."

His gloved hands tightened into fists. "You...you do not understand the dangers a woman of her age and beauty, let alone her inheritance will face, Miss Price. She cannot be left alone, even with those you believe she trusts, those who purport to be her friends."

She had to shake her head at his pronouncement. "That will make her an outsider. No one will wish to have her along on outings if her maiden aunt must always be attached to her, as though she is on leading strings."

His stance remained firm. "Nevertheless, it is what I require as her guardian."

Felicity wanted to stomp her foot and demand he see reason. Instead, she took in a deep breath and let it out again, slowly. "I cannot think why you would require such a thing. Tell me why, Halstead—tell me your reason for such a thing. Help me to understand."

Though she had made the request, she did not expect him to answer. Not really. So when the Colonel took a measured breath and spoke, his tone low and dark, she held completely still.

"I have seen what happens when young ladies are left unchecked. Society may be filled with polite manners and refined company, but behind the civility is danger." He turned away from her, and she had to strain to hear his voice once his back was turned. "I once knew a young woman much like Daphne. She was full of life. Witty. Lovely to look upon—yet she suffered the consequences of misplaced trust. Life-changing consequences for herself, for others. Nothing...nothing was ever the same for her again."

He provided no further details, but even those few words were enough for Felicity to sense his demands did not stem from unfounded fears. There was a story there; a story he was not yet willing to tell.

"It's not just propriety, Miss Price. There are men who take advantage of young ladies who trust too easily—I've seen it. I refuse to let it happen to Daphne."

Felicity took care to consider his words, but could not fully accept his argument. "I realize that by being a woman, many think I cannot know much about the world, especially as I am unmarried. But I am not ignorant of the sort of danger that you speak of, Halstead. I have prepared Daphne to recognize such dangers." She tried to smile, but his stern countenance made it wilt from her face. "I know you are concerned. But suffocating Daphne will only make her more susceptible to harm. Not less." He seemed ready to argue, but she quickly continued, "Fear cannot be her guiding principle, Colonel. She must learn to navigate the world, not hide from it."

"I am not suggesting she hide," he said gruffly. "Merely that she be guarded."

They would get nowhere without one of them giving in. At least a little. "Then I propose a compromise."

His eyebrows raised. "I am listening, Miss Price."

"Let us try to give Daphne more freedom but under watchful guidance, ensuring she is neither left to her naiveté nor wholly restricted."

He stepped closer. "How do you propose we do that without leaving her open to harm, Captain?"

She stared straight back at him, unflinching, trying not to smile at the nickname which he had given her. "You cannot loom over her and every friend she makes, every gentleman who wishes to call on her. You will ruin her chances of finding a happy life."

"Perhaps you are too willing to risk her reputation, leaving her in an unhappy situation."

Her jaw dropped open at the man's audacity. "Colonel Halstead, I have done everything I could for Daphne's happiness and security since she was a child. I want to see her happy, to see her well settled, with friends who support her and a husband who will care for her. To set her up for the rest of her life."

The Colonel shook his head and pointed at her, his finger hovering over the lapel of his coat on her shoulders. "And how do you propose to ensure such things for her, Miss Price, when you have been unsuccessful in finding them for yourself?"

The chill air struck all the harder when the heat left Felicity's body, humiliation flooding her like water from a cold spring. She swallowed back her hurt. "How—how dare you, sir?" she whispered, the words rasping out. "You know nothing, *nothing* of my circumstances."

She had survived pity before. Dismissal. Even the faint, polite scorn of Society.

But this—this man, this stranger, cutting to the quick with a single, careless observation—was nearly too much. The pain of it struck sharp and sudden behind her ribs. How dare he speak aloud the very thing she had spent years making peace with?

Colonel Halstead took a step back, his own face pale, speaking now as quietly as she had. "You undoubtedly think me cruel, Miss Price. You think I know nothing of how Society functions, but I know more than you can imagine. And I know that if she makes the wrong move, if she trusts the wrong person, it will be her ruin."

Felicity, breathless, shook her head at him, words spilling out before she could halt them. "There is more than one way for a young woman's chances to be ruined, Colonel Halstead—a thing I know all too well." She turned on her heel and marched away as quickly as she could.

He did not call her back.

When Felicity entered the house, she shed his coat at the door and kept walking until she came to her chamber. She ought to check on Daphne, but that could wait while she regained her composure. It must wait.

Standing before her looking glass, Felicity stared at her pale countenance. There was no use thinking of the past, but the memories came anyway.

His smile.

The letters that stopped arriving.

The day she heard he'd married someone else, someone younger, richer, and prettier, of course.

And now here she was, years later, with the same old ache cracking open under a soldier's careless words.

Chapter Eleven

An acquaintance from Blackstone's club had invited Edward and his ward to a garden party a few days after his most unsatisfactory conversation with Miss Price. Precisely whether or not his ward's companion was invited was unclear so, wearing a fine dark green coat and a deep brown embroidered waistcoat, he alone escorted his ward and made introductions.

The greenery of Mr. Thomas Norman's townhouse stretched out in neat, ordered rows. Every hedge clipped, every bed of early spring blooms precisely arranged—and yet, for all the effort, it looked as lifeless as the blasted rose garden at Briarwood. Decorative, cold, and utterly unremarkable.

Rather like himself, according to Miss Price.

Edward adjusted the position of Daphne's gloved hand on his arm as they strolled along the outer path of the gathering, nodding politely to a passing couple but hardly seeing them. His mind remained fixed on Felicity Price's voice, sharp as a blade, still echoing in the back of his skull. It didn't matter that she had not attended; uncertain invitations notwithstanding, she had caught Daphne's cold after the young lady recovered from it, and her words still echoed in his mind.

"You are exactly like your house. Hollow. Unwelcoming. Cold."

Heaven help him.

"Are you quite well, Colonel?" Daphne's voice, sweet and uncertain, tugged him from his irritating thoughts.

He looked down to find her watching him with polite curiosity, her brow faintly creased in the way Felicity's often did when studying him, though the expression was softer. Less judgmental. A great deal more cautious, too.

It was the first time the two of them had gone anywhere without her aunt, an occasion he ought to make the most of as he proved to his young ward he held her success as a high priority.

She looked quite innocent, dressed in a modest gown for one of her age, the soft blue fabric bringing out her eyes. She had to take after her mother in coloring, given that her father and aunt were both of a darker complexion.

"Yes, I am well," he lied. "I am only considering the layout of the grounds in comparison to my gardens."

Daphne tilted her head, clearly unconvinced, but she did not press him on it. "It is very pretty here," she offered instead, though with little conviction. "Not as large as your gardens, of course. Nor as lovely as Briarwood will be in a few weeks. Aunt Felicity says once the roses bloom, it will look as though the house is floating amid a sea of them."

Of course Miss Felicity Price noted such things. She paid more attention to his house and its appearance than anyone.

He could practically hear her voice in the remark, perhaps already plotting improvements, as if Briarwood belonged to her rather than him. Edward was not blind to the small changes to his home in the weeks since her arrival; even the hours at which the meals were served had changed. Mrs. Lane deferred to Miss Price in household matters, even when he had a question or suggestion. The staff already fully trusted her opinions on things, following her instructions without hesitation.

They all liked her.

"Aunt Felicity has a talent for seeing what something *could* become," Daphne added, as if reading his thoughts. "She did the same at home. With the house, I mean. With Papa. With me."

Edward glanced down at his young companion, surprised by the frankness of the admission. "With your father?"

"Yes. She helped him remember life after Mama died. I think he would have been perfectly content to retreat from the world forever, but Aunt Felicity refused to let him." Daphne's eyes widened somewhat and her smile grew. "She is...she is very good at reminding people to live, I think. She does not like to see people wither away when there is so much good in life. After Papa died, I was certain I could never abide anything beautiful again, but Aunt Felicity would not allow it."

Edward cleared his throat, uncomfortably aware that Felicity had said nearly the same of him. The woman had a way of making him feel exposed, as though she had scouted out his weaknesses before every one of their verbal skirmishes.

"I had thought," he said slowly, "that her primary interest was in your welfare. Your protection, your safety—"

"Oh, it is," Daphne said cheerfully at once. "But she believes life is more than simply being safe, Colonel. It's about... I don't know. Joy. Beauty. Music and gardens and all the things that make us glad to wake up each morning." She smiled faintly, her gaze distant. "I cannot explain it so well as my aunt. She says that the lovely moments are what makes all the rest worth enduring."

Edward glanced down at her. So young still, yet she spoke with the quiet assurance of someone who had already walked through life's shadows and survived them. Perhaps, in a small way she had, orphaned so young as she was.

He wished, in that moment, he had someone who had insisted on beauty when he had returned from the war. Someone who had refused to let him retreat into the cold silence of an empty house. But there had been no benevolent aunt, no Felicity Price waiting for him then. Only the ghosts of men he could not save and a father still ashamed of him. A father who had sent him to war to keep him out of sight.

A tightness formed in Edward's chest. He hadn't intended to have his convictions challenged by a seventeen-year-old girl with freckles across her nose and lingering grief in her eyes.

But there it was. It felt rather like standing on a battlefield with the wrong map and realizing, too late, that you'd underestimated the enemy. Except Daphne was not his enemy in the least; she was his responsibility. He had agreed that her aunt was his ally, though he hadn't exactly acted that way during their last private conversation, either. They had been polite to each other, at meals, the way one was civil to a distant relative. It was excruciating.

"Oh, Miss Banhurst." Daphne slowed to greet another young lady, curtsying with a graceful ease that was almost startling. When she had first arrived at his door, he hadn't seen the confidence in her she bore now.

Felicity's doing, no doubt.

And where was Felicity now? Home, recovering from her cold, no doubt commanding the servants of Briarwood from her sickbed and rearranging his life without asking permission.

Rather ridiculously, he almost missed her presence.

"I suppose," he said, after a pause after pleasantries with the Miss Banhurst had been exchanged and the young lady had continued on her way, "that your aunt is more formidable than I gave her credit for."

Daphne gave a soft laugh. "Oh, yes. Most definitely."

They continued walking in silence, but Edward's thoughts churned. The weight of Felicity's words, and her quiet power in his household, settled over him like a heavy, immovable cloak.

He still intended to protect Daphne, that mission would never alter. But *perhaps* there was more to protection than vigilance and rules. Perhaps there was something to Felicity's belief in joy—and perhaps he ought to consider the shape of his role, not just as Daphne's guardian, but as the man standing across from Felicity Price.

They had not gone three more steps before a lady Daphne's age approached with a bright smile and an airy curtsy.

"Miss Price! We were just about to play a game of lawn bowling. Would you care to join us?"

Daphne's face lit with pleasure as she cast a quick glance up at Edward. He felt the weight of it immediately, the silent question of permission.

He gave a short nod. "Of course. Enjoy yourself."

"Thank you, Colonel. Oh, this is delightful, thank you, Miss Anna." Daphne linked arms with the other young lady and they walked rapidly to the back of the garden, where a small rectangle of grass held the game.

Edward walked along behind her at a slower pace. As he slowly approached the group, he caught the tail end of an exchange between Daphne and one of the young men. He was a dark-haired fellow, well-dressed and with the easy posture of someone accustomed to laughter.

"—and I tell you, Miss Price, if you cannot best Miss Norman at lawn bowling, I vow I shall write an ode dedicated to your defeat on the spot. A dreadful one, too, to punish you."

Daphne's bright laughter filled the air, and he was proud she took the teasing in stride. "Then I had best play well, I wouldn't want my reputation ruined by terribly written poetry."

"Then we are all in agreement," Miss Anna said airily. "No one here wishes to hear Mr. Montague rhyme 'Price' with 'precise' again."

The small circle laughed free, unguarded laughter, as young people did when they felt at ease in each other's company. It gratified him. Daphne had found her footing with ease, had made friends of these people. She was liked.

Then Edward stepped onto the green.

The laughter died, a soft, halting death.

Mr. Montague noticed Edward first, straightening with an instinctual crispness, his good humor smoothing into polite neutrality. Miss Anna's fan—half-lifted in the air—paused mid-motion before she delicately folded it shut. The other young gentleman, a fair-haired sort, cleared his throat and adjusted his gloves. Miss Norman cradled the bowling ball closer to her stomach.

Daphne, still smiling, hesitated before her expression adjusted. Just slightly. Just enough that Edward saw it.

"Colonel Halstead," Mr. Montague greeted him with a respectful nod. "I did not see you there, sir."

"I thought to accompany Miss Price to watch the game," Edward said evenly.

There was a beat of silence where no one said anything, but glanced at one another exchanging silent thoughts.

Miss Anna, the one who had seemingly taken charge of the game, recovered first. She turned to Daphne with an encouraging smile. "You do intend to play, of course?"

"Oh yes," Daphne said quickly. "I have my honor to defend, you know. Mr. Montague's poetry will besmirch me, otherwise."

No one replied. The easy rhythm from before was gone, the teasing had died. There would be no poorly rhymed poetry, no genuine mirth, only careful politeness and sidelong glances at the *guardian* spectating from the sidelines.

Edward felt the shift viscerally in his gut.

And he suddenly, deeply, regretted it. He cleared his throat, stepped back a few paces, pretending to study a shrub of all things. What could he do? He could not leave, granting an opportunity for secret conversations or maneuverings by anyone present. He had a duty to watch over Daphne. No matter what.

Felicity Price would have a great deal to say on the matter if she heard about it, he had no doubt of that.

Edward took another step back, the damp grass pressing against the soles of his shoes. It could not be more clear that he did not belong here. Not in this moment, not with these young people, not even at a garden party where men of his standing escorted their daughters and sons to ensure they made friends with the correct set.

A soft laugh, somewhat forced and breathless, cut through the silence. Daphne, bless her, trying to recover what had been lost. "Goodness, we needn't worry too much about the Colonel. He will hardly subject poor players to a court-martial."

Stiff politeness already held them all in its grasp. Mr. Montague smiled, but it was mechanical, the ease gone. Miss Anna flicked open her fan again, filling the empty space with the soft rustling as she waved it. The other young gentleman reminded them of the rules of the game. Miss Norman asked politely who would go first.

Edward clasped his hands behind his back, watching, feeling keenly the change his presence had on the atmosphere.

The same as when a commanding officer appeared where the men tried to relax between assignments.

This is what Felicity meant.

She would not have stood there, looming like a headmaster waiting to bring order to unruly children. She would have laughed. Charmed them, perhaps, with some quick-witted remark to smooth over the awkwardness he had caused. She would have made herself belong, rather than standing stiffly at the edge, reminding them all of his presence by sheer force of it— and she most certainly would have taken him by the arm and none too gently steered him away, to leave the young people to their game.

But Felicity was not here. She was home, nursing her head cold in her bedchamber, and instead of sparring with him over breakfast, he had sat at the head of his too-long dining table, making stilted conversation with Daphne about the day's forth-coming entertainment.

"—if you'd like, Colonel?"

Edward looked up sharply.

Mr. Montague stood near him, holding a lawn bowl in his palm, his expression nothing but polite. "Would you care to play?"

It was a kindness. An offering. A way to turn him into some-thing other than a looming giant at the edge of the gathering.

Edward looked at the ball. Then at the expectant, if slightly wary, faces turned his way.

He should say no.

He did not.

Instead, he nodded. Anything to relieve the tension.

"If Miss Price does not mind my joining."

Daphne's eyes widened slightly. But then, bless the girl, she beamed. "Of course not, Colonel. Perhaps I shall best *you* instead —and I shall have to be the one to write an ode."

A few nervous laughs sprinkled the air. The tension in the group did not vanish, but it eased. At least a little.

For the first time in longer than he cared to remember, Edward Halstead rolled up his sleeves and prepared to play.

Chapter Twelve

S pending three days in bed while sneezing, coughing, and feeling as though someone had stuffed her head with cotton had not made Felicity any more mild a person than she had been before her cold. She knew this about herself. Though she did her utmost to care for others when they were ill, she found it insupportable to be the one needing the same sort of care.

So as she walked through the house, gray shawl wrapped around her black dress, she felt like a storm cloud as surely as she must have the appearance of one. Confined to the indoors, sleeping at odd intervals, her head aching and her limbs chilled, her mind had not found much for easy distraction. She blamed her cold and that state for the odd dreams she had experienced.

Several of them about Colonel Halstead.

"He has no business barging in where he doesn't belong," she muttered as she descended the stairs to the ground floor, where he kept his study. "Not in my dreams nor Daphne's outings."

Horrid man. Daphne had told Felicity all about the garden party and his insistence on joining the game of lawn bowling. What had he been thinking, intruding in that way? Had her niece not possessed such a compassionate soul, she likely would have expressed more annoyance and dismay at the circumstance.

Despite the lingering effects of her cold, Felicity could stand it no longer. She had to speak to him, and the invitations arriving every day were as good an excuse to seek the man out as any.

Not that she truly needed an excuse—but it felt better to have a sheaf of papers in her hand to shake at him the moment she saw him.

Felicity entered the quiet corridor leading to Halstead's study, but she did not realize the door to that room was open until she was nearly upon it. A voice drifted out from within, unknown to her, but masculine.

"—I have found substantial information that supports this line of inquiry, sir. The letters and witness statement are promising. I think I need but another month to be certain, unless you wish me to approach directly."

"No," Halstead's voice said with its usual firmness. She had to roll her eyes. Always the expert, wasn't he? "I do not want anyone aware that I am making this search. Not until I have all the information about his present circumstances."

"Yes, Colonel, I understand. If that is what you wish, your patience may have to stretch a little longer yet."

"Patience. After nearly twenty years, I suppose a few more weeks or months will be nothing. It is not as though he is yet a child in need of guidance."

He sounded so resigned in that moment that Felicity had to blink back surprise. She had never heard that tone from the Colonel. He always sounded so...so certain, so full of confidence.

"Even if you choose not to make yourself known," the other man said, something like kindness in his tone, "in another year or two, you may change your mind. Surely you will want some sort of contact with the boy?"

When Halstead answered, he sounded tired. As though he had said these things too many times before. "I will not decide on a course of action until I have the picture in full, Mr. Wright, as we have previously discussed."

Felicity listened, transfixed, as they discussed a budget and transportation. Her cold-muddled mind could not quite make sense of all she had heard, and she swayed slightly on her feet as she considered what she ought to do. She hadn't ever been one to eavesdrop before. Why hadn't she walked away? Or knocked?

Shaking her head at herself, Felicity took a step back. She glanced down the long corridor, but before she had decided to fully withdraw, she heard the other man's voice taking his leave. She turned instinctively, heart beating rapidly, and ducked into the room across the corridor, though she had only been in that room once, and had found a poor excuse of a library within, filled with empty bookshelves and uncomfortable furnishings. A perfect place to hide, especially given the darkness inside with the curtains drawn closed.

Standing in the semi-darkness, Felicity closed her eyes and tried to sort out the conversation again. Contact him…the boy… The emotion she heard in Halstead's voice had shocked her. He wasn't a man prone to sentiment, that she had learned over the weeks she'd lived here—but the sorrow and restraint in his tone were unmistakable.

Here was yet another thing about him that did not quite fit with what she thought she knew. The picture of him, the details of his past, did not yet tell a clear story.

As she heard the footsteps of the visitor withdraw down the corridor, Felicity wondered what she ought to do. Did she confess to overhearing a private conversation? Slink away and pretend nothing happened?

Shaking her head, she stepped out of the darkness and crossed to the door, raised her hand to knock, and hesitated. Her plan to pester him about the invitations felt quite juvenile in that moment.

She needed to leave. Rethink things. Perhaps spend another three days abed, hiding—no, resting. Resting.

Decision made, Felicity turned to go—and the door to the study opened at the same moment.

The Colonel stepped out, a weary expression on his face, his eyes heavy with thought and his posture less than perfect. He was in shirtsleeves again, too, looking not at all put together.

His shoulders tensed the moment his eyes fell on her. "Miss Price." One corner of his mouth went upward. "Captain. How are you this day? You must feel somewhat better to be walking about." The weariness melted away into something almost fond as he spoke to her, confusing Felicity all the more. "I had no hopes of seeing you today when you did not come down to breakfast."

Her mouth opened to respond, but closed again having uttered nothing. She had expected irritation from him, given their last interaction. Not this solicitous behavior and inquiry about her health.

"I am well. Erm. Better. Better than before, I mean." She held the invitations against her chest. "Are you in good health?"

What a ridiculous question. He was obviously fit as a fiddle, as handsome and healthy as ever. Felicity winced. Why did she have to note his attractiveness every time she saw him? It was becoming a terrible habit.

"Tolerably well," he said with a chuckle. "Oh. Here—I have wanted to show you this." He moved by her, but then his hand closed gently on her forearm as he tugged her across the corridor to the very room in which she had hid a moment before. "I hoped to ask your opinion before now, but it was not a matter of great urgency."

She heard him walk through the darkness, saw his outline approach the curtains, then he pulled them back to flood the room with light.

It was most definitely not the same as the last time she had seen it.

The wooden floor was now covered in several rugs. There were two armchairs by the empty hearth and a couch near the opposite wall, and a painting of an old castle hung over the fire-place. The still-mostly-empty shelves now had books scattered within them, and there were two crates next to the shelves open, more book spines showing within them.

"I haven't the first idea how to decorate a house, but I do know the importance of a good library. Keeping all the best books to myself in the study struck me as selfish. I have already asked for Daphne to give me a list of her favorite books to add to the shelves in here. I hope you will have suggestions, too."

Felicity walked numbly to the shelves, looking down into the crate, then up at him with a frown. "You—you are filling your library? Now?"

"I started ordering things from London shortly after you brought my attention to the—shall we say—bland contents of the rooms in my home." The Colonel's eyes crinkled at the corners as he looked at her, a brightness in them she did not expect. As though he were amused, or actually happy for once.

She hugged the invitations closer to her chest. The feelings of confusion curled cozily around her heart, changing into some-thing else. Something warm and satisfactory, like a stand-offish cat curling up in one's lap.

He had listened to her.

"I should not have said all that I did," she whispered. "It isn't my place."

Halstead's smile faded into something smaller, less enthusi-astic and gentler. "You are concerned for your niece's happiness," he said, his voice low. "You were within your rights, in that regard, to be concerned about her home. Besides, you are not the only one who regrets words spoken that day. I apologize."

She nodded once. "That is kind of you to say. Apology accepted. Thank you."

He came a step closer. "Miss Price. Are you certain you are well enough to be up and about? Perhaps you ought to be resting —you do not seem yourself."

"Neither do you," Felicity muttered softly, rubbing her forehead with her free hand. She could not convince herself to dredge up the indignation she had felt when she had planned to confront him about the garden party, and the game of lawn bowling, and the invitations.

She did not want to soften toward him. She wanted to remain annoyed with him, with his high-handedness—but something about his expression, the steady gaze he kept upon her, the concern in his eyes and the way he shifted, as if resisting the impulse to come closer...it unnerved her.

When he was like this, when he showed such gentleness, he was more handsome than ever. A thing which immediately dismayed her, and it gave her the ability to find a touch of tartness. "I assure you, Colonel, I am not so delicate that a mild cold will confine me for days on end."

Given that she still felt the last of the illness clinging to her, befuddling her usually quick mind, it was a horrid lie.

Nevertheless, Felicity held her chin high and tried to regain her composure. "I came to discuss something of importance, unless you are too occupied with other matters."

Colonel Halstead studied her for a long moment, then gestured to the chairs in front of the cold hearth. "Would you like to sit while we talk?" He glanced at the door. "Or we could return to my study if it is a matter of great seriousness."

Felicity looked to the door and tugged her shawl closer to her shoulders. "It is rather cold in here, without a fire."

"Of course, I should not have suggested it. Come, the study is warm." He led the way back to his domain, and she hesitated a moment before following.

When she stepped inside the study, the air was warm and laced with the scent of ink parchment, along with the faintest trace of his scent, a mix of soap and other things she found far too pleasant and familiar.

His desk was still cluttered with papers, ledgers, and an abandoned cup of tea. She resisted the urge to glance at whatever notes might be scattered there from his meeting with the stranger. Ill, she might be, but ill-mannered, she was not. Instead, Felicity took her seat and kept her eyes on him until he settled on the other side of the desk in his large leather chair, putting his elbows on the desk and folding his hands on its surface.

"What is it you wished to speak with me about?"

Best to get straight to the point. "There are several invitations here for various parties and balls. If you are going to insist on being overly protective of Daphne, I require clarification. I am certain you will have an opinion on which invitations ought to be accepted and which declined."

He leaned back, crossing his arms over his chest. "Of course I will."

Felicity straightened her spine. At last, she felt her ire return to her. "Then I must ask if I am to run every social decision through you now, Colonel, or will you allow me to do my duty and guide Daphne without interference?"

His gaze sharpened. "I think I ought to be consulted with regards to where Daphne spends her time. Once at such events, it would be ridiculous for every detail to need discussion."

"Especially since you will be acting as her shadow at every turn."

"Indeed. One of us should always be with her."

He was to be as stubborn as ever on that point, drat him.

Felicity put the invitations on the desk and pushed them toward him. "Very well. Here are the invitations. Do let me know which you find acceptable. Perhaps you would also like to choose which gowns she wears, and what jewelry adorns her? To ensure that her clothing does not offend your sensibilities. Perhaps letting her decide between ivory and lilac is granting the girl too much freedom."

His brows drew together in a most disapproving frown. "Miss Price—"

"Then there is the matter of her hair. We will consult you about which ribbons and pins to employ."

"Miss Price, I—"

"Then there is the matter of fans. Lace? Paper? Silk?" She raised her voice, continuing despite the childishness of it. After all, he'd started it. "Then there is the matter of which books—"

"Felicity!" he barked sternly.

Her lips parted in surprise as the rest of her words fled.

He had used her given name.

"I know what you are doing," Halstead said, tone still stern yet he did not sound angry. "You think I have made a ridiculous request, so you mean to make it more so by adding one thing after another—I am not a fool. I can see we will not agree on how best to chaperone Daphne. My ward, your niece. But I trust you to see to the rest, Felicity. I trust that you know best how your niece presents herself, and how she navigates the world, and who she spends her time with. Why does this one instance of our disagreement cause you such distress? Why can you not bend to my reasonable request?"

Felicity's stuffy and muddled head made it all too easy to grow petulant, but she retained enough of her sensibilities to recognize that as an unwise course of action. Instead, she studied him, and closely. "Will you truly listen to my explanation this time? Without interruptions, Edward?"

Well, he used her Christian name. She might as well use his.

As it passed her lips for the first time aloud, Felicity felt herself relaxing. To address him thus made things feel less tilted in his favor.

He was just a man. Not a Colonel. Not above her. They were both simply people who were joined unwillingly by the circumstance of caring for the same young woman.

He sighed and ran his hand over his face before cupping his chin in his hand. "Contrary to what you may think, Felicity Price, I value your opinion."

His words made her pause, collecting her thoughts as she

would a scattered deck of cards as she prepared to address his question. "Edward," she said, her voice calm, "my resistance to your request is not borne of a mere desire for disagreement. I am not rebellious by nature." She straightened, meeting his gaze directly. "It is about the manner in which we prepare Daphne for her future role in society. She is no longer a child, and after she marries she will need to navigate the complexities of social engagements on her own." Felicity's hands rested lightly on the stack of invitations. "If we shadow her at every event, scrutinizing each interaction, forbidding her from making slight faux pas which will surely be forgotten, are we not at risk of undermining her ability to discern and decide for herself? Such constant oversight might suggest to her that she is incapable of any independent judgment or action—or imply to others we do not believe her competent in that regard."

His eyebrows raised, but he kept his word and said nothing, giving Felicity encouragement to continue with a softer tone. "You have led men in battle, sir, where obedience and vigilance are essential. I would not question you on the battlefield of war— but on this particular battlefield, I do. Daphne's challenges, though less perilous, will require no less courage and the ability to trust her own decisions. Is it not our responsibility to prepare her to meet these challenges with confidence?"

Edward's features remained neutral, watching her intently, giving her no idea how he received her careful reasoning.

Felicity continued in earnest. Well, in for a penny… "I value your guardianship, Edward, and your protectiveness towards Daphne. Truly, I did not expect you to concern yourself so much with her. But we must also trust her to grow, to learn from her own experiences. To make minor mistakes now, when we are at hand to help right them." She sat back, folding her hands in her lap.

Had she said too much—or not enough?

Felicity watched the Colonel closely as he seemed to weigh his words, he winced as though pained when he looked down at the surface of his desk. At the myriad of invitations. "Miss Price... Captain. Felicity. I understand your desire to see Daphne flourish under less stringent supervision." He paused, lifting his head but looking past Felicity as though seeing into his own distant memories. "I must confess, my insistence on vigilance is not solely the product of an overprotective old soldier." His gaze returned to hers, filled with a seriousness bordering on sorrow. "When I was younger—much younger—I learned a hard lesson about the consequences of youthful mistakes. My whole life, and the lives of others, shifted paths because of my mistake." Edward shifted uncomfortably in his chair, the creases in his brow deepening. "There were repercussions which followed me long after, repercussions from a moment of folly easily avoided with more prudent guardianship." His voice was low, almost hesitant.

An unexpected pulse of compassion went through Felicity as she felt the pain behind his words. Something awful had happened, then.

When he continued, it was with a voice of compassion. "All I wish is to spare Daphne from such potential pitfalls, to ensure her safety and well-being."

"We cannot protect her from everything," Felicity murmured. "Even if we wished to do so—and your mistakes will not be hers, Edward. Surely." She hesitated a moment, then said quietly, "It seems to me that you are still carrying the weight of your past mistake with you. They must be grave indeed to remain prevalent so many years later."

He sat back. A muscle ticked in his jaw. "Indeed. But such is none of your concern. Some things are not meant to be spoken of, Miss Price."

She raised her eyebrows. So, she was Miss Price again? She tilted her head to the side, studying him. "And yet some things weigh heavier when carried alone, Edward."

EDWARD PULLED IN A STARTLED BREATH. HER WORDS SETTLED OVER him, a warm compress on an old, aching wound. Surely, she was not asking him to speak of his past? She could not be offering such a thing. They barely knew one another. And yet…

"I cannot deny the truth of your statement." Edward watched her, noted her still pale countenance from her illness and its contrast with the stubborn tilt of her chin. Her eyes, dark and intelligent, remained leveled on him. Waiting. "It is not your burden to bear, Captain. Felicity." It was so easy to say her name, to let it leave his tongue, and he wanted to examine why. He had only called one other woman unrelated to him by her given name.

Pamela. The woman he had ruined with his own recklessness. His selfishness.

Her focus moved to her lap, and he relaxed even as he felt a prickle of disappointment. She hadn't really known what she asked. Truly, how could she want to know any details of his past beyond what was necessary for them to work together in the present? No, there was no more to be said on the matter. She would apologize for her intrusive question. She would leave the study. They would argue about handling Daphne's social forays later, after this awkward ceasefire had passed.

"I fell in love when I was Daphne's age," Felicity said, her words startling him for all that they were softly spoken. "I loved, I pined, for a full year, dreaming of the one I cared for coming to see that I was the best choice for him. I put off my coming out into Society so I could stay in his vicinity, in the country. I told my parents, I insisted to them, that I was not ready for an experience in London."

She looked up at him again, a sad smile curving her lips. "Finally, he noticed me. His approach was cautious at first. He was a younger son, I thought he was shy. But now…now I wonder if he was merely reluctant. He was a younger son, for one thing, and though my dowry was of decent size, a marriage settlement would be much less. Not enough to live on in the way he was accustomed."

Ought he to stop her words? Tell her she need not relive something that obviously pained her? But Edward had not asked a question to lead to this. Felicity revealed her past of her own volition...and the more she spoke of this younger son, of her first love, the more intrigued he became.

"I told him I would wait for him." A laugh with a note of bitterness escaped Felicity's lips before they pressed together in a grimace. "As long as it took. I believed I loved him enough to wait, that his mutual affection would in turn be patient. He accepted my promise, and he went away. To stay with an uncle, to study the law. We were not permitted to write to one another directly, of course. I could only receive news of him from the letters he wrote to his family, and they were sparse indeed. My parents thought him weak willed. They spoke against him in my hearing...but they loved me, and they wanted my happiness. It was a difficult balancing act, especially with Anthony going away to fight in the war and men like...like *him* remaining home. Younger sons fill the military, as I am certain you know."

He felt himself agreeing with her parents, given he already suspected what the end of the story would be.

Felicity sat before him, unmarried still, after all.

When she looked up at him, he felt he should smile, should respond; he had been silent for so long while she unearthed a painful history to him. Edward cleared his throat. "I am aware. Anthony was quite an exception to that. Despite his place as eldest son, he truly believed he fought for the good of others, that it was a duty and a calling."

"I miss him," Felicity said, pulling her shawl tighter about her shoulders. "I wish he had been home when my...when the man I thought I loved came home at last. Unexpectedly. Already married."

Edward hadn't expected *that* ending. He sat straighter in his chair, hands splayed on the desk. "What? I thought you were going to tell me he had died!"

She blinked up at him, eyebrows furrowing in evident confusion. "No. No, he's quite alive. And married. She was a young widow, her husband died at war, and she had a substantial income."

"The cad," Edward said, shaking his head in utter disbelief. "You were waiting for him, honorably and patiently, and he returned home already married? Without warning? Felicity, why do you still mourn him?"

She blinked. "I...I do not mourn him."

"You looked heartbroken the moment you began the story," Edward pointed out, looking into her eyes heavy with emotion. With... "No. You cannot still wish for him? Not a man who would behave so dishonorably toward you."

"Your defense of my feelings is kind, Edward." The puzzlement on her face made him sink back into his chair. "But it is not necessary. I know he did not behave honorably. Truly."

"Yet you remain unwed?" He winced. "That is truly none of my business, I apologize."

Felicity's lips twitched upward and the darkness in her eyes receded a little, making way for a twinkle of amusement. "No, it is not. You see, by the time that gentleman—" Edward snorted at that term, for surely it could not apply to such a scoundrel, "— returned home with his bride, and after I recovered from my hurt, I did not wish to face more disappointment. Not right away. I was but three and twenty." Her somber expression returned, a flicker of pain passing over her face. "Around that time, Anthony's wife, Margaret, fell ill. Daphne was only seven years old. I stayed with them to help, and Margaret died a few months after Anthony came home from the war. I stayed on, for my brother and niece's sake. My parents passed away a few years ago. I had made myself so useful, Anthony said I ought to continue on with him until Daphne wed, and...that brings us to now." She gestured with both hands, palms up, to the study and then to him.

"To this very moment." Edward took in her soft features, the set of her chin, the dark hair that framed her face and the plain gray gown she wore. He had yet to see her outside of mourning colors. The sharp lines of her face, the depth of her eyes, the delicate movements of her hands, were enough to make her a stunning woman. But what if she wore the deep greens he was himself fond of?

He cleared his throat. That thought had no business in his mind. It did not matter what she wore; all that mattered was that they worked well together to set Daphne on a path of success and happiness. In honor of her father's memory, and for the girl's own sake.

"Thank you for sharing your history with me, Felicity." He had not expected that sort of confidence from her. She had struck him almost as an adversary in their first days and weeks together; fierce in her defense of Daphne, in her demands for her niece's needs, but never asking for anything for herself.

That realization struck him hard in that moment. He had taken each of her demands, her instructions, and honored them, but always with the feeling that he was capitulating, giving in to her wants and her ways. But in truth, everything she asked for was on Daphne's behalf.

"What do you need?" he asked, moving to the edge of his chair.

Felicity blinked at the abrupt shift in conversation. "I-I beg your pardon?"

"Surely there is something you need that you have not expressed. You have been here a month with your niece, and I have seen bills for her upkeep and her wants. But what of you? What do you need, Felicity?"

As her shoulders relaxed, the woman before him shook her head. "I need nothing from you, Edward. Nothing except your trust." She stood and a slight smile, not precisely warm but at least not adversarial, curled her lips upward. "Let me know which of those invitations are acceptable soon, please. Daphne's schedule is important." Without another word she curtsied and left the room, with him staring after her.

Edward remained seated, the memory of Felicity's story lingering in the stillness of the study. He stared at the door through which she had vanished, grappling with the shift in their relationship.

What she shared: it had peeled back layers of her own guarded past, revealing vulnerabilities he hadn't expected to discover. It wasn't the past itself but the simplicity with which Felicity had shared it that unsettled him. Her raw honesty was a thing he often avoided within himself. Though an honorable man, Edward kept much of what he felt to himself. Let the world see his good cheer, not the dark shadows of his history, of what the war had done, what life had done. What he had done to himself.

The room seemed somehow emptier after Felicity had left. As if her presence had filled it more than her slight form ever could. Why was he so often in this single room, alone, when he had a whole house at his disposal? A house he could easily fill with friends and neighbors. But instead he sat behind this desk, his back to his garden and the rest of the outside world.

Edward rubbed his temples where the beginnings of a headache throbbed. A physical manifestation, perhaps, of the emotional pains the conversation had stirred.

"Trust," he murmured to himself. The word hung heavily in the air. It had been neither a challenge nor a plea when the word had fallen from her lips. No. Felicity's request was simple.

He stood, pacing to the window, where the view of his gardens brought little comfort. Even though the roses had put out new growth, they remained without blooms. Roses made one exercise a great deal of patience, a thing he had thought he possessed in abundance before Felicity and Daphne entered his life.

How was he to reconcile what Felicity asked for and still keep Daphne safe?

His thoughts wandered back to Pamela. How different things might have been if there was better oversight; had his parents cared what he did, had they kept watch over him. And here was Felicity, sharing the pains of past regrets with him yet still standing resiliently, still willing to support her niece with all she had.

Resting his forehead against the cool pane of glass, Edward closed his eyes and wondered once again why Anthony had chosen him as guardian to his child...and why he could not seem to dismiss thoughts of Felicity Price's soft smile, even in the midst of one of their disagreements.

Chapter Thirteen

HYDE PARK, APRIL 8, 1817

With the observation of Easter the Sunday previous, London came alive at last as spring reached her pinnacle. Nowhere was this more evident than in Hyde Park, where Felicity took in everything around her with quiet appreciation. The grasses were as green as ever, the trees had new growth in vibrant hues, and flowers peeked out of carefully manicured garden beds.

Felicity, along with the Colonel and Daphne, were attending part in a picnic arranged by the Normans. Mr. Norman seemed disposed to like Edward—Felicity had tried but failed to think of him as Halstead since their conversation in his study. Miss Norman had befriended Daphne. The outing suited everyone involved, including Mr. and Miss Montague, who were once again chatting amiably with Daphne.

"I have always liked the park away from Rotten Row," Mrs. Norman said, sipping delicately at her tea. Felicity sat on one side of the lady, Mr. Norman on the other, and Edward beside that gentleman. "There is so much more to this place than the crowds all vying to be seen in their slow promenade."

"Such as the ducks," Edward said, gesturing to the water glimmering before them.

The group looked over. The Serpentine boasted its usual swans, geese, and ducks, but if one knew where to look they would find nesting spots tucked here and there in the park.

Felicity shaded her eyes to better look across the pond where a few couples rowed about in small boats, rented out on fine days, her eyes seeing more than was before her. "My father brought me here years ago, to hunt for nests. We never disturbed them, of course, but it was always great fun to poke about in the weeds to find them."

Mr. Norman chuckled before making his own observation. "In a few more weeks, the water will be full of goslings, signets, and ducklings. All of them driving their parents to distraction." He nudged Edward with his elbow. "You are getting a fine taste of that yourself, Halstead. Guardianship of a young lady is no small thing."

Felicity adjusted the corner of the blanket nearest her, somehow resisting the desire to watch Edward respond to that particular comment. Instead she glanced toward the other picnic blanket, a few yards away, where the younger people were enjoying their tea and sandwiches. Daphne's laughter sounded sweetly from where she sat between Miss Norman and Miss Montague, prompting a smile from her aunt.

"I am fortunate that I am not alone in the work of caring for a young lady," Edward said, tempting Felicity to turn her attention back to their conversation. "Lord Blackstone advised me to think of ladies as I would think of geese."

"Oh, that man." Mrs. Norman sounded more amused than annoyed. "Every time my husband comes home from the club, it seems he has another wild tale to tell. What do you think of Lord Blackstone, Miss Price?"

Felicity looked up, meeting the woman's curious gaze with raised eyebrows. As she was more chaperone than guest, she had not expected to be brought into the conversation properly. She had whiled away the first quarter hour of the picnic reading a book which now lay open beside her on the blanket—yet Mrs.

Norman had invited her to contribute several times already. The other woman was closer to forty than Felicity was, with just the barest of lines showing around her eyes and a cheery disposition that made her think the woman a pleasant person.

"I am afraid I have not heard much about him," Felicity admitted. "I know only that he founded and patronizes the club where Colonel Halstead is a member." She glanced at Edward to find him watching her, his eyes bright with amusement.

He inclined his head. "I suppose I have not spoken of him often —he is a rather peculiar man, to say the least."

Mr. Norman leaned back on his hands, an easy smile on his face. "Peculiar is a mild word for it. Have you made peace with his eccentricities yet, Colonel, or has Lord Blackstone's fondness for taxidermy made you regret joining our unusual club?"

Edward's low chuckle made something inside Felicity squirm, though certainly not unpleasantly. She tried to direct her attention away again, to the more youthful members of the party, when he spoke.

"The giraffe in the billiard room was quite a surprise."

A laugh escaped her as she turned toward him. "A giraffe? Colonel, that cannot be true." She looked at Mr. Norman, expecting him to deny such a thing. She had seen a live giraffe once, at the Tower Menagerie. The creature had stood marvelously high, the entire of one being found in a billiard room—

"Well. Not an entire giraffe," Mr. Norman said with a broad grin. "Just the neck up."

Felicity started to shake her head, unable to help looking at Edward with wide eyes. "I should very much like to know why a man would look at a giraffe and decide its final resting place ought to be inside a gentleman's club, billiard room or otherwise."

The corners of Edward's mouth twitched upward. "Perhaps I will have the pleasure of introducing you to Lord Blackstone soon. I have heard rumor of his hosting a gathering at his home for club members and their families." He sat up, leaning slightly in her direction as though to impart a secret. "You ought to know, Miss Price, that Lord Blackstone claims all his specimens died of natural causes."

Mr. Norman chuckled. "A most convenient truth, if I have ever heard one."

Edward laughed again. "Who do you think provides him with all these creatures, offering such reassurances to him?" He shook his head. "I cannot fault him for wishing to believe such things. He seems a good man in every respect."

"Indeed." Mr. Norman moved closer to his wife, stealing a biscuit from her plate while she playfully swatted at his hand. "He is a good sort, from all I know of him—and particular about the men who join his club."

"A thing for which I am thankful," Edward said, his tone still bright. "Acquaintance with you and your family has provided Daphne with a good friend in your daughter."

A breeze came through at that moment, pushing the blanket up in such a way as to nearly unsettle a dish of berries. Edward moved quickly, saving the dish and moving to sit on that side of the blanket to keep it down.

"Heavens." Mrs. Norman adjusted her bonnet. "I do hope the wind will not become disruptive. I am so enjoying the afternoon out of doors."

"A stray breeze, I am certain," her husband said genially.

Edward looked up at Felicity, sitting much closer to her now. His smile returned, warm as the sunshine.

She liked him like this. At ease. Cheerful. Among friends.

He looked down at her book, its pages rustling, and put his hand upon it to pin them in place. "You will have lost your place, Miss Price."

She looked down, realizing her hand was mere inches from his where it rested on the blanket—and bare, she had not yet put her gloves on again after eating. She drew back, tucking her hand in her lap, but not before her pulse skipped traitorously.

"It—it is of no consequence," she said, somewhat belatedly.

148

His gaze found hers, his eyebrows raised. When he spoke, his voice was lower, meant for her ears alone. "Are you feeling unwell again? Your cold has not returned?"

"No, not at all. I am quite well, Colonel." Felicity forced a smile. How had she sounded unwell when she spoke? Had he sensed the hesitation in her words?

"Good." He smiled at her, then plucked a clover from beside the blanket. He placed it in the book, closed it, and handed it to her. "Perhaps you ought to rest more, Miss Price. To ensure you remain in good health."

She accepted the book, putting it in her lap, not caring he had marked the wrong page. "I believe you mistake me for someone who listens to such advice, sir, when that is quite impossible. There is a young lady to manage, you see."

A soft laugh escaped him in a breath of air, the twinkle in his eyes returning. His lips parted as though he had more to say, but another voice spoke before Edward could.

"What book is it that you are reading, my dear?" Mrs. Norman asked, and Felicity nearly started in her surprise. For a moment, she quite forgot that they were not alone.

She hastily handed the book to the other woman, her tongue struggling to catch up with her actions. "The third Waverley novel, by Scott. *The Antiquary*. I admit, each book has fascinated me, but have only just acquired this one."

Mrs. Norman met Felicity's eyes as she accepted the book, and Felicity read clearly the other woman's curiosity. It had nothing to do with the novel, and everything to do with what she had observed between Felicity and Edward. Or thought she had observed.

Felicity relaxed her shoulders, carefully softening her expression. "Do you enjoy reading, Mrs. Norman?"

After a quick glance at Edward, who remained seated next to Felicity, the woman nodded. "I do—and I have read this one. Though all the dramatics surrounding the romances agitated me at times. The ladies never seemed to have happy endings."

"I am not one to let my thoughts linger on romance," Felicity said, keeping her gaze level with Mrs. Norman. "I consider myself quite on the shelf, and all my energies are taken up with Daphne. When my niece weds a good man, I will consider my work complete and pack myself off to some seaside village and count myself happy indeed."

The conversation was less about books and reading than it was about Mrs. Norman's curiosity. Her frequent glances at Edward told Felicity the woman was curious, perhaps even concerned that Miss Daphne Price's spinster aunt had found herself the recipient of unwanted advances.

Edward had closed his eyes, tilted his head back, and seemed completely lost in his own thoughts and oblivious to the ladies. Mr. Norman had covered his face with his hat.

Mrs. Norman handed Felicity's book to her. "Your niece is lucky she has you to look after her. I am certain her guardian does well enough, but there is nothing a young lady needs so much as the guidance of an older, wiser woman in her life."

Accepting the book, Felicity held it to her chest again. "I agree. Thank you."

"You ought to come to my home with Daphne for tea," the woman added, her voice lower and a smile on her lips. "I would enjoy a conversation with you, I think. We could discuss Scott and the perils of readying girls for womanhood."

Felicity relaxed. This was no warning of gossip, but an offer of friendship. It had been a long time since she had received enough notice from anyone to think such a thing possible. "I would like that."

A sudden movement at the other group brought Felicity's attention there as Mr. Montague leapt to his feet with the energy of a young, enthusiastic man.

"Ladies, it seems a crime to sit when we might be walking along the Serpentine." With Mr. Montague's declaration, he held his hands out; one to his sister to help her up, the other to Daphne, who immediately looked toward Felicity and Edward.

Her eyes were wide, hopeful, but her words were somewhat hesitant when she spoke. "Oh, Colonel, might I please—"

"No," Edward said, eyes still closed.

The single word cut through the warmth of the afternoon. Daphne's expression turned immediately contrite, and she lowered her gaze to the blanket.

Felicity gave Edward a sharp look, full of disapproval, but he had barely cracked an eye open to look in Daphne's direction.

Still, it appeared her silent censure was nonetheless felt. Edward sighed. "Not without a proper escort. You cannot wander about without protection, Daphne."

Despite what sounded like little more than a practical note, a heaviness remained on the gathering. Felicity felt it keenly as the young ladies exchanged glances, and Mr. Montague stared evenly at Edward.

The young man, no more than twenty years old, smiled and offered a small bow to Edward. "Colonel, I should hope my sister and I, along with Miss Norman, are considered adequate company. While I am not so equipped as a soldier to protect Miss Daphne, I think myself equal to the task of looking after her long enough to enjoy an afternoon's stroll in the environs near the picnic."

It was quite a diplomatic speech, but Daphne's crestfallen expression spoke well enough of what she and Felicity already knew. Colonel Halstead had no intention of letting Daphne out of his sight or hearing. The other young people had already grown more reserved, and even Mr. Norman and Mrs. Norman exchanged a glance.

This was what Edward did not understand. And unless she could explain it to him—

"Unfortunately, Mr. Montague," the Colonel began stiffly.

Felicity put her teacup on its saucer with a clatter. "Oh, a walk does sound lovely. Daphne, darling, do not forget your parasol. Where is mine? I should like to feed my crusts to the swans." She stood and fluttered about. "Here is your parasol, I have mine.

Would you like me to feed your crusts to the waterfowl, Mrs. Norman?"

The married woman chuckled and held her plate out to Felicity. "Indeed. I will stay put, I think."

Edward rose to his feet. "Miss Price—"

She cut him a sharp glance and smiled brightly. "You needn't trouble yourself, Colonel."

He narrowed his eyes, glanced at the young people, and nodded. "Of course. I will come with you. Daphne, enjoy your walk."

Felicity watched her niece's eyes brighten as she finally took Mr. Montague's offered hand to come to her feet, parasol clutched in her other gloved hand. The young people started forward, their steps light, and laughter floating back on the breeze.

Holding the crusts in one ungloved hand, Felicity propped her parasol on her shoulder as though it were a rifle and marched directly to the water. Edward fell into step beside her.

"That was hardly necessary," he muttered, keeping up with her quite easily given his much longer stride.

"On the contrary, it was entirely necessary." Felicity forced a wide smile onto her face as she caught Daphne peering back at them. "We cannot deny Daphne every bit of independence, nor can we allow her friends to think you a tyrant."

He grumbled, "I do not care what they think—"

"You need to, Edward," she said quietly. "Would you rather be the villain who ruins an afternoon for a young lady, or the gracious guardian who trusts her friends?"

He shook his head. "We have discussed this numerous times, Felicity. I have made my opinion quite clear—"

"And they are within your sight, Edward." She nodded to the little group. "And I sincerely doubt there are any secretive plans being discussed between three young ladies and a young man, who is brother to one of them. See, he escorts Miss Norman, as is right since she is the hostess. The other two ladies walk behind him. There is nothing amiss there. They are also in full view of

Mr. and Mrs. Norman, a respected couple of your acquaintance. What is there to fear?"

Edward stared at the young people, sighed, then held his hand out to Felicity. She blinked at it. He hadn't taken the time to put his gloves on, either, it seemed.

"May I have a crust of bread?" he asked, tone gruff.

"Oh. Of course." She dropped it into his palm as they reached the edge of the Serpentine, her fingertips brushing his warm skin.

"Thank you." He began breaking it into smaller pieces, tossing it outward to the water where the birds floating on its surface rushed to claim the scraps. Felicity did the same. His frown remained.

With a sigh, Felicity turned her attention to a mallard brave enough to waddle up to her and quack, asking for a crumb. She tossed him a piece. "Have you ever seen a man frown so crossly on such a fine day?" she asked the duck.

"I have reason enough for it," the Colonel muttered.

Felicity, hands empty of bread, closed her parasol before she shook it at him. "Colonel Halstead, if you refuse to enjoy the afternoon all because Daphne wished to take a walk with her friends, I may very well put you up for court martial. It ought to be a crime, as Mr. Montague said, not to enjoy such a fine spring day as this."

He stared at her for a long moment, his expression solemn. "Are you threatening me with your parasol, Captain Price?"

She looked at the instrument, then back up at him resolutely. "Yes," she said, quite aware of the foolishness of such a thing. "I shall run you through with it if you do not start enjoying the day, immediately."

He stepped closer, so the tip of her parasol pressed against his chest, right above his heart. "A sad fate for a man who survived the war with the French. Yet if you think it necessary, I submit myself to this most dishonorable death."

Felicity gasped, then nearly choked. The man had teased her! In the next moment, a grin broke free on his handsome face, with a low chuckle that turned into a soft laugh, a most entrancing sound that pulled an answering smile onto her face.

Laughter bubbled up with her, too. "You are terrible, sir," she said at last, shaking her head.

Edward tapped the parasol still pressed against his chest. "Truce, Miss Price?"

"Truce," she agreed, dropping the parasol to her side. "I did not know you could be ridiculous."

"Really?" He tilted his head to the side. "I am convinced you must often think me so." He held out his arm, glancing toward Daphne's group of friends. "Come. You have had your way, and Daphne has enjoyed her independence. But I should like to walk in that direction, in case she has need of me. Of us."

Us. At the sound of that word from his lips, that comfortable warmth wrapped itself around her heart again. She took his arm as he smiled, and Felicity realized the sight of his smile stirred an odd, hopeful feeling in her chest. Her cheeks warmed, and she swiftly turned to watch a swan glide across the water.

Something rather strange, and certainly quite dangerous, was unfolding in her heart. She needed to put a stop to it—for Daphne's sake, if not for her own. She had resigned herself to spinsterhood, accepted it long before she had met the Colonel. Once Daphne's future was secure, there would be nothing left for Felicity except a quiet set of rented rooms near the seaside, and the occasional Christmas visits to her niece and, hopefully, her children. That was her future.

The warmth faded into cold certainty.

Colonel Halstead was a necessary ally until then, and nothing else. He could be nothing else.

Chapter Fourteen

"Forty-nine days," Edward murmured, staring at the reading room shelves. He sat in Blackstone's, of course, whiling away the hours while Felicity and Daphne paid polite calls in London's finer neighborhoods. Despite his estate's nearness to Town, he had no intention of sending them off on visiting days without him. When they were ready to depart for home, they would bring the carriage and the coachman would fetch him.

Mr. Harold Marlowe, the man responsible for Edward's introduction to Lord Blackstone, looked up from his book. They were not yet friends, in truth, but they did not mind one another's company. "Did you say something, Colonel?"

Edward shook his head. "Oh, nothing of consequence. It has been forty-nine days since I received the letter about my ward." In forty-nine days, his whole life had changed. His responsibility to Daphne necessitated a complete adjustment of his priorities, putting her well-being first and foremost in his mind and plans.

He only hoped Anthony Price's trust hadn't been misplaced.

The same amount of time had passed since he learned of Miss Felicity Price, a woman who had immediately set about to prove he had no idea what it meant to provide for her niece; a woman who by turns frustrated and fascinated him as they learned to work together for Daphne's sake. Captain Felicity Price had never shied away from speaking her mind to him, from being direct; instead she squared her shoulders and delivered her thoughts to him as though used to facing down men far more intimidating than himself.

Of late, he could not seem to get the image of her out of his head. If Edward looked out the window, he remembered the day he put his coat on her shoulders while she argued vociferously with him. If he trained his gaze anywhere indoors, especially in his study, he pictured her sitting across the desk with her slight, knowing smile and intelligent eyes.

Thank goodness for Blackstone's. In a place full of gentlemen, he did not need to think about Felicity. Nor did he need to worry overmuch about Daphne while she was out making social calls. Instead, he refocused his mind on his own business: tasks at the estate, the progress of his investigator—

The door to the reading room burst open and several men spilled in, most of them holding glasses of spirits and the one leading the fray grasping a familiar tome.

The club's betting book.

Every gentleman's club in London had one, though not all were treated as holy books. Blackstone's book in particular seemed to be more a bit of fun than something to seriously concern oneself with.

"What are all of you doing in here?" the man with the book, one Lord Henry Philbrook said. "The Season has started properly, and we must get down all the names of the poor souls the mamas of the *ton* have in their sights."

Marlowe groaned and sank into his chair. "Not this again. Every single year..." He held his book closer to his face in an attempt to hide.

The man with the book sighted him. "Marlowe, dear fellow! Haven't you a cousin on the list of bachelors?"

"The boy is only twenty," Marlowe said, snapping his book

shut and shaking a finger at them. "Far too young to wed, no matter what the scheming women of London may think."

"A good age for a debutante," someone argued. "Better an eighteen year old wed a man of twenty than someone old and feeble, like Colonel Halstead."

A round of laughter filled the previously silent reading room.

Despite his finer feelings, Edward forced himself to chuckle and shook his head. "I assure you, I have no intention of robbing schoolrooms or nurseries—nor do I have any plans to wed this Season or any other."

Several of the men booed, a few cheered, but Lord Henry opened the book and took out a sharpened pencil. He ceremoniously licked the tip of it, grinned at Edward, and spoke aloud as he wrote. "Colonel Edward Halstead, bachelor of mature—nay, advanced age." He looked around at the other men. "Who thinks he will be the target of the mamas themselves? Perhaps a widow with six children?"

Mr. Norman walked into the room then, looking about as he ran a hand through his hat-flattened hair. "What is all this noise? I heard you lot bellowing like bull calves as I came in downstairs—the neighbors will complain to Lord Blackstone again."

"It is the Season, Norman." One of the men pushed a glass of brandy into the newcomer's hand while Edward shook his head. The men had all gone mad. "Widows and ambitious mamas are sharpening their claws—and our dear friend here, the Colonel, is unattached."

"With a fine estate," Marlowe, the traitor, added with twinkling eyes. "He bought it outright with his prize money from the war, it was in the papers."

Lord Henry waved the book under Edward's nose. "You will have every woman over thirty years vying for your attention, Colonel. Leave some for the rest of us!"

Edward pushed the book away, unable to help his grimace. The idea was distasteful, and hopefully far-fetched. "Spare me. My interest in women begins and ends with seeing my ward happily settled. I want nothing more to do with their world."

Felicity's knowing smile appeared traitorously in his thoughts.

The men were all laughing—but then, mercifully, they focused on someone else, a lone man in the corner trying to hide behind the newssheets, and the mob moved in that direction. Marlowe shook his head as they went, and Norman gave Edward a consoling pat on the shoulder.

"I am sorry for you, friend," Norman said.

Edward looked up. "Whatever for?"

"Despite them saying it is the women at work in this mart of theirs," Marlowe explained, his nose wrinkled, "every one of those fellows has an unwed female relative. You are in their sights now. They will tell their wives, sisters, mothers, cousins, and so on and so forth, all about Colonel Halstead's bachelorhood."

"You will be a fine prize." Norman's understanding sympathy froze on his face. His eyebrows raised. "Unless, of course, you already have a lady in your sights?"

Edward groaned and closed his eyes, rubbing the bridge of his nose. "No, I do not. My focus is on my ward's happiness. This is her first Season—she is young. There will likely be more Seasons for young Daphne, I *hope* there will be more. I have no matrimonial thoughts beyond making certain she is well settled. In time."

A new voice chuckled with a plummy voice from behind Edward's chair. "A man who concerns himself only with the happiness of others, and not his own, soon finds himself a ghost haunting the edges of a life he ought to have lived."

Edward opened his eyes and bolted to his feet. "Lord Blackstone—I did not see you come in."

Marlowe had stood as well and all three of them bowed to the viscount, who waved aside the formalities.

Norman spoke first. "Forgive me, my lord, but what you said sounded quite philosophical. I did not know you dabbled in such things."

"Only when I see someone in need of it do I dispense my

wisdom." He chuckled and winked at Edward. "Colonel, you remind me of that owl over the fireplace. Stuck in one place, frozen in time, watching the world move on without him."

The other two chuckled, but as Edward looked at the owl in question—someone had put a pair of tiny spectacles on its beak— he felt something shift uncomfortably in his chest. He shook his head. "I have been far too often away from my comfortable chair in front of my own fire, my lord. The comparison is not apt."

"Hmmm. I am not certain of that." Norman chuckled and leaned against the back of Edward's chair. "I must be a decade older than you, but you were the one acting like an old codger at our picnic two days' past."

Marlowe had not returned to his seat, and when the viscount gestured, the younger man quickly stepped aside to allow Lord Blackstone to take it for himself.

Their host settled into the chair, eyes on Edward the entire time with a maddeningly knowing expression. "You mistake me, Colonel. It is not about movement, it is about stillness. The owl watches the world, but it does not live in it. Tell me, when was the last time you did something simply for the joy of it?"

Edward scoffed. He opened his mouth to speak, then paused. "That…is a good question, my lord." What had he enjoyed lately? The picnic at Hyde Park had been tolerable. Especially after he and Felicity fed the ducks, then walked along the Serpentine. But he had found the afternoon pleasant because of her company, and he could hardly admit such a thing to these men. They gossiped terribly, it seemed.

"I wonder that you only mention the younger of the two Miss Prices in your concerns, Colonel." Norman walked around where Edward sat to stand behind Lord Blackstone's chair instead, raising a quizzical brow as he did so.

It was as though the man had somehow read Edward's mind, and his stomach twisted uncomfortably. Nevertheless, he spoke with as much coolness in his tone as he could manage. "Miss Felicity Price is not on the marriage mart."

"And yet she is a handsome woman, is she not?" Norman asked, eyebrows raised. Marlowe and Blackstone both seemed intrigued by this line of questioning.

"I do not think she would take kindly to such discussions about her person." Edward kept his tone even, yet that seemed to make the three men in front of him all the more curious. *Blast.*

"Now that is a fascinating response," Lord Blackstone said, tapping his fingers on the arm of the chair. "Absolutely fascinating."

Edward scowled at all three of them. Though he need not trouble himself, truly. Felicity had said herself she had no thoughts for marriage. She was independent, headstrong, and she did not need him as a defender. He had never asked to occupy that role. Except... Well. He had told her she was part of his household, therefore he concerned himself with her happiness and safety.

"Ah well. As I am a happily married man, and Marlowe too, you have nothing to fear from us." Norman patted Edward on the shoulder one more time. "But brace yourself, old fellow. It will not be long until people note the charming woman chaperoning your ward, living with you to boot, and will ask more questions."

At that moment, a footman appeared with a bow. "Colonel Halstead, sir. Your coachman has arrived."

Edward stood and bowed, saying his farewells with a certain amount of relief before he left in as unhurried a manner as possible. When he stepped out of the club onto the street, he remained unsettled.

Blackstone's comparison to the stuffed owl sat stuck to him as Marlowe and Norman's words bounced between his ears like a billiard ball struck too hard against the side of the table.

Pushing the conversation as firmly from his mind as he could, Edward rolled his shoulders and fixed a pleasant expression on his face to greet the ladies in his waiting carriage.

He looked up at his carriage only to see that it was empty.

His brow furrowed. Where was Felicity? What was she doing

at that moment? And why did her absence when he expected to see her annoy him so much?

"Where are Miss Price and Miss Daphne?" he asked the coachman, not even moving to step inside.

The coachman winced. "Erm...my apologies, Colonel, but Miss Price accepted an invitation to accompany another lady on an outing. Didn't seem like she could get out of it?"

Edward stiffened. An outing? With whom? Where? He narrowed his eyes. "Take me to them at once."

THE WARMTH OF THE PARLOR FIRE PROVIDED A COMFORTABLE contrast to the brisk April air outside, though Felicity hardly felt at ease with the brisk direction of the conversation. Mrs. Norman's needle threaded smoothly through her embroidery hoop, her voice mild but pointed.

"You must forgive me, Miss Price," she said, glancing up with a cheery smile, "but I cannot help but remark upon the way you and Colonel Halstead worked together so delightfully during our picnic."

Felicity adjusted the tray of biscuits on the table in front of her, carefully composed, though her stomach twisted at the remark. "Worked together?" she echoed lightly. Her mind raced to recall the details: the way Edward had spoken to her, moved to help stay the pages of her book, walked alongside her as they trailed the young people. Nothing about their conduct had been inappropriate, surely?

Mrs. Norman's smile deepened, revealing a dimple in one cheek. "Yes. I watched you two closely. It was quite...instructive." Nothing about her tone seemed malicious. Her words at least seemed sincere.

That gave Felicity leave to relax somewhat, but her soft laugh still came out rather forced. "I should not think instructive is the correct word. We merely ensured Daphne could enjoy herself, a thing we somehow manage despite our disagreements on how best to keep an eye on her."

Across the room, Daphne and Miss Norman sat close together near the window, speaking in hushed tones, the occasional giggle breaking through. Their conversation was their own, the youthful ease between them entirely natural. As it should be. They seemed completely unaware of the older women's conversation.

Mrs. Norman set her embroidery aside, watching Felicity with something akin to amusement. "He listens to you, you know. More than he realizes, I think. More than either of you realize."

Felicity's fingers twitched against her skirts. "The Colonel and I are allies, nothing more. We have a shared interest in Daphne's success, her happiness."

"Of course," Mrs. Norman agreed with good-natured mildness. She tilted her head, watching Felicity as though trying to look beneath the surface. "I imagine there is nothing more frustrating than a reluctant ally. And yet, I saw something else between you. Something companionable."

"I suppose we must get along, to an extent, for Daphne's wellbeing." Heat was rising up her neck. She needed to keep the blush away, and sipping the tepid tea hardly helped. "It is not a permanent arrangement."

The married woman hesitated a moment, her expression turning almost pained. "My dear, I do not mean to imply anything untoward."

Felicity's lips pressed together, but she refused to answer with anything other than politeness in her tone. "Governesses and companions often reside in bachelor households," she pointed out, her voice even. "I am not unique in my situation."

Mrs. Norman gave a soft hum. "No, you are not. But forgive me for being so blunt, Miss Price—you are unmarried, and while the circumstances are clear enough, there are those who may whisper. You know how Society is, Miss Price."

Felicity did know. Far too well. She folded her hands neatly in her lap, nodding. "Which is why my focus remains entirely on my niece. Once she is settled, I will move on. Colonel Halstead under-stands that."

Mrs. Norman's expression softened. "That may be, but I hope you will allow yourself to make friends while you are here. If nothing else, I should like to be counted among them."

Felicity blinked at the genuine kindness in the other woman's voice. A quiet warmth settled in her chest, and though it was foreign and unexpected, she did not reject it. Instead, she gave a small, sincere smile. "That is very kind of you, Mrs. Norman."

The lady returned her smile. "I do like what I know of you, Miss Price. I intend to prove myself a true friend. Women need each other in this world, you know."

Before Felicity could respond, Daphne and Miss Norman's hushed conversation dissolved into another fit of giggles. She turned slightly, catching the unmistakable brightness in Daphne's expression. The laughter, the carefree way she spoke at a rapid pace; it was a sight Felicity had worried she would never see again after Anthony's passing.

Mrs. Norman followed her gaze. "You see? Even the young ones need each other," she murmured. "And I must say, your niece is flourishing under your care."

Felicity exhaled, the tension easing from her shoulders. Yes. That was what mattered.

The rest of the visit passed quickly, and without any more uncomfortable topics broached. Their social calendars had been compared, aligned, and advised upon. The young ladies were happy. They could climb into their carriage and fetch the Colonel from his club at last.

Now why had she thought that—at last?

Ignoring the thought as best she could as they left the Norman home and stepped into the brisk air, Felicity let out a slow breath, still mulling over Mrs. Norman's words. But before she could settle her thoughts, a familiar voice called out.

"Miss Price! Miss Daphne!"

Felicity turned to see Lady Kendal and Lady Louisa

descending from their own elegant carriage, both dressed in the highest of fashion. The mother fairly glittered with tiny jewels at her throat and ears while her daughter's ringlets bounced perfectly around her face.

Lady Kendal was all smooth authority, her gaze as sharp as ever as she approached. "What a fortunate coincidence," she said with a faint smile. "We were discussing our meeting of the Ladies' Charitable Society, and thought you and Miss Daphne might care to join us."

Felicity hesitated, glancing toward Daphne, who looked between them with a mixture of interest and uncertainty.

The polite refusal formed swiftly in her mind, but before she could utter it, Lady Kendal added smoothly, "I am certain Colonel Halstead will not object. Indeed, according to my Louisa, he seems quite dedicated to ensuring Miss Daphne's social engagements are appropriate. What better company than ourselves, and for such a good cause?"

Felicity's spine stiffened. It was a challenge, lightly spoken but unmistakable. To refuse would seem ungracious, but to accept without consulting Edward could be construed as her overstepping.

It was a puzzle, but if she explained the situation to him later, she was certain he would understand. Turning away an invitation from a peeress was never a wise course of action.

"Of course, my lady. We would be honored."

Lady Kendal's smile widened just slightly. "Excellent. We are gathering at Lady Denton's home this afternoon. Come, ride in our carriage with us. We are but a street away."

Felicity turned to the coachman, giving quick murmured instructions. "Take our carriage to Colonel Halstead. Let him know where we are, and that we shall return home later."

The man nodded, touching his hat before climbing into the driver's seat.

As the ladies entered Lady Kendal's carriage, Felicity forced down her dislike of the altered course of the afternoon. She was not one to throw out plans, and the impromptu invitation struck her as calculated in some way. And, if she was being truly honest, she was rather curious to see what Edward would do about it, given his need to remain informed and in control of Daphne's comings and goings.

But she could not think of that now. When they arrived at the home of the countess hosting the committee, Felicity could not help admiring it. The drawing room of Lady Denton's home was pleasantly warm, the scent of beeswax polish and freshly brewed tea mingling with the faint perfume of the well-dressed women gathered within made it feel like a haven of femininity. It made her long for her brother's home, or her parents'. She could not help contrasting the welcoming decor with the sparseness of Briarwood.

Felicity sat beside Lady Kendal on a lovely scarlet settee, her hands folded neatly in her lap as she listened to an elderly dowager, Sarah, Countess Whitby, speak of charitable funds allocated to widows of war veterans. Daphne sat across from her, engaged in polite and demure conversation with Lady Louisa. Though her niece had initially seemed nervous about the visit, she now acted perfectly at ease, nodding attentively and offering quiet smiles.

Felicity should have felt content...and yet she could not shake the lingering tension in her chest.

Lady Kendal had made the invitation seem effortless, a mere polite suggestion. But Felicity knew better. The woman was testing her; testing how pliable she was, how well she understood the delicate games of Society.

Her fingers tightened around her teacup as she considered her position. As Daphne's aunt, and a gentlewoman with her own income, albeit small, she ought to act as an equal in the company of fine women. Filling the role of companion to her niece put her lower in status, true, yet kept tongues from wagging about her living arrangement.

Was Lady Kendal prying? Or was her attention to the Price ladies innocent?

What was to be gained either way?

The rules of Society were often interpreted by the powerful in whatever way they wished. All she could truly do was wait and see what came next.

She did not have long to wait.

"I understand, from what Lady Kendal tells me," a woman named Mrs. Plumpton said from another chair, "that you reside with your niece at the home of her guardian. Is that so, Miss Price?"

Felicity kept her hands delicately folded in her lap. "We do. My late brother's will specified that I was to remain with my niece until she no longer had need of me."

"Her guardian is a Mr. Edward Halstead, is he not?" another woman asked.

"Indeed, though he maintains his rank as his title. Colonel Halstead has been adamant about honoring my late brother's wishes and has ensured only the best for my niece." Felicity glanced to where Daphne sat, noting her niece was watching with a curious expression on her face. Dangerous ground indeed, but navigated well...so far.

Lady Kendal laughed airily and unnecessarily. "Of course he would. What man knows anything about launching a girl into Society? The man needs you, my dear."

Although she had made that argument herself a number of times, it felt condescending when the Countess spoke that way. Felicity could hardly claim him capable on his own, though, without making her presence seem either superfluous or suspicious.

"Halstead," the older dowager murmured. "Halstead. I know that name. His father had two sons, did he not? The elder inherited, of course. The first for the family, the second for the country, the third for God." She seemed to drift away in thought. "That is what we always did, you know."

Lady Kendal seemed impatient for the woman to finish speaking, as she quickly said, "Of course the name would be familiar,

Lady Whitby. Were you not saying to me, a scant three days past, that you remembered some sort of rumor regarding that family?" She cut a sharp look at Felicity. "From ages and ages ago, I am certain."

"Rumor? Oh, you mean with regards to that lady, oh, grand-niece to one of my friends. Yes. There is a story there, I believe. Though I cannot recall all the details, it was so long ago."

Felicity found herself both hoping the dowager would fall silent and curious as to what the woman might be speaking of— but before she could secure one of the other, the doors to the parlor opened, and the air itself seemed to shift as the footman announced to the room, "Colonel Halstead, my lady."

Edward had not, evidently, returned to his estate to await their return.

The room quieted as he entered, his dark green coat crisp, his cravat tied with military precision. When his gaze finally settled on Felicity, something flickered behind his expression.

Not anger. Not quite. Something closer to frustration mixed with reluctant amusement.

Lady Denton approached him at once, and the Colonel bowed perfectly to her. "My lady, forgive my intrusion on your meeting. I have merely come to look after my ward. I am afraid, as I am newly made a guardian to a young lady, that I am somewhat overzealous in my duties."

The Countess fairly beamed up at him, and Felicity did not blame her in the slightest. Edward towered over all the women in the room, and it would be a difficult thing to find many men able to match him in height—or in looks. His attractiveness likely granted him all sorts of favors.

"You are welcome, of course, Colonel Halstead. The important part of our meeting is concluded, and if you do not mind the company of mere ladies, I happily welcome you to join us. Please, help yourself to some refreshment. If you spend all day at a club, as my own dear husband does, heaven only knows that you are unlikely to be sustained by the dishes they serve *there*."

"You are most kind, my lady." Edward bowed again, then turned his gaze pointedly to his ward's companion.

Felicity set her teacup down delicately, then stood and moved to one of the tables bearing refreshment, arranging little delicacies onto a small plate. Her stomach was so completely in knots she would not be capable of eating any of it.

Edward approached, picking up his own plate. "I was not aware," he said, his voice measured, "that my ward's afternoon itinerary included a visit to Lady Denton's home."

"It was a spontaneous invitation, one I had not anticipated. I sent word to you." Felicity kept her voice low and soft. *Please, don't make a scene...*

Edward took a measured breath and turned to look at Daphne, his expression softening as he watched her. "Is she enjoying herself?"

"I believe so. But you really should ask her," Felicity said.

Daphne, having caught his gaze, rose and approached at the quickest possible speed while still being polite before she curtsied to him. "Good afternoon, Colonel."

"Good afternoon, Daphne. I was just asking your aunt how you are enjoying your afternoon."

After darting a quick glance at Felicity, Daphne answered, "It has been rather wonderful, though I do find myself growing fatigued. Might we return to Briarwood soon?"

"Of course. Perhaps you ought to say your farewells?" Edward gave an approving nod before glancing back at Felicity. "As for you, Miss Price," he said quietly, "a word?"

Felicity arched a brow but did not object. Setting her plate down, she followed him to stand near the windows with effortless grace.

He tucked his hand behind his back and pretended to look out the window. "You are playing a dangerous game, Miss Price."

Felicity lifted her chin, schooling her expression into perfect indifference. "I am not playing any games, Colonel." She turned to face the room as she spoke. "Would you have me decline a kind invitation from a Countess, made in public and to the betterment of your ward, merely because it was given at the last moment without advance notice? Lady Louisa likes Daphne, and her mother indulges her daughter's whims. An earl's daughter is a suitable friend for—"

"I am not certain I like Lady Louisa," he muttered.

Felicity's lips curled upward. He sounded like a petulant little boy. "Your likes and dislikes are not as important as what is best."

Edward grumbled, a low hum of irritation, eyes flicking toward her in clear disapproval.

But she refused to apologize, even when he scowled like that. "I am ensuring Daphne makes the right connections. You cannot fault me for that."

"Are you always right, then?"

"I am about this."

Felicity expected more argument, but instead something else flickered in his gaze. Not anger. Not frustration. Something that looked suspiciously like admiration.

Edward made another sound of annoyance. "You are far too stubborn indeed." But to her great surprise, the corner of his mouth quirked up ever so slightly before he turned around again, leaving her to take leave for them with Lady Denton.

Chapter Fifteen

APRIL 19TH. 1817

E dward had promised himself he would not be overbearing tonight. It had been a conscious decision made before he stepped into the grand ballroom of Lady Kendal's townhome: he would try, truly try, to allow Daphne some measure of independence, to grant her the freedom Felicity so often argued she deserved.

And so he did his best to remain at ease, rather than trailing Daphne's every movement like a hound. Felicity remained close when Daphne was not in the company of a friend or on the dance floor, and for Edward's part, he observed from a respectful distance, noting the way she laughed with her new friends and the genuine delight in her expression when Mr. Montague asked her to dance. His hands twitched at his sides, but he forced himself to remain in conversation with the gentlemen around him, only occasionally letting his gaze sweep the room to ensure all remained well.

"Have you been accosted by marriageable widows yet, Colonel?" Marlowe grinned as he stood beside him, sipping at tepid lemonade. "Ever since that crowd of ne'er-do-wells put my cousin's name in their books, he has been inundated with match-making mothers. You must be suffering the same fate to a degree."

"I am not," Edward said evenly, refusing to rise to the bait. "No one has approached me for introductions, beyond those with sons near Daphne's age."

Marlowe gave him an incredulous look, eyebrows raised. "Perhaps it is your formidable appearance. Ladies likely have no wish to expose themselves to a curmudgeon."

Edward cut him an unamused glance. It was true, he hadn't stood about smiling like a fool, and his focus was certainly not on the other guests that evening. He hadn't come to the ball for himself, though. He came for Daphne's sake.

"I am starting to remember why I counted my departure from Society as no great loss." Edward tucked his arms behind his back, his stance more in keeping with a soldier at ease than a gentleman amid splendor. "The crowds are terrible."

"After a man weds, these things do seem superfluous." Marlowe sipped at his lemonade and grimaced. "But it is always good to be seen in the right places, and by the right people—and my wife does enjoy dancing. Perhaps you will be so kind as to ask her for one? These ridiculous rules against dancing with one's spouse prohibit me the pleasure, of course."

The request was not inappropriate, and Edward liked Marlowe enough to grant it. His wife seemed a pleasant sort for conversation. However… "I had thought to remain without partners this evening, the better to watch after Daphne. Should she need anything."

"Your ward will be fine, Colonel." Marlowe chuckled and shook his head, his smile broad. "You worry too much. Besides, she has her aunt to keep an eye on her too. Try to enjoy yourself—let the girl have a little freedom from your ever watchful eye."

"That is what her aunt says." Edward winced when he heard the complaint in his tone.

"Do you not trust her?"

"I trust Miss Price completely. She has her niece's best interests at heart—"

Marlowe cleared his throat. "I meant, do you not trust your

ward? But I suppose trusting the aunt is important, too, given that you have to place so much faith in her. Amazing, really, that you have not minded her interference when the girl's future is your responsibility."

"It is hardly interference. She practically raised Daphne."

"Yes, but the girl is grown now. Or nearly so. And your duty will end when she is wed, which may not be this Season, but it will surely not be long." Marlowe shrugged carelessly. "It is not as though you are her father, after all."

Edward stared at the man, uncomprehending his argument. "She is my responsibility. Her own father entrusted her well-being to me, now he is no longer here to protect her. I take it very seriously."

"Oh." Marlowe shrunk somewhat. "Of course. Very honorable. Yes." He cleared his throat. "Ah—I see someone I need to speak to. Excuse me."

Watching him go, Edward shook his head as slightly as he could manage. What a thing, for a man to think so little of duty. Perhaps others would see Daphne as merely a thing to pawn off on another, or indeed her aunt as an unwelcome complication, but Edward could not contemplate such things himself. His duty to Anthony Price's memory and trust was one thing, but compassion and human decency certainly reinforced his decisions in those regards.

He straightened his black coat and checked the watch tucked into his deep green waistcoat. They had not even been at the ball for an hour yet, and the blasted thing went well past midnight. How would he get through it?

He was doing precisely what Felicity wished him to do, and yet a gnawing sense of unease would not leave him be. The room's size made it difficult to see everything and everyone at once. The music, combined with chatter and laughter of guests, overwhelmed him with sound, not to mention the scent of many bodies wearing all sorts of oils and perfumes assaulted his nose at every moment.

He had been among unwashed soldiers and not minded the pungent odor as much as he minded it here. Why did everyone have to reek of rose oil and jasmine? There were subtler scents. Felicity often wore a lighter, citrus scent that cut through other things most pleasantly.

"Probably shouldn't notice that," Edward muttered to himself and gained a sideways look from two older women for his indiscretion. He forced a smile and nodded to them. One raised her fan and spoke behind it to her friend while both of them stared.

He turned away. For his own sanity's sake, he needed to stop thinking about smells and sounds if he wanted to get through the evening without a headache...or without people thinking him stranger than they already did.

Perhaps a distraction was in order.

His gaze landed on Felicity, standing just beyond the dance floor, ever watchful, ever composed. She had dressed appropriately for the occasion, but still wore mourning colors—though not the deep blacks of fresh grief. Her gown was a simple, elegant chocolate brown, a rich shade that only made the warm depths of her eyes more striking.

Without examining the impulse, he crossed the room. "Miss Price," he greeted, allowing himself the pleasure of seeing the flicker of surprise in her expression before she hid it away. "Would you do me the honor of a dance?"

Felicity's lips parted before her brow drew down. "You—you wish to dance?"

He did. "I do." Especially if he could secure a waltz with her.

"But in the carriage—you said you disliked dancing."

"Ah. Yes." So he had. "I should amend the statement. I do not mind it, if my partner is an enjoyable companion."

"You find my company enjoyable?"

Why did she sound so surprised?

Edward lowered his gaze to the ground for a moment. "Is that so astonishing?" Then he raised his eyes, but kept his head tipped

A BACHELOR'S LESSONS IN LOVE

down, trying to win her over with a smile. Hoping to see *her* smile.

Her lips curved, but the expression did not quite reach her eyes. "Chaperones do not dance, Colonel. Especially when it is a waltz, which is what I believe is next."

His chest tightened at the quiet refusal. "I see." He shifted slightly, acting as though the rejection had not affected him. "And that poses a problem."

"I do not think you ought to be seen dancing with me, either," she added, a flush that was not a flush gracing her cheeks. "Best if we maintain a respectable distance from each other. In public, especially."

That was an entirely different matter, yet he understood. "I imagine you have no desire to give anyone the wrong ideas?"

Felicity inclined her head, but something in her gaze softened. "I think it best we not invite speculation or gossip. For Daphne's sake." She glanced away as the music swelled, beginning another song, another dance. When she spoke again, he had to strain to hear her. "I have already had to quell well-meaning comments on the matter."

Had she? That didn't please him. "I understand," he said quietly. And he did. But that did not mean he had to linger. In fact, it was best if he did not. "If you will excuse me, Miss Price."

"Of course, Colonel."

Did he imagine the disappointment in her eyes?

Edward left her at the edge of the ballroom, stepping out through the terrace doors and into the cool, crisp air of the gardens. The distant strains of music and laughter filtered through the hedges, but he ignored them, focusing instead on the peace of the evening.

"Get hold of yourself, man," he muttered, then cursed at himself for speaking aloud again. He was not in his own gardens, free to speak his mind as he beheld his flourishing roses.

Edward walked deeper into the garden and the night air. He took in several deep breaths, and closed his eyes. Despite the relative tranquility of the gardens, his inner state tumbled with confusion. He had known for some time that his feelings for Felicity were not strictly appropriate. Not for a man in his position, not for a woman in hers. But tonight, with the warmth of her rejection still lingering, the truth was far more difficult to ignore.

Did he want her?

The answer was undeniable.

Did he care for her? Or was this merely surface level, physical yearning?

Edward exhaled sharply, shaking his head as if the gesture might dispel the thoughts entirely. He had come outside to clear his mind, not to sink deeper into the confusion she so effortlessly inspired.

And yet here he was, once again, wrapped up in thoughts of the woman with dark eyes and a stubborn chin. A woman he respected, who lived beneath his roof. A woman who showed a strength of intelligence and compassion, even toward him when he did not bend to her will.

Goodness, he had not let his thoughts get this tangled over a woman in a long time—and never to this extent. How had he allowed this to happen? And what could he do about it now?

Before Edward came anywhere near solving the problem, he heard a murmur of voices drifting through the neatly trimmed hedges behind him. Edward stilled, recognizing one of them immediately.

Daphne.

Had she slipped out of the ballroom when he left? Had Felicity accompanied her?

He took a quiet step forward, ears straining to catch the words, hoping treacherously to hear Felicity's voice.

"You must admit, Colonel Halstead is rather overzealous in his concern," came Lady Louisa's voice, amusement evident in her tone.

"You needn't tell me," Daphne replied, exasperation and humor woven through her words. "He watches me like I am bound to tumble down a well at the slightest provocation."

Lady Louisa giggled. "Even my father does not watch me so," the Earl's daughter chimed in, her voice dripping with condescension. "My mother rarely pays attention to what I do, even within her sight. I should go mad if I were you, Miss Price."

A male voice, the young Mr. Montague's, spoke next. "He is a concerned guardian. I think he means only to keep you safe, Miss Price. I know I have felt overly protective of my sister on occasion."

"Yes, but that is your sister," Lady Louisa said, annoyance in her tone. "She is your blood. The Colonel is not Miss Price's father."

"I am grateful to him," Daphne said quickly. "I only wish he would—"

"Loosen the reins?" A new voice entered the conversation, one Edward did not recognize. Male, smooth, filled with an easy sort of charm that immediately put him on edge. "There are ways around that, you know," the stranger murmured. "One must simply learn how to be discreet."

"You are not proposing Miss Price act deceitful," Mr. Montague inquired, his tone cautious.

"Discretion and deceit are not the same, my dear boy." This new man's voice dripped with disdain. "And Miss Price strikes me as a clever young lady. Certainly, mature beyond her years. I am certain, should she wish it, she could find a way to pursue what she pleased without her guardian knowing."

"I slip my leash all the time," Lady Louisa said lightly with a laugh. "Come, Daphne. You must wish to seize more freedom for yourself. It is delightful to do as one pleases."

Edward's blood turned to ice.

Without another thought, he stepped through the hedge, emerging into the candlelit garden path before Daphne could answer.

The conversation halted instantly.

Daphne turned, eyes widening. "Colonel!"

"Daphne." Edward's gaze did not leave the unknown gentleman, his stance deceptively relaxed. "I do not believe we have met. I am Colonel Halstead. And you are?"

The man smiled, but it did not reach his eyes, and he did not incline his head. "Mr. Richard Arnold. My father is Lord Dalton. A pleasure, Colonel Halstead."

Edward did not return the pleasantry. His voice was quiet, but no less dangerous for it. "I imagine we shall see about that." He held his arm out to his ward. "Come, Daphne. Your aunt will be wondering where you have disappeared off to."

His ward lowered her gaze as she accepted his escort, walking with him back through the garden along the most well-lit path. After a moment of silence, he said quietly, "Did your aunt give you permission to walk in the garden?"

Daphne shook her head slightly. "I—I was with Lady Louisa and Mr. Montague. Since you both know them, and it was only to take in a little fresh air, I did not think I needed to ask—"

"No. You did not *think*." Edward did not mince words. Escorting Daphne back into the ballroom, he maintained a composed facade but his jaw remained tight and his blood still pounded in his ears from that encounter. The gall of that man! To suggest Daphne deceive him; worse, that she had been allowed to wander into such a situation and such an acquaintance in the first place.

His gaze swept the room until he found Felicity, still near the edge of the dance floor, speaking with another woman he did not know.

Good. At least he did not have to search her out, even if she was not with Daphne as she ought to have been.

With a measured breath, he approached and spoke to his ward in a low voice. "Daphne Price, do not leave the ballroom again without speaking to either me or your aunt."

Daphne swallowed, a blush staining her cheeks, clearly aware that an argument would be futile. "Yes, Colonel."

He gestured to Miss Montague and Miss Norman near the refreshments. "Go to your friends. We will leave shortly."

She lowered her head and nodded, releasing his arm to walk the short distance to the refreshment table.

Redirecting himself toward Felicity, Edward closed the space between himself and the woman with slow, deliberate steps. They were in public, it would not do to draw attention. The woman she spoke with stepped away before he obtained a place at her side, and Felicity looked up at him with a smile which instantly shifted to an expression of concern.

"What is it?"

He kept his voice low, his words meant for her alone. "Did you know Daphne was in the gardens?"

A flicker of something passed over her face. Did he imagine it was more guilt than surprise? It was gone in an instant, replaced by her usual calm expression. "No," she admitted calmly. "But she was with Lady Louisa when last I looked. She was not out there alone, I take it?"

"No. But Lady Louisa's company wasn't all she kept." His tone hardened, though he remained mindful of others conversing and moving about nearby. "Mr. Montague was there as well, and a Mr. Arnold. That particular fool was instructing her on how to sneak about without my knowledge, how to avoid our watch and do—do what she—tell me, Miss Price, do you also believe Daphne should learn how to deceive us? How to slip my watchful eye?"

Felicity's lips parted slightly, and hurt flashed in her dark eyes. "Of course not," she whispered as that chin lifted. "But I do not think you should speak to me in this manner. Not here."

The firmness in her voice should not have surprised him, but it did. Even so, it did not temper his frustration. He exhaled sharply through his nose, his fingers flexing at his sides before he could curl them into fists. Fists he would greatly like to use on the Arnold boy.

"Then we will discuss it later," he said, the words clipped. "But understand me, Miss Price. I will not have Daphne influenced by those who would encourage reckless, dangerous behavior."

Felicity's smile was forced and brittle, but her composure was steady, despite the tension between them. "And I will not have you imply that I do not have her best interests at heart."

The silence between them crackled like the air before a lightning strike. His shoulders remained rigid, his breath controlled, but the sharp gleam of disappointment in her eyes unsettled him in ways he did not wish to name.

The music swelled behind them as the orchestra began anew. A waltz.

For a fleeting moment, Edward wondered if she regretted refusing him. His eyes stayed on hers, trying to read her. She would not dance with him, would not allow herself to be seen with him in any way that would spark gossip. And yet this moment between them, thick with unspoken words and frustration, felt far more intimate than any dance could have been.

Felicity broke the stare as she inclined her head in a graceful, measured way. "If you will excuse me, Colonel."

He had no choice but to incline his own head in return. "Miss Price."

With that, she turned and walked away, leaving him to grapple with the bitter taste of frustration and something else.

Something that felt dangerously like regret.

180

Chapter Sixteen

Felicity hadn't meant to watch for him. Yet here she was, standing at the music room window, eyes on the path she knew Colonel Halstead took to return to the stables. It simply happened that way.

The morning sun warmed the music room, where Daphne's fingers flitted with ease over the keys of the pianoforte. Then the melody faltered, slowed, and resumed at the correct speed. Her efforts were earnest but unpolished.

"You are doing well, darling. Try again," Felicity said, somewhat absently, her attention drawn beyond the window's glass. Then she saw him.

Edward rode along a path tucked behind tall hedges, his dark coat fitted close to his frame. He guided his towering bay gelding with a precision she could not help admiring. She had seen him ride before, he was an elegant horseman, utterly at ease in the saddle; but something about the sight of him unnerved her this morning. Perhaps because, for the first time, she realized how much effort he put into that measure of control.

Felicity had spent half the night trying to resent him, nursing the sharp sting of his quiet rebuke. She wanted to be angry with him, offended—insulted. Anything that would make her feel unlikely to forgive him for his slight against her abilities.

Now, in the daylight, watching him move so naturally on horseback, she had to admit another truth entirely.

He had been worried. More so, he had been genuinely afraid for Daphne's well-being.

That did not excuse his words, to be sure, but it made her understand them. Still more, it made her compassion for him overcome her own frustrations. Which was, in itself, frustrating.

"Daphne," Felicity said as she pulled her deep gray shawl tight around her shoulders. "I need to step out. Keep practicing until I return." She walked at quite a normal speed to the door, which was very much on purpose.

"Yes, Aunt Felicity." Daphne did not sound enthusiastic, but she would do as asked. She always did. She was an obedient and responsible girl.

Once the music room door clicked shut, Felicity lifted her skirts and walked at a brisk pace through the house. In all honesty, one could call her movement a run if one was not feeling charitable.

Making her way outdoors, she increased her speed to gain the stables quickly. After all, Felicity knew an opportunity when she saw one. Everyone in the household knew that Edward preferred to care for his horse himself. The servants thought it an odd habit left over from the war, but Felicity suspected it was something he did to soothe himself as much as to care for the beast he rode.

She preferred to stroke a cat purring in her lap, but why wouldn't an enormous man derive the same satisfaction from brushing an enormous animal?

Entering the stables, Felicity placed her hand over her chest, slowing her breathing as her eyes adjusted to the semi-darkness of the building. The scent of fresh hay and saddle leather filled her senses and had a subtle calming effect. Adjusting her shoulders, she strode inside with her head held high, making her way to Voltaire's stall.

Yes, the Colonel had named his battle steed after a French philosopher. When she had initially heard the name, she had giggled, but the housekeeper, Mrs. Lane, had warned her that Edward was fond of quoting the Frenchman every time he was brought up. Felicity kept her lips pressed together rather than ask questions. Men quoting philosophers rarely entertained anyone.

Now, as she approached, she wondered what about the philosopher Edward had admired.

But she was not here to hear him quote anyone, or to placate him. They needed to talk.

Felicity halted outside of Voltaire's stall, peering over the high wall. Edward stood inside, his back to her, one hand brushing the gelding's neck in slow, methodical strokes. The animal stood patiently beneath his touch, shifting only to snort softly when he caught sight of Felicity.

She hesitated a moment, admiring the breadth of Edward's shoulders as he worked. The careful way that he moved. He had to have sensed her there, surely. "Colonel."

"Miss Price." He did not turn as he addressed her. "Are we on formal terms again?" His voice was calm. Level.

"We needn't be." It was infuriating, how easily he contained himself while she had spent the last several hours simmering with emotion. Still, she kept her voice measured. "Edward, I believe we need to have a conversation."

The man continued brushing Voltaire's coat in long, firm strokes at a steady rhythm. "Are you here to remind me that I spoke out of turn last evening?"

She lifted her chin. "If I thought it would make a difference, perhaps."

He paused. Then, finally, he turned to look at her holding the brush in both hands. "I was harsher than I meant to be."

It wasn't precisely an apology, but the acknowledgement helped.

Felicity let out a slow breath, her fingers curling around the edge of the stall. "And I do not believe you meant to imply that I have no care for Daphne's well-being."

Slowly, he shook his head. "No. I did not."

Well. That was some progress.

But she was not finished. "Still. You cannot watch her every moment of the day, Edward—nor can you control the choices she will make, nor the people she will encounter. All you can do, all either of us can do, is guide her and hope she chooses wisely."

Turning away again, Edward resumed brushing Voltaire, his focus seemingly on his horse. But she knew better. "A man who hopes is a man who has already lost control of the outcome."

Felicity narrowed her eyes at his back. "Control?" She shook her head. "Is that what you value most?"

His hand slowed, but he did not answer.

"Why do you insist on seeing the worst in people?" Felicity leaned slightly over the wooden edge of the stall. "Mr. Montague is a fine young man, and Daphne appears to enjoy—"

"Montague is not the one who concerned me," Edward cut in smoothly, voice still calm, though she caught an undercurrent of something else. Something sharp and protective. Only then did understanding dawn.

"The man you met last night," she said urgently. "This Mr. Arnold—you recognized him? Or know something of him?"

His shoulders tightened. "No. But I recognized his sort."

He did not elaborate, and she did not press him. She knew the type, too.

"Did you let Daphne explain matters to you?" Felicity asked quietly. "Have you asked what she made of the conversation you overheard?"

"No." He was quiet for a long moment. "I...I did not give her a chance to say much at all."

"Perhaps you should have."

"Perhaps."

For a long moment, Felicity simply studied him. She watched and admired the steady, gentle way he worked the brush over

Voltaire's coat. The methodical care in his hands. The way he did not rush, even in his frustration.

"You do this often." She surprised herself by speaking aloud. When he looked over his shoulder, eyebrows raised, she clarified. "You care for the horse yourself. Mrs. Lane told me."

Edward exhaled, the brush slowing to a stop. "Since the war." He glanced up briefly. "Most cavalrymen had to replace their horses often, as did the officers. I did not."

Felicity frowned, her brow furrowing. "Voltaire was with you —in France?"

A nod. "For the last five years of my service." The Colonel put his empty hand on the horse's shoulder. "He had more patience than I do."

Voltaire, as if knowing himself the subject of conversation, let out a soft huff of breath, lifting his head almost regally.

Felicity could not help but smile at the animal. "That is not difficult," she teased.

Edward released a quiet chuckle, a low and unexpected sound that warmed her inside and out. "Perhaps not."

A small shift in the air between them made her relax. She rested her hands more fully on the wooden door, the tension in her body finally easing. "You named him after a philosopher."

His answer was a small shrug, then a pause before he said, "Seemed fitting. Voltaire's philosophy was rooted in reason, which I once thought I valued above all else."

"Once thought?" she echoed the word, puzzled.

The man's gaze lifted, his eyes meeting hers, and the moment stretched between them. Long, and heavy with something unspoken. For the first time since the previous night, Felicity saw something as potent as anger and frustration, but an entirely different emotion. Something more dangerous. Something she did not dare name, even as her heart sped up.

Edward was the first to look away, returning his attention to Voltaire's mane. "I will do better," he said at last, his voice quieter than before. "For Daphne's sake. But I cannot, will not apologize for protecting her."

Felicity considered him for a moment, letting her pulse slow to normal. Then, slowly, she stepped away from the stall. "Then I suppose we understand each other."

"It seems we do, Captain."

"Good." She turned. "I will see you at dinner, then." Felicity walked down the central walkway of the stables and back into the morning light. She didn't look over her shoulder once. But she felt his gaze following her long after she left the stables.

HOURS LATER, FELICITY AND HER NIECE WERE IN THE DRAWING room, Daphne seated by the window, embroidering handkerchiefs with colorful flowers to match the younger woman's gowns for the season.

For Felicity, it was slow going. She enjoyed embroidery, generally, as it let her mind rest while her fingers worked. Today, however, her thoughts kept distracting her. Every jab of the needle made her think about Edward—not that she wanted to stick him with a pin or anything. Not anymore. But it felt somewhat satisfying to think of his stubbornness every time she pushed the needle through the cotton.

Except when she lifted the handkerchief to examine her work, her apron came up with it.

Felicity groaned. She hadn't made such a novice error in... Well. She didn't know how long it had been.

"I suppose it serves me right," she muttered, giving the hoop a tug and realizing it would be best to remove the thread more delicately. "Daphne, darling. Your scissors?"

Her niece did not answer.

Felicity looked up. "Daphne?"

The young woman's embroidery hoop lay cast aside on the table beside her. Her hands were folded in her lap, fingers twitching as though she wished for a more interesting way to employ them.

Felicity had seen that exact expression before, years ago; when Daphne had been eight years old, made to sit through an unbearably long sermon, and had nearly vibrated with impatience in the pew beside her.

But this was not the same child who had once tugged at Felicity's sleeve and whispered shy complaints about the length of the vicar's droning voice. Daphne was nearly grown, and her frustration was not born of childish restlessness but of something far weightier.

"You're brooding," Felicity said lightly, putting her hoop and apron down.

Daphne huffed, her breath fogging the glass where she leaned against the windowpane. "I am *thinking*."

"Thinking usually requires less glaring at the garden below."

Daphne turned her head slightly, enough to give Felicity a sidelong glance. "Does it?"

Felicity smiled despite herself, but she knew better than to tease overly much. She had been a young woman once, hemmed in by rules, watched too closely, told that everything was for her own good.

She rested her hands over her skirts, studying the profile of her nearly grown niece with a tender heart. "Shall I guess the subject of your brooding thoughts?"

Daphne sighed, finally turning fully from the window. "Do you think I am foolish?"

The question took Felicity aback. "Foolish? Of course not. I have always thought you rather level-headed. Intelligent, too."

"That is not how *he* treats me."

Felicity did not need to ask who she meant.

Daphne crossed her arms, her expression tightening. "He— Colonel Halstead—watches me as if I am a child who might put a pin in her mouth and swallow it. It is growing intolerable."

Felicity inhaled slowly, considering. Though she agreed with her niece, it would not do to encourage such thoughts about the girl's guardian. They were, after all, supposed to be united. "You are frustrated," she said at last. "That is understandable."

Daphne let out a short, breathy laugh. "I have been almost continually frustrated. I must be beyond that by now."

"Very well. You are absolutely seething with indignation."

That won a slight smile, though Daphne quickly smoothed her features again.

Felicity leaned forward, softening her voice. "But the real question is this, my dear. Do you think he watches you because he believes you are foolish or because he is afraid?"

Daphne's brows pulled together. "Afraid? The Colonel?"

Felicity pressed on. "You lost your father not long ago—and while Colonel Halstead may not admit it, I believe he is terrified that something might happen to you, too. That he will fail you in some way, and thus fail your father's trust. He is a soldier, Daphne. Soldiers protect what is theirs, 'tis what they are trained to do."

"I am not his," Daphne muttered, but the bitterness in her voice was less prevalent than before.

"No," Felicity agreed softly, "but he has made you his responsibility when he could have ignored you. He could have done almost naught to aid you in coming out, and see how he has changed his routine, his habits, his expenditure. We have certainly seen he takes responsibility very seriously."

Daphne lowered her gaze to her hands, tracing an invisible pattern along the folds of her skirts. "I do not mean to be ungrateful," she said at last. "But I want to be trusted—to be seen as more than a charge to be managed."

Felicity's chest tightened. Was that not exactly how she had felt years ago? When she had still harbored hope that she might have the love she wished for? Her voice was gentler now. "Then prove you can be."

Daphne looked up, startled.

Felicity tilted her head slightly. "If you wish to be trusted, then show him you are worthy of that trust. Obviously, you will not be sneaking about or practicing deception—but you need to make it absolutely clear, through your actions, that you are not reckless."

Daphne frowned. "And how am I to do that?"

Felicity leaned back. "That, my dear girl, is for you to decide. After all, it would be no demonstration if I instructed you how to do it."

Another moment of thoughtful silence passed.

Then, unexpectedly, her niece's gaze turned sharp, almost assessing. "And what of you?"

Felicity had started gently tugging the thread out of her apron. Perhaps she did not need the scissors. She only needed patience. "What of me?" she asked without looking up.

Daphne's tone did not waver. "What will you do when I marry?"

Everything within her stilled a moment, then she continued plucking at the thread. "I will find rooms to rent in a quiet seaside village, perhaps buy a cottage. I will pass my days gossiping with the locals, and I will visit you and your new husband whenever you wish."

She had rehearsed the plans often to herself, and she knew Daphne had heard them before. So why these questions?

Daphne pressed on, though, lips turned down. "You came with me because you would not leave me alone with a stranger. But I am beginning to wonder, Aunt Felicity, are you only here because you think I need you? Or are you here because you do not want what comes next?"

Felicity's breath caught in her throat. She met her niece's stare. *Surely not...* "Do you wish me to leave?"

Quickly, Daphne shook her head. "No—no! I would keep you with me always. But Aunt Felicity, there must be more for you. More that you want." She gestured to Felicity's person. "Even now, you forget yourself too often for me. When will you put off your mourning? Father would not like to see you dressed so. He used to say mourning kept one's heart aching, but color—"

"—color returned cheer and warmth to the soul," Felicity finished for her, smiling as she remembered her brother's words. He had spoken them to her after they lost their parents, Daphne's beloved grandparents, and repeated them frequently since then until his own passing.

"I do not want you to fade into the shadows of life." Daphne stood and crossed the room to her aunt, leaning down to kiss her on the cheek. "You have always been so happy. Always telling me to explore the world around me, to find the things I love and surround myself with them. You ought to do the same, Aunt Felicity."

Uncomfortable to be on the receiving end of such sage advice, Felicity shifted in her chair and released a dramatic sigh. "Alas, my Daffodil, I am but a spinster. Not a young woman with the world at her feet."

Her niece crossed her arms and scoffed, in much the way the Colonel had done several times since their meeting. "Aunt Felicity, really! You are a lovely woman of independent means. You could marry, if you wished, or travel. Stop speaking as though you are an old woman with life already spent. Please." Daphne looked down at her aunt's apron, and her eyebrows drew together. "Did you sew the hoop to your apron?"

"Um." Felicity winced. "Yes?"

After giving her a confused glance, and then a smile, Daphne fetched her scissors. Together, they undid Felicity's mess, and the topic shifted, much to Felicity's relief. Yet the conversation stayed with her throughout the rest of her day...and then it followed her into her dreams.

Chapter Seventeen

Why on earth had Edward agreed to this?

He should have put his foot down, insisted Daphne find a more reasonable afternoon diversion. Instead, he now found himself stalking the edge of the Serpentine, his boots grinding against the path as he kept a wary eye on the boat bobbing across the water. Daphne sat laughing at one end of the rowboat, her bonnet tipped back slightly, a cheerful smile on her face. Miss Montague sat beside her, ever poised, while Mr. Montague manned the oars with an ease that irritated Edward for absolutely no logical reason.

"A person can drown just as easily in calm waters as in a raging sea," he muttered aloud.

Beside him, holding her bonnet to her head as she tried to keep up with his rapid pace, Felicity laughed—actually laughed. "They are perfectly safe, Edward."

Edward did not look at her. "I do not like it."

"You rarely like anything that is beyond your control."

That won her a sharp look, but she merely smiled.

Edward huffed and kept walking, his stride quick, as though he could escape the ever-growing knot of worry in his chest.

Felicity kept pace. "There are no signets yet," she mused, glancing along the shore. "Nor ducklings or goslings. But soon, I expect." Edward frowned at the apparent change in subject, but she only continued, her voice softer now. "You care about Daphne," she said, "but I think there is more to it than that."

He exhaled through his nose. "You think too much."

"Oh, dear. Is that why we do not get along?"

That brought him to a halt. Edward looked down at her, lips parted. "You think we are not getting along? Right now?"

Her smile broadened. "I think we are doing better now than previously, Edward."

He snorted and started walking again, gaze drifting to the young people in the boat. Ridiculous.

His ward's aunt fell into step beside him, but this time she put her hand on his arm. "What happened, years ago, that has made you so protective? What did you see?"

His steps slowed. Felicity did not press. She only waited. And somehow, that was worse. Edward kept his eyes forward, watching the shifting ripples of the Serpentine.

He did not know why he finally spoke. But he did.

"There was a young woman," he said, his voice carefully flat.

Felicity remained silent, looking ahead, but he felt all her attention focus on him. They kept walking as he formed the words, seeking to explain. But could he explain? Were there even words for such an experience?

He swallowed hard. "You will think differently of me, after this."

"Perhaps not," she said lightly, as though they discussed the weather. "But you will not know unless you try."

He did not like that. He wanted reassurances that her opinion of him would not change; or would not, at least, grow worse. But one look at her expression told him she would not make such a promise.

So, with a sigh, Edward continued. "She was a gentleman's daughter. Not well connected, but not without means. I was—I am a second son, and I was young. Foolish." He closed his eyes a moment and stopped walking, his mind dizzying with memories pouring back against his will. "I thought myself in love, and I thought love the best reason in the world to cast off the strictures of Society. I convinced her to meet me, time and again...in the privacy of the wood between our parents' properties." A muscle in his jaw ticked. "Each time I pressed the bounds of propriety more than the last. Until..." He swallowed and shook his head. "My parents found out about my indiscretion."

Felicity stiffened slightly, but hopefully not in judgment.

Edward did not cease his tale. He opened his eyes and looked at her. "They sent me away to war, as you know." The words came out without inflection, as though he were relating someone else's fate.

Felicity's brows drew together. "They forced you to leave?"

"They purchased me a commission," he said, almost absently. "A quick, quiet way to remove a son who had embarrassed them. I was not the first, nor last."

Felicity exhaled sharply, even so, she let him speak.

"Their letters those first years were full of disappointment, with no word of the young woman except to inform me that her parents arranged a more appropriate match for her. She did not write to me, either. I had thought, of all the rules we broke, that would have been an easy one—to correspond, to tell me what had happened. What she felt." His voice tightened slightly. "It was not until two years ago that I learned the whole truth of the consequences she faced for our—for my recklessness."

Felicity's lips parted, but she said nothing. Shock had drained the color from her face. He could read no other emotion there.

Edward forced himself to continue. "As I said, she did not remain unwed," he said, staring hard at the rippling water. "That much I knew. Her family sent her away and married her off to her distant cousin, a man with wealth enough to wipe away any stain to their reputation."

Felicity's hand clenched the fabric of his sleeve.

Edward exhaled slowly, deliberately. Her presence was somehow a greater comfort than he could have imagined. "I had no idea," he said, his voice quieter. "For eighteen years, I did not know the most altering part. It was two years ago, on my father's death bed, that he finally told me the whole of it."

Felicity stared at him, her expression unreadable.

He forced himself to look at her, forced himself to meet her wide, dark eyes. "She had a child, early in her marriage." he said quietly. "Too early. A boy."

Felicity gasped softly and released him. "Oh, Edward."

His chest felt like a vise had closed around it. "I have a son," he said, voice shaking. "And I have never met him." The words hung in the air, weighty and impossible to take back.

For a long moment, Felicity only looked at him. The shock had faded and in its place he had expected to see disgust. Judgment.

Instead, he saw something deep and quiet—something he hadn't expected. Compassion. A moment later, as she stepped closer, understanding. Her fingers curved around his forearm. The touch was not light. It was steady.

His throat worked, but he did not pull away.

"You have paid for your mistakes, Edward—more than you ought to have. And now, I can see you wish to protect others from making those same mistakes."

He looked out to the rowboat. He took in a deep breath. "I cannot fail Daphne, or her father, or you. History will not repeat itself."

For a moment, Felicity leaned her head against his shoulder. The touch sent warmth through him, as though she had embraced him. "Thank you for telling me."

He nodded tightly. "You see now why Daphne must be watched."

"I see why you feel that way, yes," she said, tone still soft, still understanding. "I think there is more we ought to discuss. But later. At home."

"I agree." And he did his best to ignore the way his heart fluttered in that moment. He was too busy feeling relief because she had not rejected him.

He did not have the energy to recognize the delight that she had called his house *home*.

Chapter Eighteen

I t had taken far too little effort for Daphne to convince Edward to take her to Hatchards. He could not say no to visiting London's most popular bookshop, a most respectable establishment. As the carriage left his country home and he observed her genuine enthusiasm, Edward wondered if she might possess more excitement than the literary pursuit merited. Perhaps Hatchards was *too* respectable, as it gave her an easy excuse to request an outing under the guise of wishing to read more.

Perhaps he *should* have said no.

But the way his ward's face had lit up when he agreed had kept him from thinking anything was amiss, at first. It was rare that Daphne made requests so earnestly, and he had thought there could be no harm in it.

When they arrived, and she practically skipped through the shop door, Edward's suspicions grew. He did not have any true reason to suspect her of more than wishing to leave the house, did he? He was being overly cautious, something Felicity had in her way attempted to warn him about. Surely that was all.

As Daphne drifted deeper into the shop, moving past the polished wooden shelves with the delighted ease of a young girl granted unexpected freedom, Edward could not quiet the unease settling in his chest.

She had been so keen to come here. Was it truly for the books? Or was she meeting someone?

Edward exhaled, flexing his hands at his sides. Felicity had been very clear—Daphne deserved trust. So why not test that theory? He would hang back, allowing her to move freely through the shop. He would let her wander without shadowing her. And he would see exactly what she did with her freedom.

Moving to the front of the shop, he set himself up near a shelf of periodicals where he could observe her without being too obvious. His back to the front door, he watched her go through a doorway farther back in the shop. Daphne browsed the rows of books, seemingly utterly absorbed. She lingered over a table stacked with poetry volumes, laying her hands on the slim books with quiet reverence. One could paint a portrait of her in the moment and capture a true reverence for the written word.

For a moment, he felt foolish. And then, the door chimed. Edward turned enough to see who entered from the corner of his eye.

Mr. Montague.

The young man entered, utterly at ease, glancing toward the counter before striding purposefully into the shop.

Edward's pulse picked up. *So. Here was the truth of it.*

Young Montague had not looked around for books, he had not drifted among the shelves like a man intending to browse. No. He had walked straight through the front room, straight past Edward without giving him a second glance, and—

Straight to the clerk.

Not through the door to the back room, toward his ward. What was this, some predetermined signal? Had Daphne and Montague arranged to meet here, in this shop, believing themselves clever enough to outwit his watchful eye—or to feign an accidental meeting to petition for an afternoon in one another's company?

Edward shifted, readying himself to intercept them if necessary.

But Montague did not glance toward the bookshelves, nor did he look toward the back room where Daphne still wandered. Instead, he exchanged a quiet word with the clerk, placed a few coins on the counter, and accepted a pre-wrapped parcel.

As swiftly as he had come, he left.

Edward's hands uncurled. Montague had not so much as glanced around the shop; he had not lingered, nor even noticed Daphne. The entire exchange had been utterly innocent.

The realization settled over Edward like a slow, creeping wave of shame. His eagerness to catch Daphne acting deceitful or manipulative had overcome him to such a degree, he had almost forgotten that he was here to care for her, not trap her in wrong-doing or suspect the worst of her. He had built an entire dramatic encounter in his head, like a man directing a play, but none of the principal actors within it had even known the roles he cast them in.

What the devil was wrong with him?

A few moments later, Daphne emerged from the back rooms, a book tucked cozily beneath her arm. She spotted him, her smile lit up her expression, and she hurried to his side.

"I found exactly what I wanted," she said, holding up the volume. "It's a collection of essays on ancient history. Aunt Felicity recommended it to me—she believes my classical history is somewhat lacking."

Edward exhaled slowly. He had been ready, eager even, to catch her in some deception. Instead, she had done exactly what she had claimed she would. She found a book to read.

He was a distrustful fool.

Daphne tilted her head, examining him with mild curiosity. "Is something wrong, Colonel?"

Edward studied her for a long moment. Then, at last, he relaxed his stance. "Not at all. Are you certain that is all you need?

I know there are quite a few collections of poetry you might enjoy, too."

She held her book to her chest. "I may get another book?"

"You may get an entire stack of them, if you wish." He chuckled and took the one she held. "We have a library to fill up, you know."

She took his arm, to his surprise, and pulled him eagerly along behind her. "Oh, then you must help me choose. I have a few I would very much like to add to the shelves at home."

Now both she and her aunt had referred to Briarwood as home. The last of Edward's unease melted away, and he submitted himself to Daphne's whims, letting the young woman put book after book in his arms as she chattered away about how much she enjoyed reading this author or that subject. Almost as though they were…family.

They left with several brown paper packages, almost all they could carry, and Edward had put in an order for several more to be delivered to his home later.

The street outside was bustling with carriages, gentlemen, and finely dressed ladies making their way along Piccadilly. Edward kept Daphne close to his side as they began the short walk to where he saw his carriage waiting, his grip on his wariness loosened.

After a moment of debating with himself, he finally spoke. "I saw Mr. Montague enter the shop."

Daphne looked up at him in surprise. "Did you?"

"Yes."

She frowned, clearly puzzled. "Oh. But I didn't see him."

Edward nodded slowly. "No. You did not. You were in the back, absorbed in your exploration of books."

Daphne let out a small laugh, and her amusement made his own resurface. "Then I assume that means he was not there searching for me?"

Edward did what he could to keep his visage unchanged. "No. He was not."

A pause stretched between them, and then—

"I like him," Daphne said, tone steady and expression calm.

Edward slowed and raised his eyebrows at her.

She glanced up at him, her expression open and thoughtful. "Mr. Montague, I mean."

"I assumed that is who you meant." Edward kept his voice carefully even as his chest tightened. "In what manner?"

Daphne smiled a little at that. "I do not know yet." She looked ahead to the waiting carriage. "I enjoy his company. He is kind. He is intelligent, and he makes me laugh."

Edward listened carefully, his mind already pulling at arguments about forming too quick an attachment, about her youth, about young Montague's prospects—

His ward's voice softened. "But I am young, and I have much to learn still. I would prefer not to form any serious attachments. Not yet."

A flicker of something unfamiliar came to light in his chest, a warmth that was equal parts relief and pride. Daphne was not reckless. Nor was she naïve. She was a thoughtful, capable young woman. How could she be anything else, with Felicity as her guide?

Perhaps it was time he started seeing her as she was, and not what he imagined her to be.

Daphne stepped lightly along the bustling pavement until they stood in front of his carriage. Edward, having finally shaken the worst of his guilt over doubting her, allowed himself to relax. Just slightly.

The conversation about Montague had been unexpected, to be sure; but what had struck him most was Daphne's self-awareness, with her admission that she wasn't ready for a serious attachment. That she had time. She was not rushing toward some reckless decision.

It unsettled him in a way he hadn't expected.

"Perhaps we need not return home yet." Daphne, with a

curious little smile, glanced sideways at him. "I have been think-ing," she said, her voice carefully light as her words trailed away.

Edward arched a brow. "A most dangerous pastime."

She giggled, nudging him with her elbow. "You sound like Aunt Felicity."

He pressed his lips together and cleared his throat even as his ears warmed. He hoped they hadn't turned pink.

Daphne did not seem to notice his reaction. Instead, she pressed on. "I only mean that you and I speak often about my future."

Edward made a low sound of agreement. "That is my purpose, as your guardian. To think on your future."

"Yes, but..." His ward tilted her head slightly. "But we never speak about Aunt Felicity's."

Edward's brows drew together. "What do you mean?"

"I mean..." The young woman hesitated, perhaps choosing her words with care. "Well. What will she do when I marry?"

Edward exhaled slowly. This again. "That is not something for you to worry over, Daphne. Nor is it my business." He handed the books to the coachman, who had opened the door for them, though he had the feeling they were not going home, though. "Your aunt is not without options," Edward said carefully. "She has an adequate inheritance. She may choose to establish a home of her own, or travel, or—"

Daphne huffed, cutting off his weak listing of ideas. "You make it sound so simple."

Edward shrugged, though some of his frustration had returned. Not at the girl, of course. "Is it not?"

"No," she said, exasperated. "Aunt Felicity has been looking after me nearly my entire life. And if I do not need her anymore..." She trailed off, but the meaning was clear.

Edward let out a slow breath. This was more than simple concern; this was guilt. Daphne felt responsible for Felicity's happiness.

Well, he could not blame her. He had felt responsible for

others before and burdened himself with their well-being even when it was not truly his duty. But he would not let Daphne bear that same weight. She was so young; let her stay young, while she could.

"She will always have a place at Briarwood," he said evenly.

Daphne stole a glance at him, her expression thoughtful. "That is kind of you to say," she said, her voice carefully neutral. "But it would not be appropriate for her to stay, or even visit, without me present. Would it?"

Edward considered. "No. I suppose not." They already skirted the bounds of true propriety with the living arrangement they maintained. Had Felicity been widowed or considerably older, less pretty, Society would have nothing to say on the matter.

Because Society was run by hypocrites.

Besides, Felicity was fiercely independent. She had fought to remain part of Daphne's life, and once her charge no longer needed her, she would undoubtedly seek a new purpose. Perhaps elsewhere—at a cottage by the sea, as he had heard her say before. Alone.

The thought was most unsettling.

Daphne, watching him closely, hid a knowing smile—not before he caught sight of it, though.

He glanced at the coachman. "I think we are going to walk for a few more minutes."

"As you say, Colonel." The coachman touched the brim of his hat, then climbed back into his seat.

They walked in silence for a few paces before Daphne said, with studied nonchalance, "It would be nice if she had a reason to stay nearby, would it not?"

He raised his eyebrows at that, looking down at the slip of a woman on his arm. "Are you not reason enough, child?"

"Well. Aunt Felicity will not wish me to feel smothered. She has said as much. Brides need to make their home and their life their own. Or so I have been informed." She batted her eyelashes innocently. "It is such a shame. I should like to keep her close. I doubt I would feel smothered. Especially if she lived in a place familiar to me."

Edward snorted. "Daphne."

"What?" she asked, voice sweet as honey.

"You are many things, but subtle is not one of them."

She grinned. "I do not know what you mean, Colonel."

He gave her a look.

His young ward, utterly unfazed, continued speaking while looking directly ahead. "She is very fond of you, you know."

Edward sighed. Honestly! "I should have left you in the bookstore to live out your days, especially if you are going to start plotting romances."

She laughed, seemingly utterly delighted. "No, you should not have! But if I am to plot a romance..."

Edward shook his head, hiding a small smile.

Daphne had struck him as clever from the first, but it had been smothered by grief. This was a new level of mischief. She continued to smile teasingly as she turned her face toward the sun, as though the afternoon were too lovely for serious conversations.

Edward, however, was still considering her earlier words. It would indeed be nice if Felicity had a reason to stay. The thought lodged itself in his mind, stubborn as a burr; but Felicity was not a woman who waited for things to happen. She would stubbornly stick to her word. She would not linger where she was not needed.

If Daphne no longer needed her, she would go. It could be in a matter of months, or a matter of years. A time he had no control over.

Edward frowned. Felicity was right about him resenting a lack of control...but how could he help it when he thought of her leaving? He simply did not like where that thought led.

Daphne glanced at him from the corner of her eye, clearly waiting for him to say something.

Instead, Edward changed the subject. "We should return home before the streets become too crowded. You must be tired."

The young woman made a thoughtful sound in the back of her throat. "Or," she said slowly, as though weighing the thought carefully, "we might make one more stop."

Edward cast her a wary glance. "One more?"

The smile he received was far too sweetly. "My seamstress is only a few streets from here."

Edward arched a brow. "And?" Surely she had everything she needed at this point. Felicity had presented him with meticulous notes with each purchase, partly he rather thought to justify the expense. She was quite thorough on all matters concerning Daphne's needs.

"And," his ward continued, "I thought perhaps you might like to visit my seamstress, Madame Bisset."

Edward's suspicion deepened. "For what purpose?" He would not mind buying her fripperies, if she asked for them, but dancing around the subject did not seem like her.

Daphne lifted her shoulders in an exaggeratedly careless shrug. "You are always saying that my gowns are 'lovely.' I thought you might wish to see where such loveliness is crafted. And, you know, Aunt Felicity had her gowns made by the same seamstress, though they are certainly not as lovely, given how dark they are."

Edward gave her a long, level look. Daphne's smile did not falter. He sighed. "I do not see why I should like to meet Madame Bisset when—" That was when a new thought struck him.

The seamstress had Felicity's measurements.

The idea formed so quickly, so completely, he had no time to question it. Daphne had given him an opportunity. Yet it would not be seemly, surely? He ought not to act on it. And yet....

Edward adjusted the cuff of his sleeve. "I suppose a visit would not be entirely unwarranted."

Daphne's smile brightened but he was not fooled. She had intended this from the start, perhaps even when she had suggested the visit to Hatchards…and he had happily played directly into her hands.

He gave his ward a crooked grin. "Miss Daphne Price, you would make a most excellent battle advisor, I think."

"Oh?" She laughed and squeezed his arm. "Thank you, Colonel. But I think I should much rather leave that to soldiers."

"A pity." He looked back down the street and signaled to the coachman to follow them along the road. "Let us go meet Madame Bisset, so I may thank her for her fine service."

And, of course, commission something new.

Chapter Nineteen

A clock somewhere in the house chimed the hour. One o'clock in the morning.

Truly, all decent folk not out for an evening's entertainment ought to be in bed; but Felicity had left her chamber in search of nothing more than a moment's peace from her racing thoughts, hoping a short walk through the corridors of Briarwood might settle her mind. As she passed a window, the glow of the moonlight on the garden paths caught her eye, and before she knew it she found herself pushing open an outer door.

She could not regret stepping out into the cool night air, for the moment she breathed it in, her mind grew clearer. Wrapping her shawl more tightly around herself, even though the spring chill was not unpleasant, Felicity walked the garden paths, her slippers hardly making a sound on the stone. It was quiet here, peaceful, the kind of hush that made it easier to think...and harder to hide from her thoughts.

Her footsteps taking her there of their own accord, she came to the most dominant, and likely most loved, portion of the gardens. Her fingers traced lightly over the thorny branches of the rosebushes, brushing against something softer than expected.

A bud. The first of the season. She smiled to herself, despite her tangled thoughts. No matter what came, the seasons turned, and new things found life. The thought settled strangely in her chest, warm and wistful all at once.

And then a voice from behind her. "Do you make a habit of wandering alone at night, Miss Price?"

Felicity pulled in a sharp breath, surprised, as she turned. Though she had not heard his approach, Edward stood at the edge of the roses, his face shining in the moonlight. His hands were clasped behind his back, his posture deceptively casual. He was dressed as though he had attempted sleep and failed. He wore no coat, only a waistcoat over his crisp linen shirt messily tucked into breeches, his hair slightly tousled.

The moonlight carved sharp shadows along his features, his expression unreadable. His bearing, as always, firm and immovable. Most unfortunately, she found him as handsome as ever in that moment.

"I could ask the same of you, Colonel," she said, tilting her chin up.

Edward's gaze flickered toward the rosebushes she had been admiring.

"They are not late yet, you know," he murmured.

Felicity blinked. "I beg your pardon?"

He nodded toward the blooms. "The roses. They come along in their own time. It is merely April. By mid-May, they will be fully alive."

She raised her brow. "I knew you spent a lot of time here, but I did not take you for a man who took such notice of growing patterns."

Edward laughed, a quiet sound of amusement, shifting his stance. "I notice a great deal. I caused these rose bushes to be planted here. My elder brother, when he inherited the family estate, told me I could request pieces of our home to bring to my own. I asked for some of the rose bushes. My mother, even in her grief at the loss of my father, helped me select the best of them to take cuttings from. I spend time with them, watch them grow. To be certain they are cared for and do not grow homesick."

She suspected he had spent many solitary evenings among the thorns. Felicity turned back to the bushes, her voice quieter now. "Early or late, they will bloom."

"A thing utterly beyond my control," he said, a touch of humor in his voice. "Are you impressed I love them still, when they do not bend to my orders?"

She touched the tight bud again, letting her finger skim along the stem to a thorn. "Perhaps I spoke too hastily about such things."

"You spoke wisely of them. Thank you for it. I have become more aware of that trait in myself." His voice had lowered and grown softer. A silence stretched between them, filled only by the whisper of the wind through the hedges. "You cannot sleep."

It was not a question, and so did not require an answer. Yet Felicity sighed and turned to look at him. "No." She hesitated, then—perhaps because the night felt safe, or perhaps because she was too tired to guard her words—she admitted, "My mind refuses to quiet itself."

Edward studied her for a moment, before looking up at the night sky. "What is troubling you?"

She let out a short laugh. "Where shall I begin?"

He met her gaze and raised his eyebrows, but he said nothing. He simply waited.

What was there to do but speak? "I have spent my whole life in someone else's home," she said slowly. "My father's, then my brother's. Now I live in yours." Felicity traced her fingers along the back of the garden bench, grounding herself. "I thought I was content," she admitted softly. "I thought it did not matter." She looked up, meeting his gaze. "But Daphne has asked me recently a question I thought I knew the answer to. She asked what I would do when she marries."

Edward's expression shifted, but the shadows and moonlight made it difficult to read when he stood so many feet away. "And what did you tell her, Captain?"

Felicity swallowed. "The same thing I have always told myself. That I will go away. Someplace quiet. Someplace small. I will live on gossip and tea, take long walks on a pebbled beach. Do nothing of consequence."

The Colonel's brow furrowed, and for a moment, he looked as though he wanted to say something. But he did not. Instead, he waited.

"I suppose it hardly matters," she said, forcing a lighter tone. "I am far too stubborn for courtship. Too set in my ways for marriage."

That was when Edward took a slow step toward her.

Felicity chuckled softly, ignoring his closer presence. "I am too old to be wanted, besides."

Edward's voice was low and even. "Three and thirty is hardly old, Miss Price."

She shook her head as though that could alter her very age. "You are very kind."

"I am not," he said as though the matter were quite simple. "I am truthful."

Felicity glanced away, watching the ground as his shadow grew nearer. "You do not know me as well as you think. There are so many reasons I will never marry."

"Tell me. As many as you can list."

Her gaze went to his again, and a disbelieving laugh left her lips. "Edward. Really?" He folded his arms and waited. "You are alarmingly patient this evening."

"I am told it is a virtue."

"I do not think it applies in situations like this, where you needle a woman to give you consequential answers about her life."

"I am not needling. I have asked, quite politely, for you to list these reasons you speak of. Come along, Felicity. Tell me all the reasons you will never marry." He stood so close now. Close enough for her to see the gleam in his eye.

Was it a challenge?

"Very well." Felicity began listing her faults, one by one, ticking them off on her fingers. "I am sharp-tongued—"

"You are intelligent," Edward countered, startling her with the interruption. "I find it preferable to insipid conversation."

She rolled her eyes. "I argue too much."

"You argue when it matters."

Felicity narrowed her eyes at him. He was doing this on purpose. "I do not bend easily."

"You shouldn't have to. And neither do I."

"I am quite set on getting my way."

"When you are in the right, I fail to see the problem with that." He leaned a little closer. "Go on. I can do this all night."

Felicity's breath caught, her heart thudding painfully against her ribs as she stared up at him. His gaze was unwavering, steady, and open enough that she read something startling within them.

Edward cared for her.

And in that moment, she realized something. She had spent so long deciding what was wrong with her. Edward was the first person in a long time to tell her what was right.

The night air stretched between them, charged and waiting. A breeze swept through the garden, and she shivered slightly.

Edward moved apparently without thinking. Shrugging off his coat, he stepped forward and draped it over her shoulders.

"Oh, not again. Edward...." Felicity looked up at him, stunned. Not by the action itself—but by the warmth of it. By the care in his gesture. By the way his fingers lingered, just for a moment, against the fabric.

She swallowed, her throat tight. "I was so ungrateful last time you gave me use of your coat. I left it on the ground."

"It came to no harm." The man kept his hands on her shoulders, moving them slightly up and down, as though to warm her through his touch. "Even if it had, I would give you another and another. All my coats are at your disposal, since you appear unable to think ahead well enough to wear your own."

She laughed softly. "You see? Another thing that marks me ill-prepared for marriage. I cannot be bothered to look after myself."

"Because you are too busy looking after everyone else," Edward said gently, looking down into her eyes. Though the moon cast everything in a silvery-blue light, she had no trouble admiring the depth in his green-brown eyes. "Let someone else look after you for a change, Felicity. Let me look after you."

"Thank you," she said softly.

Edward exhaled, shaking his head slightly. "You have spent so long deciding what is wrong with you." He bent closer. "Have you never considered all that is perfect and lovely?"

Felicity's breath shuddered. Her fingers curled around the edges of his coat, holding it tighter around her. She could not speak; for the first time, she had no argument.

Edward's eyes searched hers—but then, with a slow inhale, he straightened. "The garden is lovely at night," he said at last.

She nodded, collecting herself. "Yes," she murmured. "It is."

A long moment of silence stretched between them.

Then, wordlessly, he took her hand and most inexplicably laced his fingers with hers. "But it is late. And you are cold."

She could hardly swallow. Everything felt charged. If she said the wrong thing, if he did, she might well combust on the spot. And what was the right thing, with her hand in his?

"I should get you inside," he said. "And send you back to bed." Her cheeks flushed as his fingers tightened around hers. "Come, Felicity. All the troubles of the world will be there when you wake tomorrow. Perhaps you will confide a few more in me, that I might help you carry them."

He gave her hand a gentle tug, and she stepped forward, walking together back toward the house. As they reached the doors, Edward gave her hand another squeeze. "I think... I think I will take one more turn around the garden. Perhaps to clear my own head." Then he bowed and at the same moment raised her hand to his lips. His lips brushed her knuckles as he said, "Goodnight, Miss Felicity Price. And sweet dreams to you."

Neither of them said another word as she withdrew, the skin of her hand tingly from where his lips had touched her.

Felicity tucked that hand beneath her cheek when she at last laid down, her cheeks warm, his coat carefully hung on the back of the chair in her room.

Chapter Twenty

E dward left home the following morning in a bright, agreeable mood. The exchange with Felicity the evening before had awoken something in him—something full of hope and excitement. The worries he carried weighed less upon him. The morning's showers hadn't lasted long, and when they tapered off, he betook himself to his club. There was a ball that evening, and he wanted to ensure Daphne would have an enjoyable evening, full of dancing and one way to do that was to speak openly about their attendance where gentlemen and their fathers would hear him.

He arrived at Blackstone's Club fresh from an unexpectedly pleasant ride. As he had passed the dressmaker's shop on his way in, he couldn't help but think on Daphne's matchmaking attempt, the memory of which only put him in a still better humor.

The club's familiar hush greeted him upon entry, the smell of pipe smoke and leather-bound books wrapping around him like an old coat. He'd grown to like the place, even with its odd taxidermy collection which seemed ever in motion. A North American beaver stood on a pedestal near the doorway today. Wearing a monocle.

He bowed to it, on impulse.

Perhaps he would take a drink in the lounge. Perhaps a game of whist. Perhaps, for once, Edward would allow himself a moment's enjoyment.

Then the doorman intercepted him. "Colonel Halstead, Lord Blackstone requests a word with you."

"Oh? Of course. Lead the way, Plockton." Edward followed the doorman with his hands tucked behind his back, mildly amused. Blackstone was an eccentric old man, fond of odd things, taxidermied creatures, and twisting a conversation in unexpected directions; but Edward had come to like the man as much as he had the club itself.

Therefore when he entered the viscount's private study, he prepared for some jest, some cryptic bit of nonsense about membership fees or the finer points of cataloging stuffed rodents.

Instead, the moment he entered the office, he knew something was wrong.

Lord Blackstone sat behind his grand desk, his expression unreadable. The usual amusement in his eyes was absent, replaced by something distant. Serious. The taxidermy menagerie loomed from the shelves—the owl with its ridiculous cap, the fox in its spectacles—but today, none of it felt remotely amusing. "If you would sit, Colonel Halstead?"

Edward's pulse shifted subtly, though outwardly, his remained composed. He lowered himself into the chair across from Blackstone. "Is something amiss, my lord?"

"A troubling matter has come to my attention," Blackstone said without preamble.

Edward did not move, nor jump to conclusions. He did not need to.

"It concerns your past."

Still, Edward said nothing as his heart sank.

Blackstone studied him. Weighing. Measuring. "I have heard a rather disappointing account of you," the viscount continued. "One I cannot ignore."

Edward's fingers curled slightly against the arms of the chair. "And what account is that, Lord Blackstone?"

"It is said that, in your youth, you ruined a young woman and immediately afterwards fled all your responsibilities. That you joined the army, rather than face the consequences of your actions."

A slow, creeping weight settled in Edward's chest. It was not rage that struck him first; it was resignation. At last, the past had come for him.

His jaw tightened, but his voice remained even, measured. "That is not how any of that happened."

Blackstone tilted his head, an unimpressed gesture. "No?"

"No." Edward's explanation was necessarily brief, his words clipped. He would not reveal all. He would not harm Pamela, not after all these years. "I did not flee—I was sent away. My commission was not of my choosing."

Blackstone made a noncommittal sound, steepling his fingers. "Perhaps. But intent does not alter the outcome, does it?"

"My only intent was to obey the wishes of my father and the express wishes of the young woman's parents." Edward's spine went rigid. "What outcome do you speak of?"

Blackstone leaned forward, his gaze sharper now. "There is another rumor, Colonel. One more recent." A pause.

Edward felt as frozen in place as the animals on display, desperate to move but entirely incapable.

Lord Blackstone spoke almost as though the words pained him. "It is said...you have been searching for a child."

Edward's breath stilled. For the first time, his control threatened to waver. "And?" he asked, his voice low. "It is no crime to make enquiries."

Blackstone studied him for a long moment. "I wonder what I am meant to make of it."

His teeth clenched together, his grip tightening the arms of the chair. "That is a private matter."

"Perhaps," Blackstone said quietly. "But reputation is not

private, Colonel. It is instead very public—and reputation is what holds this club together. I have made it a point to only offer membership to men of upstanding honor, of high moral fiber. Men I am not ashamed to know."

Edward's shoulders locked. He had always known his membership here was tenuous. Probationary. Now Blackstone was making the terms very clear.

"If you cannot satisfy my concerns," the viscount said smoothly, "I will have no choice but to revoke your membership."

It was all he could do to exhale slowly through his nose. "You mean to say, I would be expelled."

"I mean to say," Blackstone corrected, "that you would no longer be welcome beneath this roof or mine, and that your fellow members would be informed of my decision...and why. They would be free to draw their own conclusions about your character."

Edward's pulse pounded, painful and swift. He could endure such a loss. He had endured worse. But this was not only about him.

If Blackstone cast such public doubt on his honor, others would whisper of it—nay, no longer fear to whisper it, but speak openly of their distrust. And if Edward was seen as a man of poor character, what would that mean for Daphne's standing? For Felicity's?

If doubt fell upon his name, would invitations to events quietly stop arriving? Would Daphne find herself excluded from certain circles, quietly left behind as others moved forward? Would the friendships of the Normans, the Montagues, all disappear? Would Felicity's place in his home face greater scrutiny?

The worry churned in his stomach. He lifted his gaze to meet Blackstone's directly. "I understand."

Blackstone nodded once. "Good. Then you understand why I must ask: what explanation can you offer me that satisfies the matter?"

Edward squeezed his eyes closed. "None."

Blackstone sounded confused. "None? What can you mean?"

Opening his eyes and focusing them on the bright gaze of the other man, he spoke in a firm voice. In a final one. "None."

The viscount considered him for a long, long moment. Then, at last, he sighed. "That is unfortunate. But you may change your mind—I will give you a fortnight to come up with a satisfactory explanation or reason why I should not doubt your integrity, Colonel Halstead. Consider your reputation. Consider those under your protection—"

Edward inclined his head stiffly. "If there is nothing else, my lord, I will take my leave."

Blackstone waved him away, standing and pacing to the window in evident discontent.

It was a relief to rise and stride from the office. He did not look back.

But the moment he stepped out into the club's main hall, the weight of what had just transpired settled heavily over Edward. He had not spoken in his own defense, but how could he? The story was not his to tell. There were others with reputations that could be ruined, lives hurt. And now, there might be tangible consequences.

The familiar comfort of Blackstone's Club felt different now. Tighter. Smaller. Edward moved toward the exit, retrieving his hat and gloves with uncharacteristic urgency. Stepping out onto the pavement, he let the tepid London air wash over him.

For the first time in a long, long while, Edward did not know what to do.

FELICITY SHOULD HAVE BEEN WATCHING DAPHNE. SHE KNEW IT. SHE had promised to keep a closer eye on her niece since the event in the garden, and yet her attention kept drifting to Edward on the other side of the ballroom.

Something was wrong.

He was not himself. He was too quiet, too measured. His usual sharp attentiveness was there, but his mind was somewhere else entirely.

"The Colonel seems broody," Mrs. Norman said at her side, from behind her fan. "Is anything amiss, my dear?"

"I cannot think so," Felicity said, forcing a smile. Mrs. Norman might be a friend, but she was a recent one, and a lady could never keep some matters too close. "My, but Miss Norman looks lovely. That shade of yellow makes her hair look as though it is spun from gold."

Mrs. Norman let her change the subject, and soon she went away to speak to someone else leaving Felicity free to fret over the colonel again.

Felicity had spent the better part of the evening stealing glances at him, trying to read the tension in his jaw, the way his hands curled into loose fists at his sides. He appeared to be avoiding the gentlemen he had previously spent evenings speaking with. Most inexplicable.

Her first thought that something was amiss had been at Briarwood, and she meant to ask, intending to pull him aside and demand to know what troubled him so deeply.

But she had waited too long, and now they were in a public place. The Assembly Rooms. Edward had a friend who asked for a favor, and the favor meant vouchers for this evening at Almack's. Looking glasses everywhere reflected the candlelight from the chandeliers and sconces, the windows above open to let the warm air drift out and encourage cool air to come in.

Truly, it was a wonderful achievement for a woman of Felicity's age and background. Even if it was the only time she entered Almack's for the Season, most would see it as a triumph. But she could hardly think on that with thoughts of Edward's solemn expression on her mind.

But there was nothing to be done about it, presently. She took in a deep breath, nearly coughed on all the perfumes that entered her lungs at once, and turned her focus back to Daphne...and could not find her among the dancers.

Felicity's breath caught as her gaze swept the room quickly. Daphne—where was she, she could not have—then her heart slowed a moment. *There.* Her niece was not far, only a few steps beyond the main gathering, standing near the gilded looking glasses along the wall.

And she was not alone. A man stood too close, his body angled toward her in a way which appeared casual, but Felicity suspected was anything but.

Mr. Richard Arnold.

Felicity's stomach twisted. Though the gentleman was, Daphne was not smiling. Her posture was poised, but there was a stiffness in her shoulders that Felicity recognized all too well.

She instinctively started forward, but Edward was already moving. He had been across the room mere moments ago but now, he was here. He cut through the gathered guests with precision, his every movement controlled but deliberate. He and Felicity arrived near Daphne at the same moment.

Mr. Arnold did not appear to notice him at first, but when he did, his easy smile faltered.

"Mr. Arnold," Edward said smoothly, his voice quiet but full of unmistakable authority.

The horrid man straightened slightly, turning to face him. "Colonel Halstead," he said, his smile returning—forced now, a little too unsteady. "I was making conversation with your charming ward."

"Were you indeed?" Edward asked, tone pleasant but razor-sharp.

Felicity shivered. Daphne had taken a small, measured step away from Arnold and closer to Edward. It was a tiny shift, but it said everything. The way she looked up at her guardian, with trust and a tight-lipped smile, set Felicity at ease.

Edward's expression did not change, but Felicity knew he saw it too.

"I would be very careful, Mr. Arnold," Edward said, voice still too low to carry beyond the four of them. "London is not as large as one might think, nor is one's reputation so untouchable."

Mr. Arnold's jaw flexed. A challenge had been made, though he knew better than to answer it. He gave a short, stiff bow, then turned and walked away. Only when he disappeared into the crowd did Felicity move to put herself between Daphne and anyone possibly watching the exchange.

Daphne turned to Edward, her face still composed, but her voice quieter than usual. "Thank you, Colonel."

Edward studied her carefully. "Are you well?"

She nodded. "I am now." Then, she hesitated. As though debating whether to say something.

Edward waited as Felicity's heart hammered.

"I am afraid I was about to step on his foot," she admitted finally.

Felicity covered her mouth to keep a sharp, relieved laugh from popping out.

Edward's frown deepened. "You were what?"

Daphne's mouth tugged into the smallest of smiles. "It is a trick I learned from Aunt Felicity. If a gentleman stands too close or refuses to move, one need only step onto his toes, hard enough to make him shift away, but not enough to be accused of an outburst. A swift apology always follows, of course, but the pain in the toes remains!"

Edward huffed a quiet, amused breath. He glanced at Felicity, his eyes sparkling. "Not a terrible idea." He looked at Daphne again. "And if that had failed?"

Daphne lifted her chin slightly. "Then I would have asked, quite loudly, how he had enjoyed his time in debtor's prison."

Felicity's brows lifted. "Mr. Arnold—was in debtor's prison?"

Daphne's eyes glinted with satisfaction. "No. But I doubt he would have liked others wondering if he had been."

Felicity stared at her seemingly unknowable niece. Then, slowly, she smiled.

"You were going to handle him yourself," Edward said, a note of approval in his voice.

Daphne nodded. "I was."

"But I arrived first."

"You did." Daphne reached out and squeezed his arm. "Still, I was glad for your rescue," she admitted.

Edward said nothing, though Felicity saw him swallow, the movement tight beneath his cravat. Then he inclined his head. "You had better go back to your friends, my dear."

"Yes, Colonel." She beamed up at him, at his show of approval and trust. The young woman stepped back toward the gathering crowd, her usual poise returning.

Felicity watched her go, pride swelling in her chest. Daphne had not invited trouble. She had not needed rescuing, and she had been grateful for Edward's presence all the same. Felicity turned to him, ready to comment on it, but the words died on her lips.

Edward was not watching Daphne. He was staring at nothing in particular, his expression dark and unreadable.

Felicity's stomach tightened. All her concern for him returned. "Edward?"

His jaw tensed. "Not here, Captain," he said, his voice lower now. "I cannot speak of it here." Then, without another word, he turned and walked away.

Felicity watched him go, unease curling in her chest. Mr. Arnold was gone. Daphne was safe. Whatever could be troubling the man?

The worst thing she could think of in that moment was Edward's missing son. She had thought on the boy's fate several times, but she had not dared broach the subject with him again. How could she? It was such a private thing. Having a child out of wedlock was an enormous scandal for all but the highest of classes. Those with money and power, the royal princes included, propagated without care for the legality of the child's birthright.

But for someone like Edward? He would have to handle the situation delicately.

And what of the boy himself? A boy, to be sure, but given the distance of time, surely almost a man. Would he want a father who had known nothing of him for nearly his whole life? Would he be angry? Did he even know his true parentage?

It was all quite complicated, and Edward had no one to share that burden with. No one except his hired investigator and her.

She would speak to him. Tonight: she had to. Edward needed to know he wasn't alone.

Of course, he might have said she spent too much time looking after everyone, and perhaps she did. But she did not begrudge the people she loved a single moment of her time. And Edward...

She did not begrudge him those moments, either.

THE CARRIAGE RIDE HOME WAS SILENT, WEIGHTED IN A WAY THAT made Edward uneasy. Daphne sat opposite him, her weary head resting on her aunt's shoulder, her gaze drifting out the window. She seemed composed, but he knew she was still turning over the events of the evening.

Felicity, on the other hand, was not watching the passing streets. She was watching him.

Edward knew she had noticed his distraction. He had felt the weight of her gaze all night. Though she had not yet pressed him for answers, he knew her well enough to know that soon enough she would. He nearly smiled at the thought of their future tête-à-tête, already picturing the stubborn tilt of her chin when she demanded to know where his thoughts were.

What would he tell her?

He hadn't the faintest idea.

When the carriage finally rolled to a stop, Edward stepped out first, offering Daphne his hand before doing the same for Felicity. He expected the older woman to release him immediately, to follow her niece upstairs and help the younger woman prepare for bed as usual, but she lingered a moment longer, fingers cool against his palm. He swallowed against the warmth that flickered at the contact, ignoring it as he turned toward the house.

Then Felicity's voice stopped him. "Daphne, go inside and head upstairs. I will be in shortly."

Daphne hesitated long enough to glance between them, her sharp mind no doubt piecing together the unspoken tension. She gave a knowing smile and did not argue. "Good night, Aunt Felicity. Good night, Colonel."

Edward inclined his head in response, waiting until she had definitely disappeared inside before looking at Felicity. The carriage pulled away, leaving them alone in front of the house, the evening air a cool relief from the insipidity of the carriage. He already knew what she would say before she spoke.

"We need to talk."

Edward exhaled slowly. "Felicity—"

"No. Not later. Not tomorrow. Now."

He hesitated, studying her in the dim lamplight. There was no use delaying the inevitable—and there was that tilt to her chin he had anticipated. How had he come to know her so well?

Without a word he turned and strode inside, leading her through the quiet corridor to his study.

The room was dark, save for the glow of a single lamp on the mantel. He lit its mate on the other end, the light flickering over the edges of the room. He did not look at her. Instead, he moved to the lamps near his desk, lighting them one by one.

"Edward, please." Her voice was softer now, but no less insistent.

He hesitated. "I am thinking how to begin."

She snorted. The beautiful, charming woman, snorted. It nearly made him smile until she said, "You are stalling."

Apparently, Felicity had grown to know him quite well, too.

Edward sighed, running a hand along the edge of his desk, his back still to her. He did not want to do this now. Not while his thoughts were still out of order, not while the weight of Blackstone's warning sat heavy in his chest.

He heard her soft approach, the slippers on her feet whispering against the rug. "You do not have to protect me from whatever this is." Her words landed harder than he expected. He tensed, fingers curling slightly against the wood of the desk. "Tell me what is wrong," she said again, quieter this time. "Please."

"Captain—Felicity. It is not so simple."

"I care for you."

Edward froze. The silence between them stretched, humming with tension. Slowly, inch by inch, he turned.

Felicity was standing near him, no more than two steps away, her hands clasped in front of her skirts, her chin tilted upward in that way which told him she would not back down. Her cheeks were flushed. Her eyes met his with quiet determination, though he could see the slight rise and fall of her breath, the way she steeled herself for his reaction.

"I...I cannot have heard you correctly," Edward murmured, his heart stuttering in his chest at the lie. He knew what she had said. But he desperately wanted to hear it again.

She swallowed but did not waver. "I care for you, Edward. Deeply. More than I have cared for any man before."

For a moment, he could do nothing but look at her. He had heard correctly. She had taken a beautiful risk, a brave chance. And he adored her all the more for it.

Before he could stop himself, before he could reason himself out of action—Edward had crossed the space between them and kissed her.

It was not a tentative or uncertain brush of the lips. It was all consuming.

His hand came to her waist, pulling her closer, while his other traced the curve of her jaw, tilting her face up toward him. Her fingers curled into his coat, gripping him as though she might anchor herself there. The warmth of her, the way she leaned into him, the way she had said his name—it was undoing him.

When he finally pulled away, the fiery kiss tangling his

thoughts, it was only enough to rest his forehead against hers. "Felicity," he murmured.

Her voice was breathless. "Yes?"

Edward exhaled, lifting his gaze to hers, searching. "I have a deep affection for you."

Her eyes softened. "You do?"

His lips quirked in a wry smile. "You doubted it? After that?"

Felicity's slight smile answered his, and her eyes danced as she gazed up at him. "I didn't want to assume."

His thumb brushed lightly over her cheek. "My stubborn, lovely Felicity. I did not even ask permission to kiss you."

"Did I not give it to you with my words? With my look? Let me give it more clearly. You may kiss me as often as you wish."

What could he do but kiss her again, after a declaration such as that? He pressed his lips to hers, one hand around her to draw her closer, the other cradling the back of her head as he supported it at the perfect angle for his much taller form to bend and taste her.

Oh, she tasted sweet. She felt soft in his arms, delicate. When his lips parted from hers, he placed a kiss on her forehead. "You will not stamp on my toes, then?"

Felicity laughed and shook her head. "No. Not this time." She laid her head on his chest and closed her eyes briefly, a soft smile touching her lips. For a moment, neither of them spoke, content to stand there in the quiet, in the flickering glow of the lamplight.

Edward marveled at his unexpected good fortune. Felicity cared for him, as he cared for her. She allowed him the privilege of holding her. The gift of her kiss.

But peace, as always, was fleeting.

Felicity pulled back slightly, searching his face. "Edward."

He sighed, already knowing what was coming. "Must we?"

"Yes."

He dragged a hand through his hair, reluctant to let the moment go. Then, because there was no point in avoiding it any longer, he exhaled. "Lord Blackstone."

Her expression sharpened. "The man who owns your club? What about him?"

It had to be said, no matter how painful it would be. "He has heard rumors about me. About my past."

Her brow furrowed. "What sort of rumors?"

His jaw clenched. "That I ruined a young woman and fled responsibility by joining the military."

"It is an old story…with some truth to it." Felicity inhaled slowly. "Is there more?"

Edward hesitated before meeting her gaze. "And he knows that I have been searching. For a child."

Her breath hitched. "Oh no—"

"He will not stand for someone less than worthy to belong to his club," Edward stated in clipped tones. "He has informed me that unless I can prove my honor beyond doubt, provide an explanation both for my actions and the consequences, I will be removed from it."

Felicity's fingers curled into fists. "If you are removed, that would cause harm to you."

"It will cast doubt on my reputation. Yes." He did not need to say the rest. It would affect her. It would affect Daphne. Everything.

The woman he cared far too much about was quiet for a long moment. Then, her voice low and sure, she said, "That is not fair."

"It is Society."

"Ugh. Society." She shook her head, disgust on her features. "I lecture Daphne about the strictures of Society almost daily, but the unforgiving hypocrites in charge of everything are always eager to dig their claws into someone. Especially someone good. Someone like you. So what shall we do?"

"We?" Edward repeated, looking down at her in bewilderment.

Her eyebrows raised. "Yes, we. Daphne is your ward. I am her aunt. We are a part of your household, your reputation is inextricably linked to ours. We are all in this together, Edward. I am completely on your side at every turn. If you say we ride at dawn, then I will prepare my musket. Or parasol." She offered him a gentle smile. "Truly. What do you wish for us to do?"

He was silent, moved by her quick acceptance and her tender loyalty to him. It was more than he deserved.

Felicity stepped closer, resting a hand against his chest. "We will find a way through this."

He looked at her, running his thumb along her jaw. "I believe you actually could, my darling." He released a sigh. "Let me think on it. I have been given a fortnight to decide what to tell Lord Blackstone."

Felicity nodded and stepped away, immediately leaving him to curse her absence in the cool air between them. "Do not hesitate to speak to me of it, Edward. Please."

"I will not," he promised.

"I had best go attend to Daphne. Good night, Edward."

"Good night, Captain." He watched her go, his chest lighter though his burdens remained the same.

Chapter Twenty-One

For two days, Felicity could not stop thinking about Edward's dilemma. It had settled in the back of her mind, lingering like an out of tune chord, its tension humming beneath everything she did.

She had not spoken to Edward much since their conversation in the study. Not because she did not wish to, but because every time she looked at him, she saw the weight on his shoulders, the quiet way he carried his burden, quite literally soldiering on. He was still thinking it all through.

And he had kissed her. That, too, she could not forget.

Which was precisely why she had invited Mrs. Norman and Miss Norman for tea today—to distract herself, if nothing else.

The parlor was bright with afternoon light, the fire warming the chill which still determinedly clung to early spring. The tea service was laid out neatly and Daphne sat beside her, in high spirits, telling Miss Norman some amusing story about the ball two nights prior.

Mrs. Norman, however, was watching Felicity. The older woman had always been perceptive, and today was no exception, waiting to speak her mind until the young ladies crossed the room to sit at a table to play draughts while they continued to chatter about upcoming invitations.

"You seem troubled, Miss Price," Mrs. Norman said smoothly, lifting her teacup.

Felicity offered what she hoped was a reassuring smile. "Oh, not at all."

Mrs. Norman hummed in a way that suggested she did not believe her in the slightest. "You know, your niece is very important to my daughter. Their friendship has been quickly made, but it seems to be of a steady nature. I consider Daphne a dear girl, and I am most grateful you have allowed the acquaintance."

"Oh, Mrs. Norman, of course. Miss Norman is exactly the sort of friend Daphne needs at present, and I hope they are friends for many years beyond it. I give myself leave to hope that their daughters may in turn find some friendship together."

"As do I." Mrs. Norman put her cup down. She folded her hands in her lap. "As I hope that you will be my friend for many years to come, Miss Price. You are an intelligent woman, and I have the greatest pleasure in your company."

Feeling her cheeks warm, Felicity looked at the other woman with open surprise which she could not help but voice. "Truly? You think of me as a friend? I am only Daphne's aunt."

"No, my dear. You are a kindhearted woman with a most excellent taste in parasols." She smiled with good humor. "And, indeed, I hope you count me your friend."

"I certainly have wished to," Felicity admitted, a hand touching her heart. "Thank you. I have enjoyed your company, too. All of our conversations have lifted me, giving me comfort and guidance. Please, call me Felicity from now on."

"Then you must call me Rose. Now, Felicity, you are officially my friend. Tell me, please—what troubles you?"

Her shoulders fell. "It...it is not my burden to share, I am afraid. But that you noticed and wished to help, that eases my mind greatly."

Rose nodded slowly, her expression still kind. "I understand. You will tell me if I can help you, will you not?"

"Of course. For now, I am best helped with distraction. We must find something pleasant, some exciting topic to—" Before Felicity could attempt to redirect the conversation, a light knock sounded at the door and a footman stepped inside, holding a carefully wrapped parcel.

"A delivery has arrived, Miss Price."

Felicity frowned slightly. "Oh?"

The footman nodded. "From Madame Bisset's dress shop."

That was peculiar. She had not ordered Daphne anything recently. Setting down her teacup, she took the parcel from the footman, untying the string and unfolding the brown paper wrapping.

A gown was nestled inside. A stunning one.

The fabric was soft beneath her fingertips, finer than anything she had commissioned before. The color—a rich, deep green—was striking, the embroidery at the hems delicate and elegant. It was surely not Daphne's. The colors were too bold for a young woman in her first Season.

"My, but that is exquisite," Rose said, peering into the box beside her. "And how lovely. I cannot think I have seen many in this color yet this Season. You'll be setting a trend."

"I think there must be a mistake," she said, her traitorous fingers running along the neckline. "We did not order such a thing for Daphne, though I did admire the cloth when we were in the shop." Like a prickle up her spine, a slow dawning realization settled over her. She turned to Daphne, who was grinning in a way which immediately set her on edge. "You did not order this for yourself, did you?" Felicity asked, holding up the sleeve of the gown.

Daphne laughed, shaking her head. "No. The Colonel and I placed the order...but we did it for *you*."

Felicity froze. Edward had done this? For her? She tried to find the words, but her friend spoke first, amusement in her voice.

"Well, well."

Felicity turned her head sharply, half expecting censure. Instead, she found her new friend Rose looking at her with something close to approbation.

Felicity, startled, could not stop herself from asking, "You—you approve?"

Rose sipped her tea, the very picture of serene amusement. "My dear," she said, setting down her cup with a delicate clink, "we cannot control when the right person comes into our life—or how. But we should certainly seize the chance for happiness when they do." She reached out to take Felicity's hand where it rested on the soft fabric of the beautiful gown. "If this is what you fretted over, you ought not. I think he is a fine gentleman, and you will look stunning in green. This may be your moment, Felicity. Seize it."

Felicity's breath caught. *Seize the chance for happiness.* She looked down at the gown, running her fingers along the buttons in the back, heart pounding.

EDWARD HAD NEVER CONSIDERED HIMSELF A MAN PRONE TO romantic notions. He had spent most of his life focused on duty, first to his family, then to Pamela, then to his regiment, then to his household, and now to Daphne. Duty was what defined him. He had told himself, in the quieter moments, that he was content with that; that whatever other men sought in marriage, in love, in companionship, was not something meant for him. Especially not since his spectacularly terrible youthful mistake.

And then had come Felicity Price.

She had upended his life in every way imaginable: challenged him, infuriated him, and somehow, without his consent, had become a fixture of his world. And now, standing at the foot of the staircase, waiting to escort the ladies to the theater, Edward was utterly undone. He knew it. He knew himself a hopeless cause. Word had come through the servants that the gown from the modiste had arrived earlier that afternoon, but neither Daphne nor Felicity had said a word about it at dinner.

Both of them had been rather quiet, actually. Preoccupied by their thoughts, which had left Edward somewhat nervous. Had she not liked the gift? He had nearly asked, but decided it best to let her broach the subject. What if she had found it too personal? Daphne had reassured him that since it was from both of them, there was nothing inappropriate about it, and the idea of Felicity in a beautiful gown had appealed to him.

But if it had been a mistake, he would certainly apologize and—

"Oh, Edward. There you are." Felicity's voice came from above, and he glanced up the stairs with a half-formed apology ready on his lips.

There it stayed until he swallowed down his fear. Unexpected wonder filled him in its stead as Felicity descended the stairs at an unhurried pace, her gloved hand resting lightly along the banister.

She had donned the deep green gown, and she looked so enchanting, so lovely in that color that he stood absolutely stunned before her.

The dress was a shade so rich and striking that it should have been entirely too bold, yet on her it was perfection, making her brown eyes stand out and sparkle in a way that would surely turn heads. The gown fit her like a dream, the neckline modest yet devastating, the embroidery fine and elegant. She did not merely wear the gown. She sparkled in the entire room.

Felicity was incredible.

"Captain," he breathed.

Edward had always thought her handsome, in the way one admired a woman with striking intelligence and strong opinions. But this—this was something else entirely. This was the moment he knew, irrevocably, that his heart was hers.

That it had been for some time. And that it always would be.

Felicity stepped onto the second-to-last stair and looked at him, her dark eyes warm and a small, knowing smile on her lips. Before he could find his voice, she spoke. "Daphne has just informed me she has a headache," she said, tilting her head as she studied him.

Daphne. His ward. Her niece. Yes, she was supposed to come downstairs, too.

Edward looked to the top of the stairs, his mind still catching up with her words, then back at the vision before him as he frowned. "She seemed well earlier."

"She did," Felicity agreed, seemingly not at all concerned. "But she has since retired to bed." She took another step down, closer to him, and Edward's breath shallowed. "I was coming to ask if you would rather stay home as well."

Edward did not answer immediately. Instead, he reached for her, drawing her close in a way that left no space between them. Felicity let out the softest of breaths, her hands resting lightly against his chest. Not to resist him, but to keep her balance.

When he spoke, his voice was quiet but full of more certainty than it had ever held before. "I love you."

Felicity stilled. He felt her inhale sharply, felt the way her fingers curled slightly against his coat. But she did not pull away.

"In the weeks and months I have known you," Edward continued, his voice steady despite the pounding of his heart, "I have fallen in love with you—and no matter what comes next, I want you beside me. Always. As my dearest friend, my ally. My captain. As my wife."

Felicity's breath shook as she exhaled. For a moment, she said nothing. Then with all the certainty in the world, she made him the happiest man alive. "Yes."

Edward closed his eyes briefly, pressing his forehead to hers. She had chosen him. For the first time in his entire life, he felt true peace.

His future wife's fingers brushed lightly over the front of his coat. "I love you, too," she admitted.

He laughed softly, opening his eyes to look down at her. "A

very good thing. I would feel quite let down otherwise. Oh, Felicity." He kissed her forehead. "I love you." First one cheek, then the other, as her breathing hitched. "I will spend the whole of my life loving you, and I will care for you as you have taken care of everyone else." He pressed his lips to hers, and she eagerly returned his kiss. "I will always be thankful you chose me."

She shook her head, the smile returned to her lips. "How could I not? You are wonderful. A man of honor, integrity, you care so deeply about the people for whom you are responsible. You are the best of men, Edward."

"I have made so many mistakes," he reminded her, a note of caution in his voice. Best she not gain the habit of thinking him perfect.

Felicity cupped his cheek in her hand. "Everyone makes mistakes. It is how we right our wrongs, how we heal the hurts we cause, that matters. You are a good man, and I—I love you with my whole being."

That deserved another kiss, and his silent vow to never stop bettering himself. Felicity deserved the best him that he could give her.

When their lips parted, but their foreheads remained touching, Felicity asked softly, "What now?"

Edward exhaled a quiet laugh, stepping back enough to look at her properly. "You have seen to Daphne?"

"Yes, of course."

"Do you have a great desire to go to the theater tonight?"

His beloved smiled. "Not precisely. And we cannot really go alone, the two of us. People would talk."

"They are going to anyway when we announce our marriage."

"Do you mean when we announce our engagement?" Felicity teased.

"I am getting a common license first thing in the morning. I will wed you this very Sunday—if you are not averse to it?"

She laughed softly, and did not censure his eagerness. "I am not. Though people certainly will talk. You still lack patience, Colonel Halstead."

"I will learn it for you. *After* we have wed. I promise."

The joy in her eyes erased any concern he felt over rushing the whole thing. They had lived together for nearly two months, butting heads almost daily about Daphne's freedoms, agreeing and disagreeing on thousands of things, and he did not want to spend many more days unable to kiss her after a disagreement, afternoons without her seated by him at these infernal visits, evenings without her by his side at balls, nights without her curled up beside him. Not when they were both so in love. Not when they could easily remove the barriers to such intimacies through a single act.

"We cannot go to the theater," Felicity said quietly, bringing him out of his excitable thoughts. "So if *you* are not averse to it, I would like to sit with you in the library."

He arched a brow. "The library? You seemed little impressed with it when I showed it to you last."

"There is a new settee," she said, lips curving slightly. "I ordered it directly after you showed me the room—on your account, I'm afraid."

Edward couldn't help but laugh at that. "Of course you did. Daphne helped me order shelves and shelves' worth of books."

"She does enjoy reading." Felicity smiled, looping her arm through his. "Will you lead the way, Colonel?"

"I will, Captain," he teased, the title he had suggested giving her from the early days of their acquaintance making them both grin like young fools.

In short order he had the library warm with lamplight, the fire burning low in the hearth. As she had said, a new settee had been placed near the bookshelves, its fabric a rich navy, its cushions plush and inviting. Not masculine as his study was, not feminine like the fripperies of a teahouse. Something their own.

Edward grinned as he took it in. "You intend to fill my cold, empty home the way you filled my cold and empty heart?"

"Indeed. I do." Without hesitation Felicity sat, curling her legs up beside her, settling comfortably as if this were already her home.

And really, it was.

Edward watched her, something deep and profound settling in his chest. She was his home, now; she was already an essential part of his life. She had been since the moment she walked into it.

Felicity suddenly laughed, tucking a stray curl behind her ear.

He arched a brow, amused. "What is so funny?"

She looked up at him, eyes glinting with mischief. "Mrs. Norman," she revealed, grinning. "Rose, she has given me leave to call her."

Edward came closer to the settee. "What about her?"

"She suspected something between us, ever since the picnic in Hyde Park," Felicity admitted, leaning back against the cushions. "And I very much hope she will come to the wedding." She held her hand out to him and he took it. Their hands, intertwined; as their lives had been, and now always would remain.

Edward's chest warmed. "So do I," he murmured, settling beside her.

And as the fire crackled, as Felicity leaned against him, he knew: this was where she belonged. With him. Now.

Always.

Chapter Twenty-Two

F elicity had never been nervous about many things in her life. She had stood firm against Society's judgments, helped her brother raise Daphne with unyielding devotion, riled against her own brother's will when it came to her niece's choice of guardian, and challenged Edward Halstead at every turn without a second thought.

And yet, this morning, she was nervous.

She sat at the breakfast table, hands clasped in her lap, willing herself to feel at ease. She was engaged. Engaged. Engaged to be married.

It should not feel so strange to say it, to think it, but it was. Even as happiness bubbled up inside of her, it was all so new.

Edward was sitting at the head of the table, immediately to her left, spreading butter onto his toast with his usual military efficiency, as if nothing monumental had happened between them the night before. But something had...and now they had to tell Daphne.

Felicity inhaled slowly, reaching for her teacup. "Do you think she will be happy for me? For us?"

Edward glanced up at her, brow slightly furrowed, as if confused by the question.

She tapped a finger against her saucer. "It could upset her, you know. She has always expected me to be there for her, I always told her I would. What if she feels I am abandoning her? Or that I care for you more than I do her? Or—"

Edward set his toast down deliberately. "Felicity."

She glanced at him, fear evidently written all across her expression, for her future husband leaned forward slightly, lowering his voice.

"Daphne is not going to be upset. My darling, Daphne is not going to be surprised. She has spent the last several weeks attempting to play matchmaker."

Felicity's mouth dropped open. "She has *not*."

The man's lips twitched. "She has. With all the subtlety of a cavalry charge."

Her mouth immediately fell open to argue, but she stopped. She would have noticed such a thing, surely. No one knew Daphne as she did. If the young woman had attempted such manipulation, it would have been obvious. Except... Except looking back, she recalled a few oddly pointed comments, the knowing glances, the way Daphne had encouraged the two of them to spend time together.

Her face grew warm.

Edward, observing her closely, smirked. "Ah. There it is. The blush I love so well."

Felicity gave him a look of reproof, but before she could respond, Daphne entered the breakfast room. She was bright-eyed, perfectly composed, and looking not at all like a young woman recovering from an evening of a discomforting headache.

She settled in her chair. "Good morning, Colonel. Aunt Felicity."

Folding his arms, Edward leaned back in his seat. "Daphne. How is your headache?"

Daphne, already reaching for the teapot, paused. For a moment, she looked genuinely confused—then her eyes lit with understanding. She set the teapot down, lifting her chin in almost a perfect replica of her aunt. "I am fine. Of course," she said simply.

Felicity nearly choked on her tea.

Edward let out a low, amused exhale, shaking his head slightly.

Daphne, utterly unaffected by the scrutiny, reached for a slice of toast. "Did you finally propose matrimony to my aunt?" she asked blithely, as though inquiring about the weather.

Felicity stared at her. What the—

"I did." Edward—drat the man—bit into his toast, entirely unbothered.

Daphne nodded approvingly. "Good. Of course, you said yes, Aunt Felicity. You are far too clever to turn the Colonel down, especially given how much he adores you. I am glad." She grinned boldly at her aunt. "You know, I was hoping for this almost from the beginning."

Setting down her teacup with a bit more force than necessary, Felicity narrowed her eyes at her niece. "Daphne Price—almost from the beginning?"

Smiling serenely, Daphne shrugged. "Well, I needed to be sure he wasn't a scoundrel."

The Colonel released a quiet laugh. "And once you determined I was not?"

Unrushed and utterly composed, Daphne buttered her toast. "Then I knew it would only be a matter of time before you both stopped being so stubborn."

After spending the last several hours wondering how to tell Daphne, it was rather a shock. "Well. I never."

Edward, horribly smug, reached for the teapot. "More tea, my dear betrothed?"

She glared at him, but she was smiling despite herself.

The young lady, chewing her toast, sighed dramatically. "I do hope marriage makes you both more sensible."

Edward's hearty laugh filled the breakfast room, but Felicity was still staring at her niece, trying to understand how everything had turned upside down so quickly.

An unrepentant grin on her face, Daphne said, "I take it by your expression that you were worried about telling me."

For goodness sake! Felicity threw both hands in the air, a gesture of surrender at last. "Yes, well! Clearly, I need not have been."

Her niece had the good manners to look a little chagrined as he passed her aunt the tray of tarts. "No, you need not have been. Have one of these, Aunt Felicity. They are your favorite. Do you think Cook knows how to make a wedding cake? Will they have time to learn by the weekend?"

Felicity covered her face with her hands, laughing despite herself, as her future husband leaned back in his chair, entirely too pleased with himself. Eventually she lifted her head and pointed at him. "Not a word."

Edward smirked, raising his hands in mock innocence. "I would not dream of it, my love."

The entirely too satisfied Daphne took another sip of tea. "So. Have you selected a date yet?"

Felicity shook her head at her niece, then looked at her husband-to-be. "I think we are going to make quite an interesting little family." And she had never expected to be part of a true family again; certainly, not one of her own.

"As do I." Edward took her hand in his. "But a happy one."

"A very happy one," Daphne said, taking a tart for herself. "But horrible at scheduling, it appears. Do be practical, Aunt—when will we have the wedding?"

"At the first possible moment," Edward answered for her. "Yes?"

What else could she reply? Felicity looked between them both, her heart overflowing with joy. "Yes. I cannot imagine waiting another moment longer than necessary." She had never looked to her own happiness at all, in her memory. Now that it was within her grasp, she would seize it gladly—with both hands.

THE DAY BEFORE HIS WEDDING, EDWARD SAT IN BRIARWOOD'S study, glaring at the surface of his desk. The desk his father had left to him. The same desk where his father had likely written letters to him during his time in the army, never once mentioning the son Edward had unknowingly fathered.

Perhaps he needed a new desk. Or to make better use of this one. Perhaps he ought to write a letter, many letters, full of his love to Felicity? Perhaps. Later.

He had been awake for hours. Sleep proved an impossible thing. The experience hadn't been unpleasant, exactly, but charged with the weight of change.

He was to be married. Felicity Price had agreed to be his wife.

That fact alone had rerouted the course of his life overnight, but another change awaited him now, sitting on the desk before him after arriving in that afternoon's post, seemingly innocent.

A letter.

It sat on the edge of his desk, the seal unbroken, the script of his investigator's hand unmistakable. Given the nature of the man's last correspondence, this letter would hold the final report. It would tell him if his son was still living, and where.

After a soft knock on the door, Felicity entered the study without hesitation, as if this were already her house to walk freely. He had to smile at her as she approached, grateful for her unexpected presence.

"There are enough blooms in the garden for a small wedding bouquet. Daphne has already chosen which she will cut for me in the morning," she told him, her eyes bright with an excitement which made his heart turn over. "The gardener is astonished. He said he did not think we would see any blooms large enough for another fortnight at least."

"We are fortunate the roses seem to know we have need of them." Edward tried to make his tone light to match her joy, but concern weighed his words.

Felicity took in his expression, then glanced at the letter, then returned her gaze to him. "Is that what I think it is?"

Edward nodded slowly.

Neither of them moved for a moment until she circled the desk to stand beside him, her hand taking his. "I am here. I will be here as long as you need me. We can read it together, if you like."

Edward lifted her hand to his lips and brushed a kiss across the back of it. His bride. His captain. His Felicity. "Thank you, love. Now that you are here, I think I can read it." He released her hand and slowly, he reached for the letter, broke the seal, and unfolded the paper.

It was time to know what so many others had kept from him, all these years.

Felicity put her arm around his waist and leaned against his shoulder, supporting him in silence as he read the letter.

His son had been found.

The letter was brief, to the point—details on where the boy lived, with whom, and what sort of life he had been given. Edward read it twice, his grip on the page tightening just slightly before he set it down.

Felicity did not ask him what it said. She did not demand answers. She merely remained with him, solid and steady.

"They named him James." He laughed as tears fell down his cheeks. "James Thornton. A couple adopted him many years ago, a vicar and his wife. He's a vicar's son." Slowly, he lowered himself—not to the chair, but all the way to the carpet.

Felicity, his love, came with him, still holding him tight.

"He is alive and healthy, studying to be an attorney. He has sisters and brothers." Edward held the letter for Felicity to read. "And he's but a day's journey from here. I could see him. I could see him, if I wished." He buried his face in her hair, breathing deeply, trying to calm himself.

His son. He was safe. He was well. And he was nearby.

"I am so happy for you," Felicity said, her voice soothing. "And I will be with you. Whatever you decide to do, Edward. Truly, this is marvelous news. You must be relieved beyond measure."

Edward laughed again, sitting up slightly to better look into her eyes. "Thank you, Felicity. That you can rejoice with me is a gift."

She reached into his coat and took out a handkerchief. How she knew he kept it there, he did not know, but he wasn't surprised. His bride dabbed at his cheeks then pressed the cloth into his hand. "Anything that brings you happiness will bring me the same. James is important to you, whatever may come next, so he is important to me."

Truly, he did not deserve her. "Thank you." He looked at the letter again, then folded it carefully. "I will first take this letter to Lord Blackstone."

Felicity raised her eyebrows. "You mean to tell him all?"

"Some of it," Edward admitted. "Not the name of his mother. Not details—James deserves to make his own name and way into Society, as he chooses. But enough that Lord Blackstone will not think me completely without morals. If he still wishes to eject me from the club, so be it. We will still find a way to ensure Daphne's future happiness—and ours."

Felicity watched him with intelligent eyes, assessing, then nodded. "I hope he will finally see what I have always known. You are an honorable man."

Edward lifted her hand to his lips, pressing a quiet kiss against her fingers. "With you beside me, Felicity, I can endure whatever comes."

They stayed like that for a time, sitting on the carpet, reading the letter from the investigator. He told her what he would say to the viscount. She told him how she would change their honeymoon schedule so they could visit the county where the young James Thornton lived. Together, they would make plans and move forward. The thought comforted him, and it gave him the strength of mind to gather himself for a visit to Blackstone's club.

A short while later found Edward entering the familiar foyer of the building, Plockton noting the visit in his book. The familiar hush of the club greeted him as he walked up the stairs, the weight of past conversations lingering in the air.

He went to Lord Blackstone's study without delay in the hope of finding him there, and was in luck. The viscount looked up from his desk as Edward entered, his gaze sharp but not unwelcoming.

Edward wasted no time in setting things right. "I have come to offer an explanation," he said, removing the letter from his coat.

Blackstone folded his hands together, nodding once. "Proceed."

And so, Edward told him. Not all of it; not the young woman's name, nor the boy's. He had covered the names on the letter with pinned slips of paper. What he had to say must be enough.

That he had once been forced away from the life he might have had. That he had loved her, would have married her had his parents and hers permitted it. That he had wanted to stay, torn from her side and forced down a path of duty he had not chosen. That decisions had been made for him. That he had learned of her marriage, and learned not to think of her. That, years later, he had discovered a truth which had changed everything.

Blackstone listened without interruption. When Edward finished, he set the letter down and met the Colonel's steady gaze with one of his own.

"I do not ask for your approval," Edward said politely. "But I will not allow my character to be questioned unjustly. I made mistakes, and I own them, without tearing down the reputation of any others. I will see those mistakes righted, if I can. And I am not without honor."

After a long moment, Blackstone smiled. It was not a smug or triumphant smile, but one of respect—a respect earned. "You are a better man than I expected, Colonel." The viscount inclined his head. "I will speak no more of removing you from this club. You are a most welcome member."

Edward exhaled slowly, allowing the tension in his shoulders to ease.

"I also understand congratulations are in order," Blackstone added, amusement flickering in his eyes. "You are to be married?"

Edward tilted his head slightly. That wasn't exactly common knowledge, though they had informed the Normans by invitation that very morning. "Indeed."

Blackstone's lips twitched. "Then allow me to wish you well. And should you ever need advice on marriage—"

It was not perhaps polite, the chuckle that escaped him. "Will you give it, my lord? Speaking of geese and owls and I know not what else?"

Blackstone's eyes gleamed with good humor. "Most likely, I will speak of lemurs."

"Lemurs?" Edward chuckled, shaking his head. "I will keep that in mind."

As he stepped out of the office, a weight fell from his shoulders. He had not erased the past, but it had been faced.

And Edward was free.

Chapter Twenty-Three

MAY 12, 1817

The country air was fresh with the scent of earth and high springtime, the sky a clear, uninterrupted blue as Colonel and Mrs. Halstead stood beside a stone wall, staring up at an ivy-covered church. They had arrived at the village the evening before, after a long day of travel. The innkeeper's wife had answered all their questions about the church, which had stood for two centuries—and she was equally happy to tell them about the vicar and his wonderful family.

"Best minister we've e'er had," she said with a firm nod. "He's a kindly one. Not all doom and gloom and going on about our sins. He's more the encouraging sort—wants us to love our neighbors, treat people well. I always leave the Sunday meeting feeling like the world is a good place after all."

Edward had listened to every word with gratitude. He'd imagined both the best and worst scenarios as they'd traveled ever closer to this place. What if the vicar thought the sins of the father were on the head of the son? What if he had treated James poorly because of his origins?

He wouldn't feel at ease until he knew for certain how his son was treated, how he had been raised. The letter from the investigator had been too brief, too spare with details. Edward had to see it all for himself.

Thankfully, his newlywed wife understood his worries. Felicity had soothed and supported him at every turn. Even now, as they walked down the lane from the small church to the vicarage, she kept her arm pressed tightly to his and pointed out the beauty around them.

"How green and glorious it is," she said genially. "Wildflowers everywhere we look, well-tended fields, too. All the buildings in the village look as though they are well loved and kept up. This is a good community, Edward—what a wonderful place to grow up."

"Yes. It appears to be." He tried, and failed, to relax his shoulders again.

Their honeymoon had been quiet; peaceful and private. Exactly as Edward had hoped. They had spent mornings in companionable ease, afternoons exploring the countryside, and evenings wrapped in the warmth of their shared life, all while Daphne stayed with the Normans under their protection. Everything had been perfect.

And yet, today, there was a weight in his chest. Today, with Daphne traveling with them but politely declining their invitation for a walk, they were stepping toward the vicarage where his son lived.

Felicity's hand curled around his arm, her steady presence grounding him. "Everything will be all right, Edward. And if it is not, we will make it so."

He nodded again and spoke without much thought. "I know."

"Do you?" she asked, a note of challenge in her voice.

He looked down into her eyes, finding that familiar stubborn light in them. He stopped walking and drew in a deep breath. "I know that with you as my ally, there is nothing I cannot do. Thank you, my love."

She searched his eyes for a long moment, then smiled. She stood on her toes and leaned upward, pressing a soft kiss to his cheek. "I love you—and you are worthy of being loved. Never forget that, Edward."

"Never," he promised. Before he could kiss her back or offer more romantic reassurance, they heard whistling ahead of them. Edward sighed at the intrusion as his wife grinned up at him. He took her arm again and kept walking.

Ahead, the lane curved slightly and the whistler appeared. He was a young man, approaching from the opposite direction. He was tall, nearly Edward's height, with a build that suggested he was not one to sit in idleness. His hair was dark, but as the young man drew closer and his gaze met Edward's, the eyes stopped Edward in his tracks.

Coppery-green. His own eyes.

The young man gave them a polite, easy smile. "Good afternoon," he said with a nod and slight touch to the brim of his hat with respect.

Felicity stiffened beside Edward. Surely she had seen it too.

Edward cleared his throat. Speak, man! "Good afternoon, sir. It is fine country you have here."

The young man stopped walking, tilting his head slightly. "I have certainly always liked it. Are you passing through, sir?"

Edward nodded. "We are. We just came from the church and I...We are looking for the vicarage."

The young man's face brightened. "That would be my father's house."

Felicity's grip tightened slightly on Edward's arm as his chest rattled, his heart pacing far beyond its usual rhythm.

He swallowed, nodding once. "Then you could guide us there?"

The young man smiled, and a dimple appeared. Pamela's dimple. "Certainly. It is not far." He bowed. "Introductions are in order, of course. I am James Thornton."

"I am Colonel Edward Halstead, and this is my wife, Mrs. Halstead." Every time he introduced her thusly, Edward's heart swelled with pride and affection. And now? Now it was all the more potent.

His wife was meeting his son.

Felicity curtsied as prettily as ever. "It is a pleasure, Mr. Thornton. Thank you for your kindness to strangers."

He waited for them to reach him, falling into step beside Edward. They walked together, the younger man shortening his stride as Edward had, to accommodate Felicity's shorter legs.

Felicity asked, her voice clear and certain, "Do you work with your father?"

The young man shook his head. "No, Mrs. Halstead. I help with the parish when I can, naturally, but I am apprenticed to an attorney in London."

Edward glanced at him sharply.

The young man caught the look and grinned. "It is good work," he said. "I had thought of the church, of course, and have a great respect for it—but I have a mind for the law, and my father has always believed that one serves best where one's talents lie."

Edward's chest tightened. My father.

Felicity spoke when he could not. "Your father sounds like a wise man."

James's expression softened with fondness. "He is."

Edward forced his voice to remain even. "And what will you do? After your apprenticeship, I mean?"

The young man hesitated, then smiled wryly. "Well, it will take a great deal of time, as I am earning my way—so I suppose, when I finally complete my studies, where I will go will depend on where I am most needed."

Edward's throat felt too tight. How did one speak—how did one breathe?

"We have come from London to tour the countryside," his wife said quietly. "It has been a lovely journey thus far."

They rounded the next bend, where a modest but well-kept stone cottage came into view. The young man gestured toward the house. "Here we are."

A man knelt in the garden, pulling weeds near a small rosebush. He was older than Edward by at least a decade, kind-faced, his hands dirt-streaked from tending the soil.

"Father," James called.

Edward's chest tightened as the vicar rose to his feet, dusting his hands off on his trousers before looking up. The moment his gaze landed on Edward, something shifted in his expression. At first there was a moment of confusion, and then somehow, recognition. The vicar's gaze flickered briefly to Felicity, then back to Edward.

"I send you off to fetch the post and instead you deliver me guests. Was there ever so fine a son?" the vicar asked, smiling broadly as he came forward. "I am Roger Thornton, the vicar of this parish."

"Father, this is Colonel Halstead and his wife, Mrs. Halstead," James said. "They were admiring the church and have now come to admire its vicar." His tone had a teasing quality to it, and an affectionate one. "They came all the way from London."

"Welcome," the young man's father said warmly. "You have come a long way to admire churches and vicars."

Edward saw the caution in the other man's eyes—and perhaps he did not imagine the sadness there, too. "We are touring the countryside with our niece, who is resting at the inn. London is somewhat crowded and exhausting this time of year." He looked down at Felicity, then up at the vicar. "My wife and I would like to know more about the village and community. The kind people at the inn suggested we speak with you."

James chuckled. "Father is a great lover of history. You came to the right place."

The vicar nodded, giving his son an affectionate smile. "Thank you, James. Now, will you please finish taking those letters to the post? I wish them to go out on the next mail coach."

The young man nodded, excusing himself with a polite nod to Edward and Felicity before striding down the lane, whistling cheerfully again.

The moment he was out of earshot, the vicar turned to

Edward. "Forgive me, sir, but I speak plainly when I meet a gentleman with just the same eyes as...as my son. I do not know what circumstances led to my son coming into my life," he said, tone growing firm as he met Edward's gaze without judgment. "Or if you intend to take him out of it now. But I will say that I am grateful, eternally so, for every minute of being that boy's father." There were tears in his eyes, and his voice shook as he continued. "He and his sisters have been my greatest joy. They were my late wife's as well. Nothing in this world will ever change how much I love him."

Edward's eyes filled with tears and he reached out to put his hand on the vicar's shoulder, a touch reserved for only those men held close to his heart through kinship or battle. "Sir, I thank you. Thank you for loving him. I did not even know—his existence a secret, kept from me for so long—but you were there. Thank you."

It was not a brilliant speech, nor entirely clear, but the vicar stepped forward and embraced Edward as though they were brothers. Edward returned the gesture, and found he did not feel the least ashamed by the tears rolling down his cheeks.

When they parted, he looked first at Felicity to find her wiping her eyes with a handkerchief, then at the vicar, who was trying to find his own linen square. Edward handed over his, not touching the wet trails on his own face.

"Would you like to come inside?" the vicar asked hopefully. "No one else is home at present and you must have things you wish to say."

"Not say—I have so many things I wish to ask," Edward corrected, reaching for Felicity's hand. "But first I must reassure you, sir. I will not take him from you. I cannot see how that would be anything other than a terrible, terrible mistake. I have already made enough of those."

The vicar looked to Felicity, his smile slight. "You will not— but I presumed... You...you are not his mother, then?"

She slowly shook her head. "I am not. But I am here in full

support of my husband, and so in full support of young James, and of you, Reverend Thornton."

Reverend Thornton's smile grew, and he looked up at Edward with a gleam in his eye. "I am glad you found yourself such a companion, Colonel. Now, let us go inside. There is much to discuss, I think—and likely to decide, too."

They were there for an hour before James returned, with two younger sisters in tow, from visiting friends in the village. Mr. Thornton invited Edward and Felicity to return for dinner the next evening, but he did not hurry them away, instead asking James to show Edward something on the vicarage farm.

Grateful for the privacy granted him, Edward followed James eagerly, listening to every word the young man said.

He had decided, with Felicity's support and the vicar's approval, that it was not yet time to tell James of his parentage. The young man knew he was adopted; he knew that his birth mother had been unwed, and nothing more. He was intelligent and kind...and he was happy in his life.

But that did not mean changes could be made. In a quiet, steadier voice than he had expected possible, Edward offered to sponsor the boy's studies. He first asked the Reverend Thornton, but he put the idea to James the following evening at dinner.

"But why me, Colonel?" the young man asked, eyes wide. One of his sisters sat on one side of him, Daphne on the other, her eyes on his profile before turning to look at Edward.

"You strike me as someone who will make the most of your education," Edward said, his heart full that he could make this gesture. "I have no doubt you will help many in your career. Sponsoring you will be an honor—and in return, I only ask that you let me host you at my home near London from time to time. Or write to me of your progress."

"Yes, Colonel. Of course." James looked to his father. "If you approve, Father?"

The vicar chuckled, then inclined his head. "I approve. Your mother would, too. As always, use this opportunity for your betterment and the good of others. We never know who we will meet in this wide world, whether they will have need of us or us need of them, but we can walk each day in the spirit of love and gratitude. I think this will be the beginning of new and wonderful things. For all of us."

"I quite agree," Felicity said, looking up at Edward with a gleam in her dark eyes. "It is a marvelous beginning."

"Goodness," Daphne said with a little shake of her head. "And I thought the most interesting story I would ever be part of had already come to an end."

Edward raised his eyebrows at her. "And what story would that be?"

"Oh, yours of course, Uncle Edward—and Aunt Felicity. The best stories end with weddings, you know," smiled his niece by marriage. "I thought we settled yours rather nicely."

The vicar chuckled at that. "Miss Price, weddings are not endings either. Not in life. They are always at the beginning of the best stories."

After dinner, they walked back to the village, Felicity's hand in his. "This is a rather marvelous beginning, is it not? And I had thought I was close to the end, that my story had been told. I would be the spinster aunt forever, coming around at holidays to spoil Daphne's children." She laughed softly.

Edward looked down at her, his heart full, his future no longer a vast, empty thing. He lifted her hand to his lips, as he so loved to do. "You can still spoil any of her future children," he pointed out helpfully as Daphne walked ahead of them, talking animatedly with James, who had volunteered to accompany them on their return to the inn. "But I have hope you will not mind being a wife instead of a spinster."

"I will not mind in the least." She raised her beautiful dark eyes to his. "Nor will I mind being both an aunt and…and perhaps someday, a mother."

There, in the twilight of a country lane, with his wife beside him, their niece and his son ahead of him, and a future full of hope before him, Edward Halstead knew he had found peace at last.

Epilogue

FIVE YEARS LATER...

The gardens were in full bloom. Thank heavens for that.

Felicity had spent the entire morning weaving between the garden beds, tables, and chairs, overseeing the final preparations for the party. The heavy scents of flowers and warm earth had nearly given her a headache, but a light summer breeze had helped her remain clearheaded enough to see to everything.

The morning sky had threatened rain, but now everything above was a bright, unbroken blue. She looked up again, grateful for the good weather. She had worked several years to come to this moment. Rain would not have caused a tragedy, but she still liked to be prepared. Parties could be held inside as well as out, after all.

All around her, servants were setting out tables and arranging refreshments, while inside, the household bustled with preparations for the afternoon's guests.

Mrs. Lane came hurrying up to her, a list in hand. "All is in order with the refreshments, Mrs. Halstead, and we also have the stable-yard ready to receive the guests from Town."

"Thank you, Mrs. Lane. I could not ask for a better second in command." Felicity had thought the woman as efficient as a brigadier general, but had only dared say such a thing once. Mrs. Lane had immediately objected to being likened to a military man. "They are terribly inept at running households," she had said, most indignant.

Today, Felicity needed everyone to be happy—or wanted that for them, anyway. It was Daphne's betrothal celebration, and things were turning out beautifully.

Felicity smiled to herself, adjusting the placement of a table-cloth. There had been a time when she had fretted over Daphne's future, worried whether she would find a match worthy of her intelligence, kindness, and strength.

She needn't have worried. Daphne had chosen well.

Felicity turned her head, sweeping her gaze across the gardens where guests would soon gather, before moving toward the long table beneath a trellis. As she reached for the silverware, a sharp cry split the air.

"Mama!"

Felicity's heart lurched as she hurried toward the sound, skirts swishing. A small figure stood near the edge of the rose bushes, his little face scrunched in distress. Three-year-old Anthony Halstead, his dark curls tousled from mischief, clutched one tiny thumb in his other hand, tears welling in his deep brown eyes.

Felicity sighed, stepping quickly around the table. "Oh, my darling, what happened?"

Little Anthony sniffled, bottom lip sticking out. "I pickeded a flower."

Felicity knelt beside him, gently prying his fingers open. A single red mark bloomed on his thumb. It was nothing serious, but quite enough to bring a small tragedy into his young world.

Oh, that the days when soothing hurts so easily could remain forever. She reached into her bodice, retrieving a soft handker-chief, and dabbed carefully at his skin. "You mustn't grab the roses, my love. They are beautiful, but they bite."

Anthony's lip trembled. "It hurts."

262

"Yes, but it will stop soon. Here." Felicity kissed his tiny thumb, then smoothed back his unruly curls.

The tears stopped instantly as her son beamed up at her. Then he bent down and, immediately doing what he had just been warned not to do, picked up the flower which had caused the mischief, careful this time of the thorn. "For you, Mama."

"Oh, darling. It is lovely. Thank you."

A deep, exasperated voice interrupted Felicity's raptures. "I only turned away for a moment, Felicity. But I cannot find—" Edward appeared at the garden entrance, somewhat harried, his coat missing and his cravat slightly askew. His words stopped and he huffed upon seeing the little boy holding his mother's hand. "Our son escaped again."

Felicity arched a brow at him. "Escaped, or outmaneuvered his father?"

Edward bent down and plucked Anthony up with ease, settling him against his side. "Are you terrorizing your mother again, pup?"

Anthony grinned, clinging to his father's lapel. "I picked-ed a flower."

Edward kissed the top of his son's curls, eyeing the rose Felicity held. "Ah. And how did that adventure end?"

Anthony frowned dramatically. "It bit me."

Felicity laughed and held her hand up for Edward to take, relying on his steady strength to get to her feet again. It was indeed an awkward thing of late, she reflected as she smoothed a hand over her rounded stomach.

"You must sit down, Aunt Felicity." She turned to see Daphne coming quickly down the garden path with a cushion in hand and a frown across her brow. "This is utterly ridiculous. You need to let everyone else do the work for once."

Felicity sighed, reluctantly accepting the inevitable. "I am not an invalid."

"You are eight months along," Edward countered, guiding her toward a shaded bench. "Humor our niece."

"Uncle Edward, you are as concerned as I am about her over-working herself." Daphne followed them, settling a hand on a hip as she flapped the cushion in her aunt's direction. "Why am I the only one with any sense today?"

Felicity settled onto the cushion, muttering about overbearing family under her breath, but Edward simply smirked.

Anthony climbed up beside her, snuggling into her side with the complete trust of a child who knew he was adored. But as Felicity put her arm around him, her son wriggled upright, pointing excitedly.

"James is here!"

And, indeed, the familiar figure of James Thornton was entering the garden. James was taller now, broader, his dark hair catching the sunlight as he strode forward. His eyes—Edward's eyes—were bright with happiness as he approached.

"Apologies for the delay," James said somewhat sheepishly, his smile warm as he turned toward Daphne. Without hesitation, he bent and pressed a kiss to her cheek.

Daphne blushed, but did not shy away, instead jutting out her chin to present her cheek. "You are lucky you are so agree-able, or I would be quite put out with you. You may kiss me again."

Felicity's whole body relaxed as she watched the exchange, the reminder of her niece's heart kept safely by a trustworthy gentleman making some of her anxieties fade.

James turned to Edward, embracing him without hesitation. "Father."

The truth had not shocked the young man a few years previ-ous, when Edward had finally told him of his parentage, and James, with infinite kindness, had not hesitated to forgive his absence and embrace Edward whole-heartedly. It helped, of course, that the father who raised him had been present to offer his guidance and love over the last few years, too.

Edward's throat bobbed as he returned the embrace, his grip firm, steady.

264

James pulled back, turning to his stepmother next as his grin turned boyish. "And Mama Felicity."

Felicity had no chance to respond before James embraced her too, careful of her growing belly. "You are late, James," she scolded lightly.

James grinned as he stepped away from her. "You know how London is. I was waylaid by an old friend of the family."

"Stop your wriggling, pup, you will wrinkle your mother's gown." Edward picked up Anthony again. "And which old friend would that be?"

"Lord Blackstone," James said brightly. "He sends his regards, by the way. Though he will be here within the hour to give them in person. He has promised us a betrothal gift, Daffy."

Edward chuckled. "If it has fur or feathers, that means he is especially fond of you."

Anthony, hanging onto Edward with one arm around his neck, held out his bandaged thumb, waving it in front of himself. "I pickeded a flower," he informed James seriously.

James took hold of Anthony's thumb, examining the grave injury with a solemn nod. "Picked a fight with one, more like. Did you win, brother?"

Anthony sighed, ever the dramatist. "No."

James patted his shoulder. "We all must learn about thorns, eventually."

Daphne asked after James's sisters and father, the vicar, and he promised they were getting dressed in the house at that very moment. The two of them were soon discussing the other party guests, and Daphne led him toward the garden entry while reminding him of their plans. His sisters appeared, and soon laughter rippled through the garden, warm and full of love.

Felicity, watching them all, felt a contentment so deep it stole her breath. She had once thought herself destined to be alone, a woman at the edges of Society, moving through life as an observer. Unimportant.

Now, she was at the very heart of a family.

She glanced at Edward who was already watching her. He put Anthony down and pointed him toward James and Felicity, then settled on the bench beside her before lifting her hand, brushing a kiss over her fingers. She smiled and moved his hand to where their second child together grew, at precisely the right moment for Edward to feel the baby turn, adjusting—trying to get comfortable, most likely, in an ever-tightening home.

"Are you well, my love?" Edward asked softly.

"Yes. I am well." Felicity laid her head on his shoulder and knew, without a doubt, that this was everything she had ever wanted. Everything she never dared to dream of.

And Felicity would spend the rest of her life quite happily, with the people she loved around her.

IF YOU ENJOYED EDWARD AND FELICITY'S STORY, MAKE CERTAIN YOU pick up the next book in the Bachelors of Blackstone's series, A Trial of His Affections, by author Mindy Burbidge Strunk.

What's it about? Well, Miles Yardley has spent years admiring the girl next door—only to find himself in an impossible predicament. Grace Jenkins knows she can't marry for love—but that doesn't mean she can afford to fail to wed at all!

Each book in this series will have a gentleman banned from the other clubs of London, sometimes for good reason, sometimes for seemingly no reason, but all of them now have something to prove.

Bachelors of Blackstone's Series

A Bachelor's Lessons in Love by Sally Britton
A Trial of His Affections by Mindy Burbidge Strunk
A Gentleman's Reckoning by Jennie Goutet
To Hunt an Heiress by Martha Keyes
Love is for the Birds by Deborah M. Hathaway
Forever Engaged by Ashtyn Newbold
A Match of Misfortune by Jess Heileman

Author's Note

This is the part where I apologize for historical slips, both intentional and not intentional. A most intentional two slips this time have occurred, and I would like to explain them in brief.

(1) An unmarried, spinster aunt most likely would not have been allowed to stay with her niece in the home of an unwed male guardian without there being some serious gossip. Yet if the male guardian had hired a companion or governess to keep his ward company, no one would bat an eye. Somehow, it made things all right if the woman was a paid servant/employee, even though she would likely be in just as precarious a situation as a spinster aunt. It is simply a matter of the time period, that women were held to a different standard than men, and women were the ones blamed when a man took advantage of a situation. But, in this book, our hero is honorable, our heroine is honorable, and they are above reproach. It makes the story a lot more fun, writing it that way.

(2) The length of time a person wore mourning is something we have some guidance on, from books on etiquette at the time and royal decrees for mourning royal personages, but there were no hard and fast rules on the length of time a person wore black or gray. Not until a few decades later, into the Victorian era. The length of time a person wore mourning was determined by the family or individual, how close those in mourning were to the person who passed, and how much they liked that person.

I have a wonderful friend in the author world who says this about guidelines and social rules in the Regency: "Oh, 200 years from now, people will see that we had speed limit signs. And they will insist of us 'Everyone in the early 2000's always went 65 MPH on that highway.'" You see, there are certainly guidelines for things like speed limits. But how many people do you know, or do you observe, who obey them constantly? Some always go faster, some always go slower. Sometimes, people who do it one way or the other make exceptions for themselves depending on who is watching them and emergency circumstances.

We can do our best to know how people behaved in times past, and we can try to adhere to what makes the most sense, but just as speed limits are not strictly followed, we can guess that there were exceptions to who followed what in terms of social rules of the early 19th century.

Now that we have that cleared up, thank you so very much for reading this novel! It's on the gentle side of romances, and I rather like it that way. I hope you enjoyed it, too.

I am thankful, as always, to my author friends who cheered me on and bounced ideas back and forth with me. I'm grateful for my family, for their patience and support. I'm grateful for the romance of my own, which keeps me going forward despite anything else that comes about.

Thank you, to all who have helped me shape this book into what it is, I am forever grateful.

-SB-

Also by Sally Britton

CASTLE CLAIRVOIR ROMANCES:

A Duchess for the Duke | Mr. Gardiner and the Governess | A Companion for the Count | Sir Andrew and the Authoress | Lord Farleigh and Miss Frost | Lady Ivy and the Irishman | A Gentleman for Lady Juniper

THE INGLEWOOD SERIES:

Rescuing Lord Inglewood | Discovering Grace | Saving Miss Everly | Engaging Sir Isaac | Reforming Lord Neil

RETURN TO INGLEWOOD:

Romancing the Artist

DEVOTED HEARTS:

Martha's Patience | The Social Tutor | The Gentleman Physician | His Bluestocking Bride | The Earl and His Lady | Miss Devon's Choice | Courting Miss Ames | Penny's Yuletide Wish

STAND ALONE ROMANCES:

The Captain and Miss Winter | A Haunting at Havenwood | Her Unsuitable Match | An Unsuitable Suitor | Mistletoe for Felicity

LOVE UNAWARES

His Unexpected Heiress | Her Unsuitable Match

HEARTS OF ARIZONA SERIES:

Silver Dollar Duke | *Copper for the Countess* | *A Lady's Heart of Gold*

About the Author

Since Jane Austen isn't releasing any new titles, Sally decided to try her hand at writing a few stories set in the Regency period. Those attempts led to a happy career doing what she loves most: telling love stories.

Sally Britton, her husband, their four incredible children, their dogs, the cat Willow who tolerates them, and a snake named Basil live in Oklahoma.

Sally started writing on her mother's electric typewriter when she was fourteen years old. Reading her way through Jane Austen, Louisa May Alcott, and L.M. Montgomery, Sally fell love with the elegant, complex world of centuries past.

In 2007, Sally earned a bachelor's in English Literature. She met and married her husband not long after, and they're quite busy living happily ever after.

All of Sally's published works are available on multiple retailers and you can connect with Sally and sign up for her newsletter on her website, AuthorSallyBritton.com.